D0512772

A TALE FROM THE
BADLANDS

THE
BOY
WITH ONE
NAME

J. R. WALLIS

SIMON & SCHUSTER

First published in Great Britain in 2017 by Simon & Schuster UK Ltd
A CBS COMPANY

Copyright © 2017 Rupert Wallis

This book is copyright under the Berne Convention.
No reproduction without permission.
All rights reserved.

The right of Rupert Wallis to be identified as the author of this
work has been asserted by him in accordance with sections 77
and 78 of the Copyright, Design and Patents Act, 1988.

1 3 5 7 9 10 8 6 4 2

Simon & Schuster UK Ltd
1st Floor
222 Gray's Inn Road
London WC1X 8HB

www.simonandschuster.co.uk
www.simonandschuster.com.au
www.simonandschuster.co.in

Simon & Schuster Australia, Sydney
Simon & Schuster India, New Delhi

A CIP catalogue record for this book
is available from the British Library.

PB ISBN 978-1-4711-5792-9
eBook ISBN 978-1-4711-5793-6

This book is a work of fiction. Names, characters, places and
incidents are either the product of the author's imagination or are
used fictitiously. Any resemblance to actual people living or
dead, events or locales is entirely coincidental.

Typeset in Goudy by M Rules
Printed and bound by CPI Group (UK) Ltd, Croydon, CR0 4YY

MIX
Paper from
responsible sources
FSC® C020471
www.fsc.org

Simon & Schuster UK Ltd are committed to sourcing paper
that is made from wood grown in sustainable forests and support the Forest
Stewardship Council, the leading international forest certification organisation.
Our books displaying the FSC logo are printed on FSC certified paper.

This book is for anyone who has ever fought a monster, whether lurking inside you or beyond, out there in the world.

'Of the many classes of Ogre encountered in the Badlands, the Berserker or *Wédorcnéus* is considered to be particularly fierce. As with all types of Ogre, together with its appetite for human flesh, it displays acute aggression and great strength.'

'Unlike other types of Ogre, the Berserker is not indigenous to the British Isles. Originally, these creatures were bred in captivity by the Viking tribes of Scandinavia and brought over on sorties to Britain (circa 793 AD onwards) to fight alongside their fiercest warriors who were also the Berserkers' handlers.'

EXTRACTS FROM

The Badlander Bestiary

Pocket Book Version

 ENGLAND . . .

. . . at night . . .

ONE

J ones stopped. He'd felt safe enough creeping down the path in front of the cottage, in the dark. But now the moon had reappeared from behind the clouds, the world was relit with a soft silver light meaning he was much more likely to be seen.

He kept trying to focus on what Maitland had promised, that he wouldn't come to any harm. But that was less easy to believe now they were actually here. Scared to go on, Jones looked behind him, to where his Master was hiding, hoping to be beckoned back.

Maitland stepped out from the granite porch concealing the front door of the cottage and stood on the path, big as a boulder in his greatcoat. He said nothing. His craggy face remained hidden below the peak of his baseball cap. And Jones knew right away Maitland wanted him to go on, however bright the moon, because this was his big night. This was his big test. Without saying a word, Jones wrapped his overcoat tight around him, and crept on obediently down the path, the flagstones in front of him sparkling in the moonlight.

A tall wooden fence took over from the whitewashed wall of the cottage. When Jones came to a door, he lifted the latch without a *clink* and nudged it open far enough to see a lawn ahead of him, a patio to his right. Carefully, he stepped forward and peered round the door. His breath caught in his throat like a fishbone when he saw someone standing away to his left, in the centre of the lawn.

It was a man, naked from the waist up, with his back to Jones, his shirt and sweater folded in a neat pile beside him on the grass. Maitland was right. Arkell, the man they'd been following, had come to this quiet, secluded garden in the countryside to moon-bathe.

Jones had observed Arkell for just a few days. It had been quite easy. Jones had gone into Arkell's corner shop and bought sweets from time to time. He'd dilly-dallied in the street outside, juggling a football between his feet, or kicked it against a wall, counting out the seconds, the minutes, and then the hours. In fact, Jones had done so well at pretending to be an ordinary, lonely boy that Arkell had started taking pity on him, inviting him in to pass the time between customers, offering him free sweets from the big plastic pots that lined the shelves and were frosted white on the inside with sugar.

Sometimes, Arkell had asked about Jones's family and he'd enjoyed pretending to have one, inventing a younger sister called Jane with a giggly laugh, and a mother with dark, shoulder-length hair who used lavender soap. His father wore

2

his shirtsleeves rolled up to his elbows and only ever drank strong brown tea from his blue-striped mug.

But, all the time they were talking, Jones would be taking mental notes of anything that struck him as odd about Arkell, and quickly began to notice the telltale signs Maitland had taught him to recognize: a bulbous tongue and excess spittle. Foul breath. Hair that grew a little too thick around each low-set ear. But it was mostly Arkell's eyes and the sadness he saw in them that gave the man away. Jones knew the loneliness that came with being different to other people too.

Maitland listened carefully to everything Jones reported back, deciding it was worth following Arkell one night, when the moon was bright and almost full, to confirm their suspicions. And now here they were.

Jones stepped back quietly from the door, pulling it to. He was fully aware all types of shapeshifters could change without needing a full moon as long as they kept themselves charged with moonlight.

Maitland was already standing beside him. Even though Maitland was a big man he moved silently and often reminded Jones it was a trick the boy would have to learn. The stubble on Maitland's face looked silver in the half-dark. The scar on his left cheek shone red and sore. His grey eyes sparkled as they always did at a time like this.

'Is he bathing?' he whispered. When Jones nodded, Maitland grinned, as if he'd known Arkell's secret all along.

'There must be something about this spot. We need to be careful. Whenever there's one shifter bathing . . .'

'. . . there's usually others too,' recited Jones in a tiny voice, and Maitland nodded, pleased. But then his face sharpened again.

'Now remember,' he whispered, 'he's not a man, not any more.'

Jones nodded and reached a shaking hand into his overcoat pocket for his catapult as Maitland drew out an old-fashioned revolver. Neither of them seemed the slightest bit surprised when the gun spoke quietly too.

'You sure the boy's ready, Maitland?'

Maitland just nodded and stared at Jones, jabbing a finger towards the door. 'We'll be right behind you. Make your first kill and tomorrow you'll be ready for your Commencement.'

A second passed.

Followed by another.

And then another.

Jones didn't move. He knew what he wanted to say. He wanted to tell Maitland he wasn't ready for his Commencement because he didn't want to be a Badlander at all. Ordinary people fascinated him. The way they lived. The things they owned and used. He wanted to be like them. But telling Maitland face to face was difficult, much harder than lying in bed at night and imagining it.

Maitland's grey eyes were hardening.

Jones looked away. All he had to do was push open the door and take one clean shot with his catapult. *It would be impossible to be normal after that, though.* Jones heard other thoughts inside him too. *Arkell had been kind to him in the shop. The man had offered him sweets from the jars. He'd listened to the boy's every word like a friend.*

The crisp sound of tyres over gravel broke the awful silence. A light swept up from the road, around the bottom of the curving driveway, drawing a bright stripe across the fence beside it.

Maitland moved quickly, pulling Jones back down the path into the shadows beside the cottage. A succession of thoughts flashed golden inside the boy. *The people who lived in the house were returning home . . . Arkell would be disturbed . . . he'd leave . . . because there'd be no sense in revealing himself if the garden was a secret bathing spot.* Jones felt a weight lift from his shoulders as he realized there'd be no opportunity to make his first kill tonight. It meant his Commencement wouldn't happen tomorrow either.

When Maitland peered round the corner wall of the cottage and began cursing under his breath, Jones took a peek as well. His heart sank. There was no car. It was just a girl, about his age, on a bicycle, cycling awkwardly over the soft, pebbly drive, a single headlamp lighting her way. And then, as if to keep her spirits up, she started to whistle a shaky tune, making Maitland curse more loudly.

Moments later, the thatch above Jones and Maitland crackled as something landed on it. They heard a low growl. Footsteps pattered along the roof of the cottage.

Maitland grabbed Jones by the shoulders. 'What can moon-bathing do?' Jones blinked. 'Come on! What?!'

'Hungry,' whispered the boy. 'It makes 'em hungry.'

'So what about now?' asked Maitland. 'Are you ready now?' But all Jones could manage was to shake his head 'no', making his Master mutter something under his breath.

Arkell dropped from the roof, landing on the driveway in front of the cottage. As he stood up, the man was already changing. There was a crackling in his ribcage as his chest expanded. Black hair was sprouting across his back and shoulders. The tip of a white tusk glinted in the moonlight.

'Maitland,' hissed the revolver. 'Forget the boy. Arkell's an Ogre, a Berserker class. We need to go to work, now. Finish this job ourselves.' But Maitland just stood there, glaring down at Jones. He didn't flinch even when he heard the bicycle braking and sliding in the gravel, then clattering onto the driveway.

'We'll talk about this later,' growled Maitland as the girl began screaming. And then he ran out of the shadows back down the path while the revolver yelled at him to pull the trigger, announcing it had already selected the right bullet tipped with mistletoe and rowan.

Jones stood in the dark, cursing himself, wondering what Maitland would say when this was all over. Then his mind unlocked and he ran, following in the footsteps of his Master like a good apprentice should, his catapult in one hand, a silver ball bearing pinched between the fingers of the other.

TWO

R uby was still screaming as she stood up and backed
down the drive away from her bicycle, its front
wheel ticking round. When her breath finally gave
out, she stopped, astonished now by what was happening in
front of her.

Lit by the yellow beam of the headlamp stood a half-naked
man, his shadow looming large on the white wall of the
cottage behind him. At least, he had been a man because,
now, he was changing very quickly into something huge.
His lower jaw had already shot out like a drawer, revealing a
large U-bend of sharp white teeth, a short tusk protruding on
either side. His brown shoes suddenly popped like Christmas
crackers as two bulbous, hairy feet appeared with thick nails
unfurling into points. The legs of his trousers grinned before
splitting across two large grey thighs.

Ruby could hear one part of her brain yelling:
that'sabloomingogretrollmonsterthingy. The other half was
shouting that creatures like this only existed in books and
films and nightmares. With all the commotion inside her

7

head, she was not sure what to believe. Or think. Or even do. So she was rather glad when a rather more normal-looking man came running down the path beside the cottage, an old baseball cap pulled down over his eyes and his black greatcoat flapping behind him. His arm was raised. And he was holding something in his hand.

A gunshot rang out and the *creatureogretrollthingy* howled.

The noise brought Ruby to her senses, shrinking all the noise in her brain to one quiet and simple idea: *slide off your backpack and turn round as quietly as you can.* Her second thought was much louder and more to the point: *RUUUUUUU-NNNNNN!*

Maitland swore. He'd misjudged his shot in the dim light of the bicycle's headlamp and only nicked the Ogre. The gun had been right. Maitland could see from the telltale markings and its size the creature was indeed a Berserker class, a *Wédorcnéus*, of the type bred centuries ago to fight ferociously in battle and gifted with the special quality of speedy healing too, meaning a clean head shot was required to put it down.

'Gebíed mé glæm,' muttered Maitland and he conjured out of white sparks in the palm of his hand a ball of bright light, which he flung into the night sky. As it floated above the cottage like a tiny sun, illuminating the driveway below, Maitland could see blood, black as oil, glistening on the Ogre's thigh, the bullet wound already healing. Maitland took aim again and fired.

Splinters flashed from the top of the wooden fence on the far side of the driveway. Maitland had missed completely, this time.

'Maitland!' shouted the revolver. 'What's wrong, man?'

But all Maitland could manage in reply was a long, low gurgle as he dropped to the ground under the weight of a second *Wédorcnéus*, which had leapt from the roof and landed on top him, one of its tusks impaled through his neck.

Jones knew instantly that Maitland was going to die and that living to see the morning was now up to him alone. He started running again down the path towards the driveway, raising his catapult and slotting the silver ball bearing into the rubber sling. When he was close enough, he stopped and pulled back the sling until his elbow locked.

He could see Maitland's lips moving as the Ogre stood over him, its huge jaws opening to finish him off. But, sensing the boy, the creature suddenly looked up. When it roared at him, the saliva strung between its bloody tusks shimmered like a string of pearls.

Jones forced himself to look deep into the Ogre's yellow eyes, then fired.

The ball bearing arrowed like an icicle and struck the beast in the centre of its large forehead, disappearing into the skull and leaving behind a neat dark hole. The Ogre collapsed instantly onto the driveway beside Maitland, twitched and then lay still.

*

Ruby had seen Maitland's second shot splinter the top of the fence beside the driveway. The bullet had fizzed past her ear and brought her skidding to a stop. Looking round, she saw the man in the greatcoat pinned beneath a second *ogreytrollythingy*. But, when she realized the first one was striding across the driveway towards her, she willed her legs to turn her back round so she could carry on running.

It only half worked, because, as her right leg moved, the left one held firm, making her skid round in the gravel. Ruby's arms windmilled as she tried staying upright. But she failed dismally at that and toppled backwards just as the creature leapt for her. A blast of hot, filthy breath parted Ruby's long black hair down the centre as the beast soared over her head and crashed into the fence beyond.

Landing on the driveway with a *crunch*, Ruby lay blinking and frightened. A shooting star skimmed briefly across the night sky. And then a voice inside told her she'd be vanishing too unless she started running again. She sat up just in time to hear a nasty growl as the ogretrollthing pulled itself free from the broken fence.

'The *cægggggg*,' whispered Maitland, the words turning to air as he struggled to speak. 'The keeyyy!'

Maitland's neck was hot and slippery with blood, and Jones fumbled with the silver chain around it. Eventually, he found the clasp and opened it. A silver key, hooked through its eye, dangled below the boy's shaking hand. Maitland had never discussed the key required for Jones's Commencement.

So here was a moment. Here was something that had never happened before.

Blood clambered up the sides of Maitland's teeth as he smiled, eyeballing the body of the dead Ogre beside him, and tried to say something. But all he managed was a little nod. Jones laid his hand on Maitland's arm, gripping tighter as though the world was about to break apart and send them spinning into space.

A long, slow breath crept out of Maitland's lungs. The power in his body faded. And the night pressed in around Jones, creeping black fingers into his throat, forcing his eyes to fill up with tears.

'JONES!' shouted the revolver, lying on the gravel beside the dead man. 'You need to finish off here. You need to look sharp, boy, just like Maitland would have done. Or else you're going to be joining him.'

Jones wiped his eyes and managed a small nod. He became aware of a low growling off to his right and looked up to see Arkell, still in his Ogre form, towering over the girl. She was doing her best to crawl down the driveway towards the road. But, each time she moved a few metres, the creature grabbed her ankle and dragged her backwards, until suddenly it seemed to tire of the game and picked her up by one foot, making her scream.

Jones slotted another ball bearing into the sling of his catapult and picked out a point on the Ogre's large head.

The silver ball disappeared like a tiny shooting star.

Nothing for a heartbeat ...

... and then a terrible howl. The Ogre dropped the girl and swung round to face Jones, a red groove shining along the left side of its head, but already healing fast. Jones cursed and fumbled for another ball bearing in his overcoat pocket as the creature that had been Arkell a few minutes ago thundered towards him.

Ruby pushed herself up onto her elbows just in time to see the boy fire another ball bearing. The ogretrollthing landed at his feet in a spray of gravel and lay there twitching, and then its body became still. For a brief moment, there was nothing but silence. Then Ruby began to hear simple sounds. A breeze rattling the leaves of an old oak tree standing over the road ... the drumming of her heart telling her she was still alive ... the boy's black boots kicking the beast to check it was dead as the catapult wilted in his hand.

Then Ruby's eyes clicked shut on their own and the last thing she heard was the back of her head hitting the gravel.

Jones stood over the unconscious girl, her black hair gathered around her on the gravel, and watched her breathing, knowing he still had work to do. Aiming another ball bearing at her forehead, the catapult began to creak as he pulled back the sling.

But his arm stopped as she groaned and opened her eyes, and he looked down into them.

'Do it, Jones!' shouted the revolver, still lying on the gravel. 'It's for her own good. She'll make *forhwierfende* if she's been bitten. You know how it works with shifters and the curse they can spread.'

The girl's face twisted up, and she tried to shrink away as she realized what was about to happen.

'Please,' she whimpered. 'Stop.'

Different thoughts hurtled through Jones's brain as he looked down into two blue eyes full of fear.

'Are you hurt?' he asked, his arm trembling with the catapult ready to fire.

'I don't—'

'*Did it bite you?!*'

'Go on,' shouted the revolver. 'One little scratch from a shapeshifter, that's all it takes!'

Jones studied the girl, deciding she was about his age as he looked for any cuts or bites, warning signs she might be able to make *forhwierfende* and shapeshift into an Ogre, albeit a small one.

'Jones!' shouted the revolver again.

Suddenly, a connection sparked somewhere deep inside Jones's head and he pulled the catapult all the way back and fired.

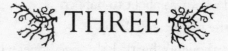

THREE

The ball bearing pinged off the gravel beside Ruby's head, making her cry out.

'Stand up,' ordered the boy, his catapult already reloaded. 'The next one won't miss.'

Ruby kept her eyes fixed firmly on him as she stood up slowly, gravel falling off her like drops of water. Something dark wormed through her guts and she wanted to be sick.

'Follow me,' continued the boy, walking backwards across the driveway towards the cottage, keeping Ruby in his sights as she followed him. He was no bigger than her. His lean face was grubby. The dark rings under his eyes made him look older than he surely was. 'Stop there,' he barked. Ruby halted in the middle of the driveway, which was still well lit by the ball of light the man in the baseball cap had thrown into the sky. 'Look up at the moon,' he instructed. 'I need to see if it does anything to you. That way we'll know for sure if you've been cursed or not.'

Ruby could see the moon above the roof of the cottage. It was bright and almost full. But, although she did as the boy asked, her eyes kept darting to the ball of light floating above the driveway. Her mind was busy, trying to process how the man had done such a thing before he'd been killed, and then a shudder rippled through her as she remembered that too.

'You've got no guts, boy,' shouted the revolver. 'What's the point in hanging around, waiting for who knows what other evil to turn up? What do you think Maitland would say about that?'

'Maitland ain't here no more,' replied the boy, who was staring at Ruby as if he knew exactly what she was thinking: *How on earth can a gun like that talk?*

'After all the time he spent teaching you to be a Badlander,' continued the talking gun. 'I mean ... you're his apprentice ... whaff ifff somefing ... '

The voice became too muffled to hear any more as the boy back-heeled a mound of gravel over the revolver and allowed himself a grin. Ruby noticed his crooked smile and a set of slightly browned teeth. When he looked back at her, he was serious again. She wanted to ask about the talking revolver and the ball of light, but she was wary of the loaded catapult creaking in his hands.

'What're you doing here?' asked this odd, raggedy boy dressed in an overcoat that was too big for him, the sleeves turned up.

'Running away,' said Ruby quietly. 'I was going to sleep here tonight. The people that own the cottage only come for weekends and holidays. I saw them leaving this morning with their car packed when I was on the school bus. I can't stay with my foster family any more.'

The boy frowned. 'I know what a school bus is. But I ain't ever heard of a "fozzter" family.'

'*Foss-ter* family,' corrected Ruby. 'One you stay with when things aren't right with your real one.'

'What's wrong with yours?'

Ruby chewed her cheek for a moment and wiped away a curl of black hair pasted to her brow. 'Sometimes, parents aren't happy with the kids they get. Life isn't always like those cheesy family shows you get on TV. But I suppose you know that,' she said, glancing over at the body of Maitland, an icy shiver rattling through her. 'Look, what—' Ruby stopped and shivered again, her lips squeezing themselves into tiny white lines. 'What the bloody hell is going on?' She grabbed her arms around herself more tightly to try and stop shaking.

The boy dug at a spot in the driveway with the toe of his boot and then cleared his throat. 'You're in shock cos you've been involved in a supernatural event,' he said. It sounded to Ruby as if he was trying to sound like an authority on the subject now the man in the baseball hat was dead.

A sudden rasping sound made Ruby's heart jump. But it was just the gun shaking off the gravel the boy had covered it with. The revolver spat out a stone that pinged off the frame of Ruby's bicycle lying nearby.

'Jones, we need to juice the bodies and leave. Now! Before anything else turns up.'

16

The boy nodded. 'The gun's right,' he said to Ruby. 'It's dangerous staying here any longer. You got lucky,' he said, lowering the catapult. 'You can't have been scratched or bitten, else the moon would've done something to you by now if you wasn't human no more.'

Ruby blinked and said nothing. There were so many questions filling her head she didn't know what to ask. And for a girl like Ruby Jenkins that was an entirely new experience.

When Jones knelt down beside Maitland, it seemed as though the dead grey eyes were staring right at him, as if the man was blaming him for what had happened. Jones whispered that none of it was his fault. But he wasn't sure he believed it. His hands trembled as he bent forward and whispered that Maitland had been the best Master he could ever have hoped for and that he would always remember him.

'Shouldn't we call the police?' asked the girl, making him start. 'Or the army?'

Jones shook his head. 'Ordinary people ain't supposed to know about any of this. It's the way things are. What we call our "Ordnung". The rules we work to.'

'Right. So what the hell's a Badlander then?' blurted out the girl.

The quiet burnt Jones's ears as he studied her, knowing there had to be lots of questions whizzing round her head. He knew if Maitland had still been alive he'd have used magic to make this girl forget everything she'd seen because secrets

17

were supposed to be kept. But Jones didn't know how to do such a thing so he was going to have to explain things even though he was more interested in talking about televisions since the girl had mentioned them. He'd seen them, blinking through the curtains of houses at night when he and Maitland had been out hunting creatures. But whenever he'd crept up close to a screen in a person's home all he'd observed was his own reflection in the black glass.

He took a deep breath before telling the girl what she wanted to know.

'Badlanders fight creatures ordinary people don't believe exist. Ones they think are just made out of imagination and locked in the pages of books. Well, they ain't. They're flesh and bones and blood too. And the Badlands is where we hunt them.'

'And where's that exactly?'

'On the edge of ordinary people's lives most of the time. Like now, at night, when they're normally fast asleep, or perhaps in the heart of a big forest or a deep valley where they never go. But sometimes the Badlands can be right under people's noses where they don't suspect a thing. There's all sorts of creatures living there,' said Jones, thinking of how he'd talked to Arkell in his shop as customers came and went. He pointed at the dead Ogre lying beside Maitland. 'Monsters like that have been around as long as us and there's always been humans rooting 'em out. Some of 'em became the first Badlanders after the Anglo-Saxons came here from Europe, bringing what they knew about hunting.

The earliest monks taught 'em things too when they arrived. Badlanders got trained in monasteries till they set up their own secret order.'

'How old are you?'

Jones blinked. ''Roundabout twelve. I don't know for sure, not like ordinary boys. I ain't like them,' he sighed as he reached into the pocket of his overcoat and drew out a small plastic pot and prised off the lid. Taking a pinch of fine brown dust, he sprinkled it over the body of the Ogre that had killed Maitland. White vapour corkscrewed into the air with a hiss as the creature's body began to dissolve. Moments later, there was nothing left except for white foam, like the curd left by a wave on a beach. Jones kicked through it, sending oily bubbles floating into the air, popping as they rose.

The small silver key weighed heavily in Jones's pocket as he went about disposing of the other Ogre's body.

It had seemed, in the moments after Maitland had died, he had no choice but to honour his Master's wishes and go through with his Commencement. It was what Maitland had been preparing him for, for as long as he could remember. And it was the reason Maitland had been so desperate to give him the key after finally seeing Jones make his first kill. It would unlock everything the boy would need to go on learning about being a Badlander and carry on his Master's legacy.

But then, as Jones had looked down at the girl pleading

for her life, another version of his future had started playing out inside him like a dream. With Maitland gone, he had an opportunity to become what he desperately wanted to be, an ordinary boy. And he knew the girl lying at his feet could help him. His decision to wait and see if she'd turn into an Ogre had already paid off. He hadn't known about foster families. He was already wondering how he might be able to find one with the girl's help. *Surely*, he thought, *I'd be first in the queue for a family, seeing as I don't have no one, now Maitland's gone.*

Something dark tiptoed down Jones's ribs, making him shiver, because it was difficult to accept his Master was dead. But there was something else too, nagging at him. Even now, disobeying Maitland and not going through with his Commencement seemed wrong. He kicked through the white foamy remains of what had once been Arkell and then walked over to Maitland.

The boy prodded Maitland's body with the toe of a boot.

Maitland ain't coming back, thought Jones to himself. *No way. Not even with the magic he knows.*

'Was he your dad?' asked the girl gently.

Jones shook his head. 'He was my everything. Grew me up from a baby after he found me in a cardboard box on the steps of a church one night.' Jones bit his lip. 'I weren't born a Badlander. No one is. You have to be taught how to be one. Badlanders find apprentices however they can.'

'What's your name?'

'Jones.'

'I mean your first name.'

'Maitland only gave me one name, so I'd grow up knowing I was different from normal people. Picked it off the first shopfront he saw after he found me. At least I ain't called *Jones the Greengrocer*,' he said, using one of Maitland's jokes, summoning his best, crooked smile to go with it. But the girl didn't smile back. Her face looked pale and small in the moonlight. Jones figured she was probably still in shock. Or scared. Or both. He decided he was going to have to work very hard at making friends with her if he was going to learn more about how to become an ordinary boy.

'You look cold,' he said, taking off his overcoat and draping it round her shoulders, opening up the collar to keep her neck warm.

'Thanks,' she said.

Jones watched her wander over to her bicycle, trying to imagine how best to ask her to come with him. His mouth opened. But then it closed. There was something else he needed to do first. Kneeling down, he searched through Maitland's trouser pockets until he found a bunch of keys, and then stood up. As he held the small plastic pot above Maitland's body, his hand was trembling. But it was part of the Rules by which they lived, the *Ordnung* they were bound by, and Jones knew Maitland would have done exactly the same to him.

As Jones began to tilt the pot of brown dust, he muttered a little rhyme under his breath:

'Do not be afear'd
It is only the *wyrd*
That says you must go
From this world that you know.

Do not be afear'd
It is only the *wyrd*
That wants you to leave
Which means I won't grieve.

Do not be afear'd
It is only the *wyrd*
That rules all our lives
And always decides

The length of one's life
All its joy, all its strife,
So do not be afear'd
It is only the *wyrd*.'

The dust sparkled as it fell.

The body began to melt.

Something was melting inside Jones too.

And then, for the first time in Jones's life, Maitland was no longer there to tell him what to do next.

Ruby hauled up her bicycle. The back wheel was bent out of shape and the whole thing wobbled as she pushed it backwards and forwards. She could ride it, just. But where would she go now? She didn't want to stay in the cottage after what had happened. But she didn't want to go home to her foster parents either. Her first few weeks with the Taylors hadn't gone well and Ruby knew she'd be moved on eventually, just like all the other times. She never seemed to settle with anyone, which was why she'd decided earlier that day that it was up to her to find a life for herself, seeing as no one else could do it for her.

She watched Jones standing over a line of foam, which was all that was left of Maitland, wondering who this boy was who'd saved her life. She was grateful of course, but what was she supposed to do now? All her excitement at running away suddenly seemed far less thrilling now she knew about the Badlands, that there were dangerous monsters in the world she'd never imagined to be real. And then, in that moment, an idea slipped into her head as though it had fallen from the night sky. What if she became a Badlander like this boy? Learnt how to do magic? She'd be able to leave the old Ruby behind and start a new life as she'd planned, and there'd be no reason to be scared of any monsters then.

Jones heard a distant howl, which he judged too loud and long to belong to any dog.

'I have to go,' he said to the girl. 'It ain't safe staying here any longer. There's something about this place that creatures like.' He clicked the top back onto the plastic pot and measured his next words carefully, unsure how best to go about inviting the girl to come with him. As he stood there, shuffling his feet, trying to work out what to say, the ball of light that Maitland had thrown into the air sputtered and started to dim.

'Look, thanks for saving my life,' blurted out the girl, 'and then for not killing me,' she added. Jones smiled and waited for more. But she seemed to be struggling to know what to say, her mouth opening then closing, then opening again.

As they stared at one another, the revolver on the driveway tutted and muttered, 'Jones, you haven't made any *mearcunga* yet.'

'I ain't bothered 'bout making a mark for the Ogres I killed.'

'Why not? They're your first kills! That makes them important.'

Before Jones could say anything else, the ball of light above them snuffed itself out and disappeared with a loud pop. Jones steeled himself. Suddenly, it felt easier to say what he wanted to the girl, without the light.

'You can come home with me if you like,' he said. 'At least, till you've worked out what you're going to do next.'

'I'd like that,' said the girl quickly. 'Really. As long as you're sure.'

'Yeah. I'm sure.'

As their eyes adjusted to the moonlight, the two of them discovered they were smiling at each other.

'I'm Ruby, by the way.'

Jones nodded as he burst an oily bubble with his boot. Maitland was gone for good. 'We're finished here,' he said and held up the bunch of keys. 'I'll drive.'

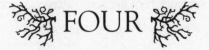

FOUR

The electric-green Volkswagen camper van was a T2 model from 1979. Maitland had restored it with great care after buying it from an old Badlander who had left it sitting around for years. Jones had helped his Master, learning as much as he could, oiling, greasing and connecting the guts of what made the vehicle work. The boy knew far more about engines than other children his age. He could remove the spark plugs and clean them. Fit hoses and test their pressure. Maitland had even taught him how to decarbonize the cylinders by releasing them first and then scraping off the carbon from the heads.

The van's interior had been customized specifically for their needs. There was a gas stove with four hobs and an oven, a tip-up white laminate table and a large number of cupboards for storage. There was even a sink and a small metal draining board. When the table was folded away, the double seats on either side of it could be pulled out to make a bed for Maitland. Jones slept on a thin mattress laid across the two front seats, usually curled up like a cat after a long day. In the case of a stake-out or a long hunting trip, the camper van was a home from home.

Jones loved it because he was allowed to drive. Using magic, Maitland had charmed the windows and windscreen to make it appear he was driving when Jones was at the wheel. The driver's seat could be levered up enough for the boy to see the road, and the pedals had all been extended too. Whenever Jones was driving, Maitland could rest, work on concocting potions and charms, or plan ahead for the next eventuality whenever they were out on a job. Being able to drive also meant Jones was useful in any emergency.

It was invaluable now.

Ruby gripped the edges of her seat and swallowed nervously as Jones turned the key and the engine growled into life. He let off the handbrake, selected first gear without a hitch, and then eased out of the field, where the van had been hidden, into the lane.

The headlights bored through the dark tunnel in front of them, an effect created by the high hedges on either side. Occasionally the moon bobbed up in the sky then disappeared again. Ruby's bicycle rattled from time to time as it rested against the table in the main body of the van next to her backpack.

The boy seemed to know exactly what he was doing as he worked the wheel gently, following the lane's twists and turns.

To test how hard he was concentrating, and to put her mind at rest, Ruby drew out a stick of gum from the pack in her pocket. But Jones didn't look away from the road, not even when she unwrapped it, and pinched it into a 'w' before placing it in her mouth, and began to chew noisily. Satisfied he was focused entirely on the job at hand, she leant back in the leather seat. So, here she was in a van at the dead of night, being driven by a boy not only about the same age as her, but one who'd also just saved her from an Ogre. It had been a dangerous one apparently. Jones had informed her on their walk to the van that it had been not only a shapeshifter partial to a bit of moon-bathing, but a Berserker class too. Had someone told her anything like this was going to happen before she'd crept out of her foster parents' house she would have laughed in their face.

Where it was all going to lead she wasn't entirely sure. But she could imagine the mayhem in the morning when her foster mother saw the empty bed. She knew people would blame her for all the inconvenience that would inevitably follow because that was how things normally turned out for Ruby.

She closed her eyes and placed her hands on her ears. The prickly noise sounded to her as though she was underwater, and in her mind's eye she imagined that she was swimming in a warm sea with a tropical island all of her own close by. It was a trick she'd learnt for whenever the world seemed too difficult a place for her to deal with, usually when things seemed to be happening that were outside of her control.

Ruby felt a tug on her arm. She pulled her hands away from her ears, allowing the grumble of the camper van's

engine back in. Jones's eyes were darting from the road ...
to her ... and back again.

'You all right?' he asked with genuine concern.

'I'm fine. It's just something I do to shut out the world.' She
chewed her gum and smiled. But it seemed to bounce off the
boy right back at her. 'When I need a time-out.'

Jones thought for a moment and then nodded. He had
never heard of a *time-out*, but he knew exactly what she
meant. He gave her another look. 'How come you never
swallow what you're eating?'

'Are you telling me you've never tried gum?'

When Jones shook his head, Ruby dug out the packet and
unwrapped another piece. Keeping both hands on the wheel,
Jones opened his mouth like a baby bird as Ruby folded the
stick of gum into his mouth.

'Keep chewing,' advised Ruby, 'and don't swallow it.'

They sat quietly, their mouths cow-chewing round, until
a muffled voice broke the silence.

'Get geee out o' 'ere.'

Ruby squirmed in her seat and pulled out the gun from
the pocket of Jones's overcoat, which she was still wearing.

'Jones!' it spluttered. 'We need to talk.'

''Bout what?' asked Jones between his chewing.

'About what happens next of course.'

'Not now. It ain't the right time,' said Jones, and the
revolver grumbled something under its breath.

Ruby had never held a gun before and she wasn't sure she
liked the feel of it. Its grumbling did little to endear it to

her either. So she placed it carefully on the dashboard, the muzzle pointing away from her.

'How come you couldn't pick it up?' she asked, looking at Jones.

The gun laughed, replying before the boy. 'Maitland put a charm on me. If Jones so much as touches me with a finger, I'll shoot him with pepper spray. Of course, Maitland never told him to start with, so the stupid boy got into trouble the first time curiosity got the better of him.'

'I was only young,' Jones said to Ruby. 'I only wanted to see how it felt to hold it.'

'What did Maitland always teach you, boy?' chuckled the gun.

'Trust is the cornerstone of any true friendship,' said Jones as though reciting it out loud in class. 'Especially for Masters and their apprentices who've got to rely on each other in the Badlands.'

'And it's a charm that means you can speak?' Ruby asked the revolver.

'It's charmed to do lots of things,' said Jones. 'Like firing any type of bullet you want whenever you need it.'

'And how do things get charmed?'

'With magic of course,' snapped the revolver. 'How else do you think Badlanders survive hunting creatures? They know how to control magic. It's their greatest secret. Once an apprentice does their Commencement, they're given the gift of magic, and then they can start to learn how to use it, charms ... spells, whatever you need. Isn't that right, Jones?'

30

'P'r'aps,' said the boy, shrugging and saying nothing more.

'Commencement?' asked Ruby.

'That's why Maitland handed over the key before he died,' said the gun. 'So Jo-wheeyyyy—'

Jones swerved the van so hard to the left the revolver hurtled across the dashboard and dropped into the pocket in the door beside him. 'Bloomin' fox,' said Jones without taking his eyes off the road, nimbly jamming a cloth on top of the gun to stop it sliding about, and muffle whatever it was saying.

Ruby sat back in her seat, wondering how different the world would be for her if she could use magic. It would be easy to be rich or have whatever you wanted. Perhaps she'd make her parents want to see her again. She liked the word *Commencement*. It sounded official and important.

Something in the other pocket of Jones's overcoat was digging uncomfortably into her hip, and she pulled out a slim red book called:

The Badlander Bestiary
Pocket Book Version

When she flicked through it, all the pages were blank.

'It only tells you things when you ask it,' said Jones. 'You could fill up three or four vans with just the basic books on creatures. There's a lot that can kill you in the Badlands.' He pointed to a newspaper cutting from the *Independent* dated

2009 taped to the dashboard with the headline: **The Missing: Each year, 275,000 Britons disappear**. 'It says most people turn up again,' said Jones. 'But there's others who don't, and now you know the big reason why. That's why Maitland stuck it there,' he said, 'to remind us how important our job is.'

An hour later, when Jones turned off the engine, the thatched cottage loomed in the headlights like something out of a fairy tale. Ruby was asleep, her head on her shoulder, and a curl of black hair hung down over her brow, vibrating as she breathed.

Quietly, so as not to wake her, Jones lifted the cloth off the gun in the pocket of the door. 'Can you hear me down there?'

'Are we finally home?' it muttered.

'Yes.'

'Then get the girl to pick me up, boy. There's enough dust and muck in here to choke me,' it grumbled.

Jones leant in closer, lowering his voice. 'You ain't to talk to Ruby about magic or Commencement or anything else.'

'Because?'

'Because none of it matters. I'm not gonna be a Badlander.'

There was a loud tutting. 'I knew there was a reason you didn't bother marking your kills tonight. I always thought you'd be a disappointment to Maitland, boy, and now you're being one after he's dead. So what about me? What's going to happen to me?'

But Jones didn't reply. He touched Ruby's arm gently instead. 'Ruby?'

The girl moved. Her eyes were big and slow when she opened them. She'd been dreaming about owning a magic wand and making every day her birthday. 'We're here,' said Jones, pointing at the cottage.

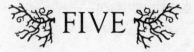

FIVE

When they opened the front door, the lamps in the hallway came on by themselves. None of them had plugs or cords. Ruby wondered what else might be different to a normal house.

'Wait here,' said Jones as he began walking away from her, 'and don't touch anything,' he cautioned, before disappearing through a doorway at the end of the hallway. Ruby had the feeling she was standing in a well-run antiques shop, or an old person's house, because the furniture looked so worn and none of it matched. She ran a finger along the wooden dresser beside her. Not one speck of dust. She put down her backpack and quietly cleared her throat.

'Abracadabra,' she whispered, twirling her arm and pointing a finger at a lamp on the dresser. But it didn't switch off. The gun in her pocket started laughing and she knew it must have heard her. Ruby's face turned red with embarrassment.

'How about doing something ordinary,' the gun said

through its giggles. 'There's a walnut case I'm normally kept in, in Maitland's study. I'd like to go back there.'

'But Jones said—'

'It'll only take a minute. He'll only have to ask you to do it eventually because he can't pick me up.'

'Yeah, but—'

'I'll show you more magic, if that's what you want?'

Keen to see as much as she could of magic, Ruby took out the gun, heaving off Jones's overcoat, leaving it in a heap on the red velvet seat of a chair.

'Go down the hallway,' said the gun. 'Then first left and keep going.'

Ruby followed the dark red carpet down the hall, turning left into another long corridor. Light bulbs wearing shades, floating below the ceiling, came on as Ruby walked beneath them, and she smiled.

'They're all charmed by Maitland to come on at night when somebody walks past, just like the ones in the hall. But that's nothing,' said the gun. 'Not compared to all the other things Maitland could do.'

'Like the ball of light above the cottage earlier?'

'Kids' stuff!' exclaimed the gun. 'There's all sorts of things you can learn if you become a Badlander.'

'Me? A Badlander?' Ruby tried to sound surprised, but her mind was racing, already imagining how good she might be with magic.

'Oh, no!' laughed the gun. 'There's never been a girl Badlander.'

'Why not?'

'It's against the *Ordnung*. Girls can't learn magic.' Ruby stopped, her face wrinkling up as if she'd just bitten into a lemon. 'It's tradition, and you can't change that, can you?'

'But—'

'However . . .' and the gun cleared its throat for dramatic effect. 'I do have an alternative proposition you might be interested in. You and me could team up anyway. Just imagine it, us hunting together. We'd show all those Badlanders where to stick their *Ordnung*. We might even become famous if you stayed alive long enough that is.'

Ruby walked on down the corridor. Working with the gun sounded exciting. But, very quickly, she decided it wouldn't be nearly as good as being able to do spells and charms. *Becoming the first girl Badlander to use magic, now that would be something really special*, she thought, immediately wondering how such a thing might be possible, given what she'd heard about this *Ordnung* so far. But she kept it to herself. 'Can I think it over?' she said. 'It was all pretty scary earlier.'

'As you wish. But remember, I'm a gun of the very highest calibre that any Badlander would be desperate to own. There's paperwork to prove it.'

They reached a heavy oak door and the gun instructed Ruby to open it which she did, revealing Maitland's study. A large chandelier floating below the ceiling began to glow, making the wood floor seem to move as the light caught it.

There was a musty smell of old parchment and ink. The

36

walls were lined with shelves crammed full of books and Ruby scanned the titles in the row nearest to her – *The Complete Guide to Goblins of Eastern Europe. Goblins and their Eating Habits. Good Goblins, Just a Myth?* Another shelf contained books all about trolls. After glancing at the first title – *Troll Teeth, a Fascinating Insight (Gums and All)* – she gave up looking and moved across to another wall where all the books had the same black spine although each one had a different number on it written in gold. She plucked out Number 27 and opened it to pages of neat black handwriting.

'They're Maitland's journals,' said the gun. 'He's written down an account of every hunt he's ever undertaken. You'll find me mentioned in many of them.'

Ruby flicked through the pages and paused at one of the entries.

Hunt 27.8
17th July, 1992
Ghoul – Marlow, Buckinghamshire

Below it was a brief account of how Maitland had hunted down and despatched a Ghoul he'd discovered lurking in an abandoned house. Careful notes had been made of what weapons had been used as well as a magic spell that had been cast, although its name was written in a language Ruby did not understand. She looked up at the shelves. The journals were numbered all the way up to Number 103.

'Maitland was a very good Badlander,' said the revolver.

'One of the best. I should know because I only work with the best of the best. It is,' it said with a slight tremble in its voice, 'very sad to know he's gone. We had so many adventures. He was the one who charmed me to talk. I suppose now at least I will be able to tell others of his great deeds. Now, if you don't mind, it's been a long day. I go in the wooden case on the desk. It's charmed to keep me clean and polished, of which I am in great need.'

The large desk in the middle of the room was covered with piles of papers and stacks of books and notebooks. Beneath the mess, Ruby could see patches of a green leather top, embossed with a line of gold around its edge. After opening the dark wooden box, she laid the gun down on the red velvet inlay.

'So we'll talk more about my offer tomorrow? About being famous, you and me?'

'Sure,' said Ruby and she put on her best winning smile. As she closed the lid, she heard the gun sigh with the sort of contentment that reminded her of getting into bed after a long day. But Ruby didn't feel tired now.

She wheeled out the chair from the desk and sat down on the cracked brown leather seat, in the depression that Maitland's weight must have made over the years. The back of the chair creaked as she leant away from the desk, making the same noise as she leant forward again. Her eyes were drawn to a human skull, sitting on the far left corner of the desk, which Maitland had obviously used as a paperweight. The bone was smooth and shiny and the skull looked in good condition, but the teeth were black and sharp, like large lead pencil points. Fascinated, Ruby reached across the desk and hooked her fingers into the eye sockets as though she was picking up a bowling ball. She placed the skull on a stack of books in front of her.

'Not so scary now, are you?' she whispered. 'No match for a Badlander.' The name sounded good rolling off her tongue. 'That's Ruby Jenkins to you. Ruby Jenkins the Badlander, the first girl to ever work the Badlands and do magic. That'd show them where to stick their *Ordnung* for sure.'

A glimmer of movement caught Ruby's eye, and she looked into a large glass jar sitting on another corner of the desk, with a grey mist swirling inside it, the lid screwed on tight. She was sure it had been empty before. Leaning across for a better look, she jumped when two green eyes materialized and blinked. A small mouth appeared and grinned, revealing tiny yellow teeth that looked like the thorns on a bramble. A single finger with a long nail appeared as the mouth breathed on the inside of the jar, fogging the glass. The tip of the fingernail drew some tiny words carefully in reverse for her to read:

LET US OUT

Ruby sat back in the chair, deciding it was probably not a good idea to open the jar. Instead, she explored the three drawers on the left side of the desk. They were largely empty except for pencils and blank sheets of paper, and in the bottom-most one was a small copper-coloured key. Trying the only drawer on her right, Ruby discovered it was locked.

When she tried the small coppery key, she discovered it fitted snugly into the keyhole, and turned it. The drawer was empty. At least, it appeared to be, until an oval-shaped black stone rolled into view. Ruby didn't think twice about picking it up because it looked so pretty, with tiny veins of silver running over its surface. It was much lighter than she'd expected, and very cold too.

The stone changed colour immediately, to a dark red, as if reacting to the warmth of her hand, and the silver veins vanished as a crack appeared around its middle. A tiny gassy sound escaped from Ruby's throat as she realized that what she was holding wasn't a stone at all, but some sort of egg.

Before she could put it back in the drawer, the top half of the egg had been pushed off by a small furry muzzle, and a minuscule puppy, the size of a baby bird, with fur as black as night, emerged with fragments of shell stuck to its coat. Ruby stared at the creature as it scrambled out of the remains of the egg, kicking it onto the floor, and into Ruby's hand. The puppy scrabbled up into a sitting position in her palm and sat, blinking at Ruby, mewling like any newborn.

Ruby wasn't sure what to make of the creature. Clearly, it wasn't a normal dog, not just because of its size but its black fur was prickly and the ears were marked with red tips that matched its red eyes. When it tried to stand up, only to fall straight down again on Ruby's uneven hand, her heart melted and she cooed at it, nudging it to get up with a finger. After managing to stand up on all four wobbly legs, it opened its mouth and Ruby thought it was yawning, and the sweetest thing she'd ever seen.

But then it bit down on her finger with teeth as sharp as pins.

Ruby gasped, shaking her hand to try and throw the creature off. But it clung on tight with its claws. When she tried picking it off with her other hand, the puppy growled, showing its white teeth streaky with blood. And it bit down on her finger again, making Ruby gag when a tiny half-moon appeared just below her middle knuckle.

In a panic, she picked up the nearest object to hand, which happened to be the skull, and swung it as best she could, hitting the tiny beast, and sending it flying through the air. It spread like a black four-pointed star when it hit the large glass jar, and then slid down onto the desk and didn't move.

The jar wobbled, then fell off the edge of the desk before Ruby could reach out to try and grab it. She heard it smash on the wooden floor.

Jones was busy under the sink in the kitchen when he heard Ruby scream. He was trying to reach for a vase for some pansies he'd hurriedly picked from the garden to try and make a good impression. He straightened up, cracking his head on the underside of a cold copper pipe, and cursed.

A gurgle of laughter floated through the house as Jones rushed out of the kitchen, and he recognized it immediately.

41

When he heard another scream, Jones hurried to Maitland's study and pushed open the heavy oak door.

Ruby was cowering, barefoot, in one corner of the room as five grey-scaled imps stood on her shoulders, pulling her hair. Each imp was the length of a human hand, with pointed ears and a forked tail, and sharp yellow teeth and green eyes. Two more of the creatures were sitting on the floor, pulling out the laces from her trainers and trying to unpeel the soles, while a further two were perched on a bookshelf, unpicking the threads of her white woollen socks with their long fingernails.

When Jones clapped his hands, the imps stopped what they were doing immediately.

'In a line, now!' he shouted and the creatures quickly made a row in front of him, arms behind their backs like naughty schoolchildren. Jones prodded the toe of a boot through the glass on the floor. He was far more surprised when he saw the tiny black dog lying motionless on the edge of the desk. When the boy picked up the creature by the scruff of its neck, it drooped like a dead flower.

'It bit me,' sniffed Ruby.

'Course he did,' snapped Jones. 'He'll have been hungry, cos he just hatched. And I wonder how that happened?' he asked sarcastically. Jones studied the creature and saw the blood around its muzzle, matching the red tips on its ears.

'Is it dead?' asked Ruby as Jones felt for a pulse in its throat.

'No. *Scucca* hounds are pretty tough, even pups. He'll live.' Jones picked out a tiny piece of dark red shell caught in the little dog's coat. 'Me and Maitland were going to study him and see if we could train him to hunt creatures. *Scuccan* have a nose for the supernatural, 'specially the undead and the like. It's very rare to find a *Scucca's ægg*,' he said rather proudly. 'You have to know where to look in a graveyard at just the right time. How much did he bite off you?' Ruby held up her finger. 'Hmm,' said the boy.

'Is it bad?' asked Ruby, who couldn't bear to look.

'No. It's not enough to make him grow much—'

'I *meant* my finger.'

'Oh,' said Jones and then he grinned. 'Well, he didn't eat all of you, did he?' he joked, hoping Ruby would see the funny side. But her face told him she didn't. When one of the imps sputtered a laugh, Jones shot it a disapproving stare.

'You three,' he said, pointing to one end of the line. 'Dustpan and brush from the cupboard in the hall. Next three, there's an empty tin box in the bottom of the wardrobe in my bedroom. Bring it down. Final three, fetch another jar from the larder in the kitchen big enough for all of you.' This last request was met with a chorus of disapproving groans. But when Jones clapped his hands all the imps scattered out of the door.

Ruby studied her finger. 'I'm sorry,' she said.

The imps swept the floor and placed the skull back on the desk. They gave Ruby back her shoes, with the laces threaded back, and one of them found her a new pair of socks. When they'd finished, Jones made them clamber one by one into the new jar, disappearing into a grey mist, and then he propped the lid loosely on top and traced a symbol on it with a finger. A flurry of white sparks rose up around the lid, which then proceeded to screw itself tight onto the jar, stopping with a loud click.

'It ain't proper magic, if that's what you're wondering,' said Jones when he saw Ruby staring, her eyes as big as plates. 'Anyone could lock those imps in if they knew what symbol to write. All I did was use the power over 'em that's already there from Maitland's magic. It's the only reason the imps do what I say. There's all sorts of charms and spells working round the house, carrying on even though Maitland's gone. He made 'em that way in case anything happened to him on a hunt.'

'So that's what your Commencement's about. Being able to do magic for yourself?'

'Yeah.'

'And that's why Maitland gave you that key?'

Jones nodded slowly as he cursed the gun under his breath for mentioning it on the journey home. Rummaging in his pocket, he held up the silver key. It was simple looking. Small. Ruby decided she would have thought nothing of it if she'd found it in a drawer or lying on the floor.

'If I use it the way it tells me to,' said Jones, 'I'll get the gift of magic. But that's the easy part. Then you got to learn how to use magic properly, and that takes years.' He held the key close to Ruby's ear and she heard the slightest whisper, a silvery voice, telling her it could unlock the secret of magic

44

for whoever used it. And then Jones whisked it away before she could hear any more.

'But it's worth it, though, right?' asked Ruby, her eyes bright. 'So you can do things other people can't?'

Jones shook his head.

'Maitland always told me once you've got the gift of magic then you have to keep your distance from ordinary people otherwise they'll want you to do things for them. Magic makes you different. And being different from everyone else ain't much to talk about if you ask me.' Jones studied the key in his hand. 'I'm going to throw this key away so I can wear proper clothes. Have friends. Go to school. I know how the world is if you're not a Badlander, bits of it anyway. There's lots of wonders in it without needing to do magic.'

'You mean you want to be an ordinary boy?'

Jones nodded. 'I thought you could show me how? I'm a good learner. Maitland wouldn't have kept me on as his apprentice otherwise.' Jones puffed out his chest proudly, like a sparrow in the cold.

As Ruby stared at Jones with his tired eyes and his narrow, pinched face, she wasn't entirely sure he'd ever fit into the ordinary world she knew. She wondered if he'd be so keen on it if he knew what it was really like being a kid, with adults telling you what to do all the time, and good friends hard to come by, as well as school getting in the way of doing far more interesting things. But she smiled and nodded. 'Of course we can talk about it.' Jones watched her eyes flitting towards the key in his hand and guessed what was secretly on her mind.

'There's never been a girl Badlander,' he said. 'That's the code. The *Ordnung* we live by. You can't Commence cos girls ain't allowed the gift of magic.'

Ruby made a face. 'This *Ordnung* sounds pretty stupid if you ask me. Girls are just as good as boys. That's how it is in the modern world. Your rules are way behind the times.'

'Yeah, I think so too, that's why I want to change. One reason anyway,' and Jones furrowed his brow. 'Maitland told me something else about magic: it's dangerous unless you learn to control it. There's Badlanders who've gone mad because of it. Done terrible things.' He tapped the side of his head. 'I reckon once it's in there it rots your brain if you're not careful. So this key's going, as soon as I work out how to get rid of it properly,' and Jones stuffed the key away in his trouser pocket.

He rubbed his eyes and did such a huge yawn he thought his jaw might split. 'You gotta be tired too,' he said, blinking at Ruby. 'I'll show you where you can sleep.' He picked up the tin box the imps had brought from his bedroom, into which the tiny black dog had been safely placed, and left without another word.

Ruby took one more look around the study, imagining what it would be like to do magic. She smiled to herself at the very idea of such a thing. When she realized the skull on Maitland's desk was staring at her, as if disapproving of everything she'd done and what she was thinking about now, her smile disappeared. 'Girls are just as good as boys,' she whispered before leaving and shutting the door behind her.

But, if she'd looked more closely at the skull, she might have realized something. That the stripe of blood she'd left on it from hitting the *Scucca* off her finger had vanished long ago into the bone and in its place now was a very fine fuzz of hair. Ruby might even have seen tiny blood vessels laced into the surface of the skull's cheeks. And, if Ruby had stared long and hard enough into the eye sockets, she would have seen a very faint orange glow.

SIX

Ruby clicked the bedroom door shut and immediately felt a great wave of exhaustion pass through her. There was a single bed, neatly made with a red blanket, in the far corner and she was glad to see it. A wardrobe stood solemnly against one wall. She dumped her backpack down and stood listening to the silence.

As she drew the curtains, she looked out across the fields rolling away into the distance, silvered by the moon. She wondered what else might be out there right now in the Badlands that Jones had described, in the places ordinary people wouldn't think to look. Perhaps there were Ogres moon-bathing in another garden, or Trolls just as vicious walking silently into someone's bedroom right at this moment, teeth bared.

After turning out the light and pulling up the covers to her chin, Ruby decided, even though she was tucked into yet another strange bed, things would be different this time. She wasn't going to be told what to do any more by anyone. Not social workers nor foster parents. Not even Jones. And definitely not this stupid *Ordnung* she'd been hearing so much about. Here was a chance to do something different and exciting for the first time ever in her life and she was going to grab it. When she rolled over and closed her eyes, she imagined the small silver key immediately, and wondered about the secrets it might unlock, before sleep rolled into her, carrying her away to a foreign, dreamy land.

Jones worked his way around the house, checking all the windows and the doors were locked, just as Maitland had done every night. Everything belonged to the boy now. That was the Rule. But he was sure he didn't want any of it. Magic was dangerous; he knew that because Maitland had told him, and he didn't want anything to do with it. Ever since he'd been old enough to start hunting with his Master he'd been fascinated by the ordinary world he was being trained to protect, where children it seemed were free to just be themselves. The more he glimpsed this world, the more he wanted to be a part of it.

By the time he'd finished locking up, he was tired, but there was one more thing to do before he went to bed.

The small bush was growing in the huge back garden, hidden behind a mass of bracken and nettles. Jones had planted its single seed there on purpose in the early spring, to keep it out of sight of Maitland as it grew. He'd watered it every day or as near enough as he could. And he'd fed it each week with his own blood, a few drops squeezed from a toe, scared that Maitland might question any marks or redness on his fingers. The bush needed his blood to stay alive because the seed had been taken from his own body, cut from inside his belly button using a sharp knife, where one of Maitland's books had told him it would be. A seed to grow a memory bush.

Jones stood in the moonlight and watered the bush as normal. But this time he tramped down all the nettles and bracken around it too to give it more space to grow, not scared any longer about Maitland discovering it. As the watering can ran dry, and he turned to go back to the cottage, he caught sight of a tiny fruit hidden among the thorny leaves of the bush. It was round and purplish, about the size of a blueberry.

Excited, Jones knelt down. Maitland's book had told him that producing a berry was very rare, and Jones explored the rest of the bush carefully for any more. But he found nothing else except for a flower, which held the promise of another fruit later on.

When he reached to take the berry, the bush folded its little branches around itself, as if scared of losing the one tiny fruit it had grown.

'I ain't gonna hurt you,' said Jones softly. 'But I got to take this berry. Maitland's gone, so I got to start finding out about who I am. I'll keep looking after you, I promise. I won't stop. But I got to try and remember where I came from before Maitland found me. Maybe I've got someone who'd like to see me.' He pulled up his shirt to reveal the little red scar inside his belly button. 'You're a part of me, remember? I wouldn't ever forget that.'

Slowly, the bush's branches parted, allowing Jones to pluck the berry from its woody stem. He held it carefully in between his fingers, remembering exactly what Maitland's book had told him to do, something he'd memorized in anticipation of a moment like this ever happening.

'I want to remember the last time I saw my mother or father,' he said firmly. 'I want to see 'em to give me a chance of finding out about 'em.' He placed the fruit in his mouth. The berry's skin popped as he bit down, its flesh sweet and sharp like a cherry. He swallowed and waited, nervous about what he might see, wondering whether it might explain why he'd been left on the steps of the church where Maitland had found him.

Very quickly, Jones had the urge to close his eyes. He stared into the black inside him as a memory started playing out, crystal clear like a piece of film, and he was . . .

. . . *staring up into the face of a woman with dark hair and green eyes. She was making little cooing noises as she rocked him gently. And then she turned and admired herself in the full-length mirror behind her and Jones could see she was holding a baby only a few months old, dressed in a blue Babygro. It was him! He was looking at himself! So the woman, this beautiful dark-haired, green-eyed woman, was his mother.*

As she laid him down in his cot, Jones caught sight of two other people in the mirror, coming in through the doorway. The first was a man, blond and blue-eyed and handsome. The second was a plump, middle-aged woman. She was about fifty years old. Her brown hair was pulled back tight in a bun.

'Angela wanted to see him before you put him down,' said the man as he embraced the dark-haired woman around her waist and they both looked down, smiling at the baby Jones in his cot. There was a mobile of silver stars and a crescent moon spinning silently above him, but the plump woman's face blocked them out as she bent down to look at Jones, a big smile on her kindly face. She had perfect white teeth and thick red lips and pure, unblemished skin. She sniffed the air like he was a pie that had just been baked.

'Oh,' she cooed. 'What a cutie. He's adorable. You must be so proud.'

'Yes, we are,' replied the man. 'But let's leave him to sleep now. We're trying to stick to a routine so we can get some sleep too,' he laughed. And then all three adults were leaving the room, a hand flicking off the light switch before the door was shut.

Jones gurgled and burbled, his legs kicking. But then he became still as, through the bars of his cot, he watched a man, wearing a baseball cap and a greatcoat, drifting out of the wall like a ghost. It was Maitland with the gun.

The baby Jones didn't make a sound as Maitland leant down and picked him up. The man began whispering words. Up and down his voice went, until he stopped abruptly and plucked a single brown hair from the baby's head. As soon as he laid it on the mattress in the centre of the cot, it started to sprout out of its root-end. A scalp materialized in a matter of moments with thousands more brown hairs growing out of it. But it didn't stop there. Soon, a baby-sized head was lying in the cot. Blank at first, but then, very quickly, the details of Jones's face appeared. The eyes. His mouth. His lips. Maitland held the real Jones close to him as the replica baby kept growing. A neck came next, sprouting shoulders and arms below it, followed by a body and legs, until a brand-new version of Jones was lying in the cot, wearing a blue Babygro. Maitland nodded, satisfied, and then he was carrying the real Jones with him out of the bedroom.

He crept down the stairs and into the hallway. He stole past a room with its door shut, beyond which voices could be heard talking and laughing.

There was a pile of open mail on a dresser. Coats hanging on pegs.

Maitland opened the front door quietly, clicked it shut behind him, and then he was running down the path into a quiet residential road lit by the orange glow of street lights. Jones could hear the rush of air around them, the sound of Maitland breathing hard, and the gun chuntering on about something.

Maitland turned down one street . . . and then another . . . and then another.

He passed a row of shops and there was a name above one of them: Jones the Greengrocer.

'Jones,' said Maitland. 'That's your new name now, boy.'

And then the memory stopped running and everything faded to black.

When Jones opened his eyes, he was still standing in the garden, the sharp taste of the memory fruit ringing in his mouth. His fists were clenched so hard they looked like little rocks in the moonlight. Everything Maitland had said about finding him was a lie. All the guilt Jones had been feeling about not obeying his Master and remaining a Badlander hardened into something else. It was anger.

Moments later, he was sprinting back to the house, his heart pounding in his ears.

The gun was snoring when Jones opened its wooden case and tipped it out onto the floor of Maitland's study.

'What the devi—'

'You and Maitland were lying all along.'

'What are you t—'

'You never found me on the steps of no church.'

'What's got into you, boy? What are you talking about? Have you been dreaming?'

Jones crouched down beside it. 'No. I've been remembering. I've been growing a memory bush. And tonight I found a fruit and when I ate it I saw the truth as clear as day. You and Maitland stole me from my parents. My mum had black hair and green eyes and my dad was blond and handsome. And you took me from 'em, right out of my cot with the stars and the moon hanging above it.'

And, for the first time, the gun was speechless.

'Tell me who they are,' demanded Jones. 'Where I came from.'

'Please, Jones,' implored the gun, turning its muzzle away from him. 'I can't.'

But Jones just growled. 'I know what some Badlanders get up to, stealing kids to train 'em up when they don't have no one and leaving a *fæcce* in their place to get ill and die. I know cos I met other apprentices what told me. And now I know Maitland was a Badlander who did it too, who stole me for his apprentice. So who were they?' he shouted. 'Tell me about my parents!'

'You can't ask me anything. You can't.'

'Why not?'

The revolver shuddered. 'Jones, don't ask any more questions. You can't—'

'Who are the—'

Before the boy could finish, the revolver fired a shot and the bullet pinged into the wall behind him. Jones kept very still for a moment. Shaking. His breathing coming in tiny bursts. His right ear was ringing. Gingerly, he touched it and found a tender graze.

Shocked, Jones opened his mouth.

But the gun shuddered again. 'Jones! No more questions. Please! It's another charm. I can't tell you or anyone else about the things you want to know. Maitland wanted it kept a secret.'

Jones closed his mouth. Even though he was desperate to

know more he knew he had no way of breaking the charm on the gun.

Furiously, he started working his way round Maitland's study, searching in drawers, pulling books from their shelves, desperate to find out more about what he'd remembered. But he found nothing.

Jones raced upstairs into Maitland's bedroom and looked beneath the mattress of the brass bed, and then he dropped to his knees and felt around for any loose floorboards that might be concealing something beneath them. Still nothing.

Remembering that Maitland's book had said the effect of the fruit would gradually wear off, he sat on the floor of his dead Master's bedroom, trying to see the memory again, hoping to spot any clues about where his parents might have lived. Eventually, after watching it through twice more, he found one. As Maitland reached the end of the street in which Jones's parents' house stood, Jones saw a wrought-iron street sign screwed to a low wall that was about the same height as Maitland's knees. Black letters on a white painted background read:

Chesterford Gardens
NW3

He found a pen and a piece of paper and wrote down this information. Then he went downstairs and let himself out into the driveway where the VW camper van was parked.

Sliding back the main door, he clambered in and pulled out a pile of road atlases stashed in a locker and started looking through them until he found the one he wanted: *The Postcode Atlas of Great Britain and Northern Ireland.* In the past, he and Maitland had used postcodes to find particular places on a hunt, so he knew exactly how to find the postcode he'd seen in the memory.

NW3, he discovered, was a postcode district in north London in an area called Hampstead. On the map, it was boundaried with a bold red line and shaped like a tiny landlocked country. To Jones, it seemed like he'd discovered the country of his birth. Eager to find out more, the boy put away the atlas and looked up Chesterford Gardens in an A–Z street map of London. He smiled when he found it, recalling how the street had looked in his memory, and the brief glimpse of his parents' house. But his excitement soon faded as he thought about the lie Maitland had told him.

After putting away the map, Jones returned to the study and knelt beside the gun. 'I'll find them,' he whispered. 'I know where they lived when Maitland stole me. London. In a place called Hampstead. I even know what street it was. So I'm going to find my parents and be a normal boy again like I was supposed to be all along. I'm going to go to school. Have friends. Watch television. And I won't have to hunt in the Badlands ever again cos I won't have to be Jones, the boy who was never loved by no one, not even Maitland who lied to him.'

'London!' scoffed the gun. 'You know full well you won't last there long on your own. Maitland taught you it's dangerous, full of creatures and people who aren't always what they seem. You should leave it well alone, boy!'

Jones turned out the light and left the gun lying on the floor, ignoring its pleas to forget about the past and focus instead on what Maitland had wanted him to do, to use the key and Commence.

As he got ready for bed, he heard a soft silver voice calling his name. It was the key in his pocket, repeating what the gun had told him to do.

'I ain't never using you,' he growled back. He hid the key away so it wouldn't disturb him, deciding to dispose of it properly in the morning when he'd worked out the best way to do it.

After the boy had climbed into bed, he lay in the dark, listening to the ticking and grumbling of the house. Then, without any warning, Jones started crying, and he rolled over and buried his face in his cold pillow, trying to stop all the hate and pain and anger coming out of his mouth and his eyes.

Jones had no idea that, down in the dark study, there was something listening to the gun muttering about Jones and his plans. It was the skull with sharp black teeth that had been on Maitland's desk, and which was now lying on the floor in a corner. Jones had hurled it there in a rage as he'd searched the study, which was why he hadn't noticed the fine covering of hair on the scalp or even the tiny eyes staring out. And not even the beginnings of a tongue that was sprouting like a tiny pink bulb. As it lay there in the dark, the thin red flesh of its slowly forming lips managed a vague smile.

SEVEN

As the early morning sun tried to peek round the curtains, Ruby crept into Jones's bedroom. She watched his face twitching as he slept and wondered what horrors he might be seeing in his dreams.

The boy's clothes from the day before were heaped on a chair and Ruby checked them, turning out the pockets of his trousers. But she didn't find what she was looking for.

She looked on top of the dresser but there was only a wooden hairbrush, nail clippers and a pair of black socks rolled into a ball. She tried the drawers, opening and closing each one as quietly as she could, but found only some clean underwear, shirts and trousers. There was no sign of the key on the boy's bedside table either.

Ruby began to panic as she wondered if Jones had disposed of it already. But then, in the silence, she heard a tiny voice she recognized calling her name in a silvery-sounding whisper. Jones rolled over in his sleep, threatening to wake up, as Ruby listened for it again.

Hearing her name a second time, she looked down. The

voice seemed to be coming from underneath her feet. When it called to her once more, she realized it was definitely coming from beneath the wooden floor and knelt down. Seeing a hole, where a knot of wood might once have been, she hooked her finger in and pulled, lifting up a piece of floorboard. Resting on two dusty copper pipes was a blue woollen sock. The voice called her name again, telling her what she knew already, that it was the key, hidden in the sock. Frightened Jones might wake up, she grabbed it and stuffed it into the front pocket of the hoodie she was wearing, and suddenly the voice went quiet. As the boy moved again in his sleep and Ruby watched him, she told herself not to feel guilty about what she was doing. Jones may have saved her life, but if he wasn't interested in doing magic then she most certainly was, so why let the opportunity go to waste? Ruby clicked the floorboard back down and crept towards the door, hoping the key would tell her what to do next as Jones had said it would for him, because she had no idea at all how to use it.

Standing on the landing, she popped the key out of the sock into her hand. Urgently, it began telling her exactly where she needed to go and what to do. Ruby made for the stairs as quietly and as quickly as she could, her heart pounding, excited that, finally, she was going to do something to make her life better.

When she arrived in front of a door downstairs, Ruby took a deep breath before opening it. Stretching out in front of her was a long room with a red carpet. Early morning

61

daylight was streaming in through a large bay window at the far end. And below the windowsill stood a large wooden chest.

Through the window, Ruby could see a large piece of lawn glistening with dew and she knew it was going to be a bright, sunny day. *A perfect day for a new beginning*, she thought as she started walking towards the wooden chest, the key gripped tight in her hand.

Stuffed animals were mounted on the left-hand wall in glass boxes. Some she recognized. Foxes. Rabbits. Squirrels. But other creatures looked like a strange mixture of different sorts of animal and were not familiar to her at all. Some had fur and others had thick brown scales, while some had both, and a pair of wings too. Every animal seemed to be watching as Ruby made her way down the red carpet towards the chest.

Even at a distance she could tell it was old, made from silvery-looking oak. The metal studding around the edge of the lid was orange and brown with rust. Ruby thought it looked like a sea chest plundered from a shipwreck. As she approached it, she remembered the caution in Jones's voice from the night before, warning her about magic and what it could do to people and their minds. But her footsteps didn't falter. She knew she didn't want to be the same old Ruby Jenkins any more.

'It's a fair swap,' she announced to the animals in their glass boxes as she knelt down in front of the chest. 'My mum and dad are drunks who never wanted me. I've been shipped all over the place, from one foster parent to another. So why shouldn't I do something to make my life better? I'll help Jones get what he wants too, I promise.' Ruby heard the key agreeing, whispering it was her destiny to Commence. Adults would never be able to tell her what to do again, it said. Not if she knew magic.

Ruby slotted the silver key into the iron lock. Before she'd decided which way to turn it, the key rotated clockwise of its own accord, completing a full circle, and was then swallowed into the lock.

Ruby wondered what was going to happen next. She didn't feel any different. After a moment or two, she tried opening the chest but it was shut tight.

She jerked back, stifling a scream, when a man's tiny face suddenly appeared on the lid and blinked at her. She saw bloodshot eyes and sharp teeth. And then the face vanished back into the wood as if it had never been there.

Ruby raised a shaky hand and tucked a lock of black hair behind her ear, waiting for something else to happen. When it did, she flinched so hard she almost bit her tongue.

A ball of wood about the size of a fist shot up out of the lid, leaving a crater, and landed on the floor in the shape of a tiny crouching man who stood up and grinned. He was only a few centimetres tall with a head of wild brown hair. Most of his body was covered with a soft, curly pelt the same colour too. Before Ruby had time to ask anything, more identical men began bursting free from the chest, like popcorn jumping out of a pan, and kicking themselves

63

upright like acrobats as they landed feet first on the floor. Quickly, they started making a line down the centre of the room along the red carpet.

In a matter of moments, the chest had disappeared and a line of small, wild-looking, hairy men stretched almost to the door. They said nothing to Ruby, whose mouth was still open in utter amazement. Then the nearest man pointed at something behind her.

Below the windowsill, where the chest had stood, was a small black book lying on the floor. The leather was supple and worn, and the spine was cracked. It looked like an old prayer book Ruby had been given in church once, when one of her foster families had dragged her along to a service.

Eager to find out what might be inside the book, she picked it up and read the title written in gold lettering.

Lak Djyð Ðl Qcfaxql Unfrtuspmb

She squinted to try and make sense of it, but that didn't work. So instead she flicked through the gold-edged pages, scanning paragraphs of text broken up with diagrams and pictures. But, like the title, none of the words made sense at all. In fact, as Ruby stared harder, she realized the letters on each page were moving, jumbling around constantly, making it impossible to understand anything. Her heart began to pound as she wondered if she'd done something wrong.

'What happens now?' she asked, looking up. But the long line of little men had almost disappeared. As the last few sprinted out of the door, Ruby slapped the book shut and ran after them.

As she reached the door, Ruby heard a low chuckle coming from somewhere she couldn't see. It was the same voice that had belonged to the key. She knew what it was now. It was the voice of magic itself and she knew it had tricked her as she began to realize the men had gone to find Jones when she heard tiny feet starting to scamper up the stairs. Ruby cursed as she ran as fast as she could to Maitland's study. The Commencement was not going as she'd planned at all.

The gun was asleep on the floor, snoring loudly, with books and papers strewn around it, but Ruby didn't bother to stop and ask why. She just picked it up and headed straight back out into the hallway, the gun spluttering awake, asking what was going on.

But, if Ruby had paused and bothered to look, she would have noticed something else lying on the floor too, hidden behind the desk in a corner.

Visible in the morning light was a bald head and the fully formed torso of a naked man, his skin a creamy, pale white, and his black teeth sharpened into what looked like large pencil points.

He licked his lips and shuddered before levering himself up with his arms to sit against the wall as the tiny stumps of his legs carried on growing.

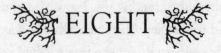# EIGHT

J ones woke with a jolt. A loud, scratchy noise on the other side of his bedroom door made him sit up, and then he heard the scrabbling sound again.

Slowly, the doorknob started to turn.

'Ruby? Is that you? Do you want something?' As Jones clambered out of bed, the door flew open and a ladder of hairy men balanced on each other's tiny shoulders broke apart and tumbled to the ground.

Jones stumbled back as they flowed across the wooden floor, his rapidly waking brain frantically warning him they were *Woodwose* as the door slammed shut. He kicked out at the first ones to reach him, but others leapt onto his pyjama legs and began climbing. The ones he managed to dislodge hit the floor with tiny *oomphs* and sat up, rubbing their heads.

Jones yelled and cursed as other *Woodwose* started punching and biting his feet. When he kicked out again, tiny hands swarmed around the ankle of his standing foot and pushed, and Jones came crashing down.

Before he could get up, his arms were pinned to his sides, and then he was being rolled across the floor. When he stopped, he realized he'd been wrapped up in the large brown rug that usually lay at the foot of his bed. He was trapped. Rolled up tight like the meat in a sausage roll.

The *Woodwose* began to chatter excitedly as a small group of them cornered one of their own and when they fell upon him he disappeared in the scrum of bodies. When a hairy, severed arm appeared in the hands of one tiny *Woodwose*, Jones choked back the urge to be sick. He watched in horror as the creature began using the bloody arm like an oversized pen, drawing something on the floor. More *Woodwose* started doing the same with other body parts. Symbols and runes, none of which Jones recognized, started to appear on the floorboards. More men were pounced upon and disappeared screaming under the weight of bodies.

'Jones!' shouted Ruby from the other side of the door. 'Jones! Are you all right?'

'Whatch du you fink?' shouted Jones angrily back through a swollen lip.

'Jones, I'll help you, okay? I promise. I didn't know this was going to happen. I shouldn't have taken the key. I'm sorry. The magic tricked me.'

When Ruby opened the door, a group of *Woodwose* rushed to close it. Ruby pushed, and the men pushed back. As Jones watched the door see-sawing back and forth, he understood what was happening now. Ruby had stolen the key and opened the chest. His Commencement was underway.

'I schould neverrr 've 'elped ewwwe,' shouted Jones. 'Neverrr.' Tears slicked down his face. 'I should've lefft uu tooo Arkellll.'

The harder Ruby pushed the door, the harder it was shoved back.

'What do I do?' she shouted at the gun in her hand. 'How do I stop them?'

But the gun just laughed. 'You can't. You've gone and done Jones a favour. You'll see. You can't stop those *Woodwose* now they've been set free. They're wild men born deep in the forests of England, hatched from the earth by magic. Unstoppable by the likes of you.'

Ruby poked the gun through the small gap between the door and the door frame, aiming it at some of the men, but when she pulled the trigger nothing happened.

'You can't make me fire if I don't want to,' shouted the gun. 'And this is what Maitland wanted so I'm not going to interfere!'

'But this isn't what Jones wanted,' said Ruby. 'I can't let this happen to him. Not after he saved my life last night.'

But the gun just laughed. 'Then you shouldn't have meddled in things you don't understand, girl. You should never have taken that key.'

Deep down, Ruby knew the gun was right, but she put it all to the back of her mind as she looked around frantically for something else to help her. A cupboard further along the landing was ajar and she could see an old upright vacuum cleaner standing in the dark. It looked defunct, like an old tractor left to rot in a barn. But an idea, however preposterous, welled up inside her.

The black book from downstairs was in the big front pocket of her hoodie. Taking it out, she opened it and wedged half of the book into the gap between the bottom of the door and the floor. Slowly, she stood up, letting the door lurch forward and then jam on the book so it remained open.

Ruby ran to the cupboard along the landing. Ignoring the gun's cries as she dumped it on a dark shelf, she hauled out the vacuum cleaner and ran back with the machine, pausing when she realized there was no cord or plug. Remembering how the lights had all come on without electricity, Ruby pressed the red 'on' switch, hoping the vacuum might be charmed too. The machine roared into life, the upright bag creaking as it swelled out, and Ruby pushed it as fast as she could back to the door.

And she was just in time. The men had removed the black book, but Ruby managed to jam the vacuum cleaner against the door before it was slammed shut. Ruby pushed the metal nozzle of the hose through the gap between the door and the door frame and wiggled her arm. She heard a cry and felt something bump up inside the tube, and then she saw the outline of a tiny face pressed against the inside of the vacuum cleaner's bag.

'YES!' she cried, her heart doing a little fist pump. 'Unstoppable by a girl like me, are they?' she shouted back at the gun in the cupboard as she started to vacuum up more of the men on the other side of the door.

Jones was unceremoniously unrolled out of the rug into the middle of the bedroom and then kicked and pushed and prodded, forcing him to cover up into a ball. As soon as he was able to, he jumped to his feet, intending to run for the door, but stopped when he was surrounded by what looked like a shimmery heat haze rising up off the floor. It was even above him too. Touching it, he discovered it was solid like glass. He had the curious sensation of being caught like the bugs he used to trap in upturned jam jars when he'd been a very little boy, before ever going hunting with Maitland.

Looking down, Jones saw he was standing inside a circle of bloody runes and symbols drawn on the floor, and he knew they were producing some sort of magic, preventing him from going anywhere. Through the haze, Jones could see a particularly hairy *Woodwose*, slightly larger than the rest, intoning a sombre prayer as blood glistened in markings on his tiny face. Other men were standing listening with their arms raised, and then they began chanting too.

The bedroom door slammed open and, through the haze surrounding him, Jones saw Ruby with the old stand-up vacuum cleaner whirring beside her. The grey bag was bulging and Jones realized why as Ruby pointed the metal nozzle at a couple of tiny men racing towards her and vacuumed them up. Ruby smiled triumphantly as she made her way towards Jones, sucking up more men as she went. But her expression changed immediately when the bag suddenly burst with a **BANG!** and a big group of *Woodwose* came tumbling out onto the floor, coughing and spluttering in a cloud of dust.

As Ruby stood beside the vacuum cleaner, trying desperately to bash some of the hairy men with the nozzle, Jones hammered and kicked at the haze encircling him. But he only succeeded in stubbing his fingers and toes.

As the *Woodwose* began chanting louder and louder, Jones slumped to the floor and awaited his fate. He put his head between his knees when Ruby's face loomed up on the other side of the haze. He didn't want to see her. It was all her fault. She'd wanted to Commence and he was paying the price for her foolishness. If he was to be given the gift of magic then the first thing he'd use it on would be her, to make Ruby pay for what she had done.

Ruby hammered on the hard barrier surrounding Jones as a point of white light appeared above his head. She banged harder, trying to break her way in.

She screamed at the *Woodwose*, pleading with them to stop what was happening. But they took no notice. As the white light above Jones shone brighter and brighter, she slumped down next to him as if the guilt inside her was too heavy to bear. Beside her was the hole in the floor she'd used to pull up the floorboard and steal the key. She wished she could rewind time and never have taken it.

71

And then an idea clicked *on* inside her.

Quickly, she wiggled her finger into the hole and pulled up the section of floorboard on which bloody runes and symbols had been painted, then threw it behind her where it landed with a crash.

Jones looked up. When he realized Ruby had broken the ring of runes and symbols, he put out his hand and found a gap in the haze directly above where the floorboard had been. He pushed his hand through further and Ruby grabbed it and pulled. But the gap was only as wide as the missing floorboard, meaning Jones was too big to fit through. As the chanting in the room grew louder, the white light above him grew ever brighter and then suddenly engulfed him.

Ruby felt a terrible burning sensation travel from Jones's hand to hers and up her arm and her shoulder into her neck and then into her head. It was so painful it felt like a red-hot poker had been placed against her brain and she saw strange symbols burnt into the backs of her eyelids. Above the rushing sound in her ears she heard a high-pitched scream and she knew it was Jones. But she was screaming too.

They were crying out as one.

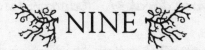

NINE

When Jones opened his eyes, he had to wait for the bedroom to stop spinning.

As the room ground to a halt, he realized he was lying on his back, looking up at the ceiling. Glancing to his right, he saw Ruby next to him, steaming gently like a just-boiled kettle. Something deep and dark opened up inside him and for a moment, overtaken by rage, Jones hoped she was dead, and then she groaned. As soon as Jones realized they were still holding hands, he let go immediately.

'Are you okay?' mumbled Ruby.

'I'm alive, if that's what you mean,' croaked Jones as he sat up slowly, noticing all the runes and symbols on the floor had vanished. His throat was dry. He could taste pears and woodsmoke and vinegar all at once.

'At least the hairy men are gone,' said Ruby brightly, but her smile bounced right back off Jones.

He stood up, groaning as his head hurt.

When Ruby caught sight of the black leather book lying

on the floor beside the door, she realized, with a little flutter in her heart, she could read the title.

The Black Book of Magical Instruction

Quickly, she tottered to her feet. The words on the pages were no longer unreadable either. Flicking through the book, she saw spells and charms for all sorts of things: levitations . . . transformations . . . weather cycles . . .

'Look! The words, I can read them! Can you?' She held up the book for Jones, who just nodded curtly and looked away.

'I don't want to see any of it,' he said.

'So I've Commenced, right, got the gift of magic, if I can read what the book says?' Jones's head was so sore he couldn't be bothered to speak. 'Well?' asked Ruby.

Jones just shrugged. 'Yes,' he said. Before Ruby could ask anything else, they both heard the sound of glass breaking downstairs. A moment later came the shrill, pipsqueak voices of the imps. And then Jones and Ruby looked at each other as they realized the cries downstairs were not happy ones. The imps were screaming.

Jones stopped outside Maitland's study with Ruby behind him. At the sound of another tiny scream, he nudged open the door.

The pale, bald man sitting behind the desk was cloaked in the red velvet curtain that had been hanging on the rail above the large window in the study. He was holding an imp by its waist and the poor creature shrieked again as the man opened his mouth. He bit off its head with his sharp black teeth and spat it onto the floor. With the imp's legs still twitching, the man drank from the creature as if it was a bottle.

The headless bodies of all the other imps lay scattered on the carpet like rag dolls, the broken jar in pieces all around them.

When the man noticed Jones standing in the doorway, he smiled.

'Where's Maitland, Jones?' His voice was hoarse and barely audible. He raised a hand to pluck something red and meaty from the corner of his mouth, his long pale fingers shaking.

'Maitland's dead.'

The man grinned slowly, as though hearing a punchline to a joke it had taken him a moment to understand. 'How terribly ...' he waved his hand as though searching for the right word, '... inconvenient for you, Jones, my boy. And for your friend too.' The man grinned at Ruby. 'Hello, Ruby Jenkins. How's the finger?'

Ruby stared at the man's sharp black teeth. She opened her mouth and then closed it again as something clicked in her head and she searched for the skull on the desk. But it wasn't there. The man nodded slowly.

'That's right, I'm all me again. A few drops of your blood were enough for me to break Maitland's grubby little binding charm. Thank you, my dear. No one likes being kept as a skull,' and he bowed his head like a prince before a queen. 'Once I get my strength back, I'm going to enjoy the rest of the blood in that body of yours, and yours too, Jones. You're both going to help me become,' and he smiled, 'normal again.'

'You need to leave!' shouted Ruby, a surge of courage racing through her. 'Or else.' She reached for the gun in her hoodie pocket and then realized it wasn't there, remembering she'd left it on the shelf in the cupboard upstairs. The man stared at Ruby with eyes that were black and yellow.

'Or ... else ... what?' he said calmly. 'Ahh,' he said, eyeing *The Black Book of Magical Instruction* in Ruby's other hand, 'Badlander magic perhaps? I know ...' The man swallowed, his throat crackling like a dirty pipe. 'I know magic too.' He held out his hand and whispered a few strange-sounding words, conjuring up faint greyish sparks around his fingers, which seemed to please him greatly.

'Actually,' said Ruby, rifling through the pages of the book, 'unluckily for you I've just Commenced. So maybe I will try some magic.'

The man laughed. 'Girls can't Commence. Badlander magic's only for men and boys.'

'Let's see about that, shall we?' Ruby started humming, to try and keep her spirits up, as she skipped through the book. But footnotes and asterisks seemed to pepper every page. The word 'WARNING!' was written on a large number of them too. Others seemed to require very long lists of ingredients. The book fell open at a spell that seemed less dangerous and complicated than others:

Healing boils, warts and ulcers

Ruby flicked over the page:

Unblocking a nose

Ruby shut the book with a sharp *clap* and addressed the man again. 'Look, you need to leave, or else Jones here is going to make you,' and she thrust the book into the boy's hands. 'Seeing as I'm new at all this,' she mumbled, 'maybe you should take this one.'

But Jones gave the book straight back to her. 'I ain't using magic,' he hissed. 'Never. Anyway, I don't know what to do.'

The man wrapped in the red curtain rose unsteadily from the chair behind the desk. The sparks he was conjuring from the fingers of one hand were much darker and stronger now. Ruby and Jones edged backwards into the hallway, extremely wary of what might be about to happen.

Muttering a string of words, the man flicked his wrist, sending a stream of jet-black sparks towards the imps. The dead, headless creatures jerked into life and stood up, swaying.

The man laughed. 'I do believe I'm getting stronger. I can feel magic returning to me and it feels . . . *wonderful*. I think perhaps I'm ready for you, boy,' and he snapped his sharp black teeth together. 'I might even be able to manage the girl as well. The blood in both of you is going to let me do so much more than I can now.'

Another spray of black sparks flew from the man's fingers and all the imps' heads took off from the floor and went flying through the air back to their bodies, each one fixing itself the right way round to a pair of shoulders.

Ruby and Jones swallowed in unison as the zombified imps ran towards them. Jones reached forward and slammed the door shut just in time and they heard the rasp of sharp fingernails, and the man laughing.

'Who is he?' asked Ruby. '*What* is he?'

'There's a big axe in the cellar,' replied Jones. 'We're going to need that as well as the gun if you think you can use it.' He looked at Ruby, but she was still waiting for an answer to her question. 'His name's Victor Brynn and he's a No-Thing. We don't have much time. He's only going to get stronger. And if he does then we're both dead. This is all your fault. All of it.' Jones turned on his heels and marched away down the hallway.

The huge axe was leaning against a wall in the cellar. It was even heavier than Jones expected as he dragged it across the stone floor, before hefting the whole thing up onto his shoulder. Once he was balanced, he made for the rickety wooden stairs in his bare feet, wishing he'd remembered to put on his boots despite being still in his pyjamas.

'Again, start again,' said Ruby. Jones looked up to the top of the steep stairs where she was standing, whirling her hand round like a propeller as though trying to get her brain up to speed.

'Victor Brynn was a Badlander once and then he became a No-Thing,' said Jones.

'And what's that again?'

'A Badlander who's Commenced, but then they turn so bad they start doing *áglæccræft*.' Jones took a deep breath and started lugging himself and the axe up the stairs.

He could see Ruby spinning her hand round faster. 'Sorry, can't you explain in English, that's where you lost me last—'

'It's Anglo-Saxon for Dark Magic,' said Jones curtly. 'The sort of magic that needs blood to work. You saw what happened after Victor Brynn drained those imps.'

Ruby's hand stopped. 'So the more blood he drinks . . . the more *áglæ-what's-it* he can do.'

Jones paused and nodded, catching his breath, realizing he was only halfway up the stairs. 'And he didn't need very much to break Maitland's binding charm, *apparently*.'

'Well, how was I supposed to know Maitland was keeping something as dangerous as that in his study?'

Jones glared hard at her because they both knew that wasn't an excuse at all.

'Okay, okay, I'm sorry,' said Ruby. 'So what do we do now?'

Jones took a deep breath and started up the stairs again. 'We'll shoot Victor Brynn with a silver bullet and cut off his head. It works most times if you're in a fix and don't know what to do. That's what Maitland taught me anyway.'

When he looked up again, Jones could see Ruby looking aghast at what he'd just told her. And then her face changed to a more questioning look. 'Most times?'

'I'm only an apprentice. Do *you* know how to kill a No-Thing like Victor Brynn?'

'We could check your Bestiary, the Pocket Book one.'

'There ain't no time to study a book while Victor Brynn gets more blood inside him and becomes more powerful.'

Jones reached the top of the stairs and tottered out into the hallway, blowing hard, and put the large axe down.

'Okay, but I don't like it,' said Ruby. 'What if your way doesn't work?'

'Well, I didn't like you stealing that key,' said Jones. 'Or breaking the charm on Victor Brynn or hatching the *Scucca* hound or letting those imps out of their jar.'

Ruby stood there, biting her tongue, before starting to flick through the pages of the black leather book. 'What about magic?' she asked brightly. 'There must be some sort of spell I can use if I really look for one.'

'No. Using magic's harder than you think. You need to learn things properly first or else you can end up doing something you don't mean. If you want my advice, don't use the book. Ever.' He closed the book in Ruby's hands. 'We stick to my plan. You're gonna do the shooting, I'll do the cutting. Chopping through the neck bone can be difficult and I'm stronger than you. Besides, I can't use the gun. Do you remember where you left it?'

'Yeah.'

'Right then, let's get on with it,' said Jones, hefting the heavy axe onto his shoulder again.

*

They appeared in the doorway to Maitland's study a few minutes later and Ruby felt a minor sense of relief when she saw Victor Brynn wasn't there.

'Looks like he's given up and left,' she said, pointing to the large sash window at the far end of the study, which was open. 'We're safe.'

'No, we're not. Things are worse than before,' said Jones as she followed him into the study, picking a path between the imps scattered on the floor. 'He'll be looking for more blood out there,' and Jones pointed to the garden. Before Ruby could ask exactly what he meant, he was clambering through the window, lugging the axe with him. 'Quick, give me a hand,' he grunted as he struggled.

Outside, the blue sky hummed one long note. The dew on the grass was cold and slimy beneath Jones's bare feet, and, once again, he wished he'd paused to put on a pair of boots as he followed Victor Brynn's footprints.

Eventually, he stopped beside an archway that opened into a walled garden. Lying on the grass was a rabbit, its neck broken and the body sucked so dry it looked like an old grey sock. Beyond it were more of Victor Brynn's footprints, leading into the walled garden. Carefully, Jones peered through the archway, the axe resting on the ground beside him.

To his left, some distance away, was the No-Thing, ankle-deep in a flower bed. Victor Brynn's face was glowing with more colour now. Around him lay the bodies of more rabbits and even a couple of crows. He raised his hands and muttered something, and fired black sparks into the soil. A rabbit burst out of the ground in a spray of dirt, straight into his open hands, and Victor Brynn bit down on the soft furry neck, sucking greedily.

Jones stepped back from the archway, stabbed his finger at the gun in Ruby's hand, and then pointed into the walled garden, making sure she got the message loud and clear. Ruby crept through the archway and when she saw Victor Brynn with his back to her she raised the revolver. But her hand began to shake as she realized what she was about to do.

'You'll be fine,' whispered the gun. 'But I need to be closer to be sure.' Ruby sneaked forward a few more steps and stopped. 'Now aim, hold your breath and pull the trigger, and I'll do the rest.' Ruby looked along the barrel, aiming at Victor Brynn's back, and held her breath. But, before she could fire, the No-Thing turned and looked directly at her. Thoughts buzzed in her head like wasps. *This was a man? At least . . . Well . . . Sort of. How could she—*

'Do it!' shouted the revolver. 'He's coming.' The gun was right. Victor Brynn was moving towards them. But, as he raised his hands and conjured up a ball of dense black sparks, more questions kept welling up inside Ruby. She could hardly hear anything above the din her head was making. This wasn't how she'd imagined being a Badlander at all. She thought she heard the gun shouting at her. Jones's voice seemed to be there too, and then she realized he was standing right beside her, urging her on. She steeled herself. Closed her eyes. Then pulled the trigger.

When she looked again, the No-Thing was still coming towards her.

'Again,' shouted the revolver. 'And this time keep your eyes open.' But, before Ruby could gather herself and pull the trigger a second time, Victor Brynn muttered something and the ball of sparks around his fingers hardened into a black sphere, the size of a tennis ball. Drawing back his arm, he flung it at Ruby and Jones.

They ducked easily, but, as the sphere passed overhead, Ruby felt a great coldness that took her breath away. The next thing she knew, she was floating six metres in the air and below her Victor Brynn was storming across the grass.

Jones was floating beside her too, puffing and struggling to hold on to the axe, his eyes bright with terror.

'Pull the trigger! He's goi—' and then he stopped when he saw the gun lying on the grass below. 'Oh ... no,' said Jones through gritted teeth.

'I know!' shouted Ruby.

Victor Brynn stopped and stared up at them with a smile that showed off his sharp black teeth. Jones dropped the axe and it landed on the turf with a dull thud. Ruby kicked her shoes off in the direction of the No-Thing. One of them hit him in the chest, but all he did was laugh.

'It's very hard to kill a No-Thing like me. Axes and shoes

won't work. Neither will guns,' and he grinned at the revolver lying on the grass. It cursed loudly back at him.

Ruby felt through her pockets for anything useful and found *The Black Book of Magical Instruction* in her hoodie. Complicated incantations dazzled her eyes as she rifled through the pages again. She saw strange foreign words she didn't know how to pronounce.

'Come on, there's got to be something easy in here!' she shouted. 'How do I get started?'

Suddenly, all the pages turned blank, and the book flipped to the beginning. On the first page appeared the words:

All you needed to do was ask!

Chapter One: Beginning to use magic

Lesson 1
Conjuring A Spark

Ruby flipped onto the next page:

Lesson 2
Ten easy spells to practise after conjuring a spark

Her eyes scanned the first one she came across:

Time Flies

A useful spell for altering the course of events

To change what's about to happen, say the following:

Andweardnes áflíeheþ

'What the hell is tha—' Ruby began, only to be uninterupted by more words appearing on the page.

All magic is spoken in Anglo-Saxon.

Below was a page of further instructions and warnings. But Ruby didn't bother reading them.

'And-weard-ne-s ahh-f-lee-hep,' she shouted at Victor Brynn, trying to get her tongue round the unfamiliar words. But nothing happened. She tried again in a foreign accent that sounded vaguely French. 'Annndd-weird-nesss ahh-fff-lee-hep.' Still nothing.

You should really practise conjuring a spark first
before attempting a spell.

Victor Brynn had been watching her curiously as if she was a dog trying to do a trick. 'Girls don't do Badlander magic,' he said, shaking his head. 'They can't. It's how the world is.' As if to make the point, Victor Brynn raised a hand and black sparks flew at Jones, forming a dark rope that looped around his waist. 'I think I'm ready for your blood now, boy!' he shouted and began dragging Jones down towards him, as Jones did his best to swim away in the opposite direction.

The book started to vibrate in Ruby's hand and she saw that further instructions had appeared on the open page.

Tip for first-time users:

You must specify whether this spell is aimed at yourself, a third party or an object.

Pointing will do.

And the pronunciation is:
And-weard-ne-s ahh-f-lee-heth.

Ruby raised her right hand and pointed a finger at Victor Brynn. 'And-weard-ne-s ahh-f-lee-heth,' she shouted.

But still nothing happened.

'Don't you understand?' shouted Victor Brynn. 'You're just a girl!' The No-Thing yanked hard on the rope, dragging Jones down. The boy grabbed onto one of Ruby's arms, causing her to drop the book, which tumbled out of her hands to the grass below. Victor Brynn pulled on the rope again and Jones slid down Ruby's arm until she caught his hand in hers.

'Good idea!' shouted Victor Brynn. 'Why don't I have both of you at the same time?' He flashed out another black spark from his other hand and a rope caught around Ruby's ankles. Victor Brynn's grin lit up something hot and angry inside Ruby as she remembered everything she'd been told about the stupid *Ordnung* and what girls couldn't do.

She pointed at the No-Thing with her free hand again. 'Annndd-weird-nesss ahh-fff-lee-heth!' she screamed as Victor Brynn yanked both her and Jones towards him.

And from her hand shot a powerful white spark.

TEN

Ruby blinked the early morning rays of sunlight out of her eyes. She was lying on the grass beside Jones. But, far more importantly, Victor Brynn was gone, and so were the black ropes he'd conjured.

'I did it,' gasped Ruby. 'Jones, I used magic!' and she grinned triumphantly.

Jones grunted. He sat up and rolled his right shoulder round in tiny circles to test it was still working. As well as the bumps and bruises from landing hard on the ground, he was aware of a slight tingle in the back of his head, rather like pins and needles.

'I don't believe it,' shouted the gun on the grass nearby. 'I-don't-be-lieve-it!'

'I know! I'm a magician ... a Badlander,' Ruby announced dreamily, beaming. Jones muttered something under his breath. Ruby wasn't entirely sure if it was at his shoulder or at her. But she didn't care. She felt good. In fact, she felt wonderful.

The Black Book of Magical Instruction flew off the grass into her hands and opened, and she looked down in surprise.

Did the spell work?

Ruby was not sure how to answer except to nod.

Excellent!
What timescale did you use for
the subject of your spell?

Ruby closed the book. As far as she was concerned, she was happy just to have performed magic.

The book flipped back open in her hands.

Beginner tip:
With no assigned timescale,
results will be random.

'Whatever,' said Ruby under her breath and closed the book again. She wasn't going to let a technicality spoil her first piece of magic.

'So you think you're a Badlander now?' asked Jones, glancing round as if still unable to believe Victor Brynn was gone. Ruby shrugged and smiled. 'Well, I don't think so. Try the same spell on that,' and he pointed at the axe, lying on the grass. Ruby twirled her hand with a flourish and pointed her finger.

'Annndd-weird-nesss ahh-fff-lee-heth,' she said. Nothing happened. Ruby inspected the end of her finger as though it might be faulty. She took a couple of deep breaths. 'Annd—'

'Hold it,' muttered Jones. He slid his hand into hers and Ruby raised her eyebrows at him. 'Try again,' he said quietly.

As soon as Ruby uttered the words, a white spark shot out of the end of her finger and hit the axe, making it disappear with a tiny *poof*. The girl heard her heart hit the bottom of her stomach with a *thump*.

'Exactly,' announced Jones as she looked at him. 'Because we Commenced together . . .' he pulled his hand out of Ruby's grip, '. . . we can only use magic together, and apparently only when we're holding hands.' He stood up, and then grinned for the first time in what seemed like ages. 'Which means as long as I stay away from you I can't use magic. I can still try to be a normal boy after all.' And with that he set off quickly across the grass back towards the cottage.

'Wait!' shouted Ruby. 'We need to talk about this.' She picked up the book of magic and the gun, which appeared to be in a state of shock.

'I've never seen anything like this before,' it was muttering. 'Never!'

'There's nothing to talk about,' said Jones when Ruby caught up with him. 'I know exactly what I need to do. Stay away from you.' And he started walking even faster.

'But what about the Badlands? What about saving people?'

'I already told you, I want to be a normal boy.'

'What about me? What am I going to do?'

Jones just shrugged. 'Stay here if you want.'

'But—'

Jones stopped and stared. 'Get it into your head. I'm not

working the Badlands with you. You can't make me. I'm getting in the van and leaving here as soon as I'm ready. I'm gonna start a new life somewhere else.' And with that he marched on back towards the house.

Ruby had composed herself by the time she was standing in the hallway. She didn't know where Jones was but the VW camper van was still parked outside so she knew he hadn't left yet.

When she heard the tramping of boots in the kitchen, Ruby cleared her throat. Jones came down the hallway in his overcoat, carrying a small bush freshly planted in a large pot. Ruby folded her arms as if making it clear she was going to have her say before Jones could go any further.

'Say what you want,' he said. 'It won't make any difference.'

'The ordinary world out there isn't everything you think it is,' said Ruby.

'It can't be any worse than the mixed-up one I know.'

'It's boring being a kid, being told what to do all the time. Everyone I know would be desperate to be able to do the things in here,' said Ruby, holding up *The Black Book of Magical Instruction*. 'You're not thinking straight. You tried to warn me off magic. Well, I'm trying to warn you off the normal, boring world.' When Jones began walking down the hall again, Ruby grabbed him. 'Where are you planning on going? You've got no one. Nothing.'

'That's my business.' But Ruby kept hold of him. 'I'm gonna be a normal boy,' said Jones. 'Find my parents. I'm gonna . . .'

He leant in as if about to reveal a secret. 'BOO!' he shouted and Ruby flinched, making Jones smirk. 'You've got to be ready for anything in the Badlands. We were lucky with Victor Brynn, and last night too. And you know the thing about luck? It runs out eventually. That's what Maitland taught me. Ain't that right?' he asked the gun, which was poking out of Ruby's hoodie pocket. 'I reckon I'm leaving at just the right time.'

'Jones,' said the gun sternly. 'Forget about finding your parents. It'll come to no good. No good at all.'

But Jones just grunted and walked on towards the front door.

'How about I come with you then?' asked Ruby, catching up with him. 'In case you need to run some spells?'

'No. I already saved your life. I don't owe you a thing.' He stopped when something else occurred to him. 'I'll give you one bit of advice, though. Don't *ever* tell anyone 'bout what we can do. Magic's not for girls. It's against the *Ordnung*. The Order'd punish us for what we've done. So it's better we stay as far apart as possible.'

Jones opened the front door, the sunshine on his face feeling like the start of something new. And then he noticed a blurry circle, about the size of a manhole, hovering in the air ahead of him beside the camper van. It looked like a little part of the world was just out of focus. Suddenly, Victor Brynn came hurtling out of the circle, still wrapped in the red velvet curtain, and landed on the drive, sliding over the gravel to land in front of Jones.

The boy staggered backwards into Ruby as the No-Thing stood up slowly, looking about him, and taking a moment to work out what was happening. And then he stared at Ruby.

'You ... you used magic, on *me*?' he hissed, his tongue darting out between his sharp black teeth. 'How can that be, *girl*?' Ruby opened her mouth, but was too scared to speak. Victor Brynn's confused look softened to an ugly-looking smile as he raised the long, spindly forefinger of his right hand and started to conjure some darkish sparks. 'You're right. Who cares? Because here we are together agai—'

Victor Brynn was jerked violently backwards towards the blurry hole, as if on a piece of elastic, and swallowed back through it. As soon as he disappeared, the hole vanished too, leaving Jones and Ruby staring at the camper can parked in the driveway.

'Jones, what *exactly* just happened?' But all Jones could do was shake his head. And then *The Black Book of Magical Instruction* opened in Ruby's hands.

Not selecting a time differential means the subject of your spell will keep appearing and disappearing randomly until commanded to stop with the correct cancelling spell.

They both stared at the page.

'Will the subject of our spell only appear if we're together?' asked Jones.

I don't understand.

'We Commenced together,' said Jones. 'So we can only do magic together. What happens to the subject of our spell if we're apart? Say for the rest of our lives,' he said somewhat sarcastically.

The book thought about that for a moment.

> Your Commencement sounds highly
> irregular; the only other known instance
> of a something similar is when Charles Instone
> of Brockenhurst Commenced with his
> rocking chair in 1564 when ...

'So you don't know then?' asked Jones.

> Of course I know!
> The subject of your spell will appear to
> both of you when together, and to each of
> you in turn when apart, until the correct
> cancelling spell is used. Since you used magic
> together, both of you must benefit equally
> from the effects of the spell cast.

And with that the book banged shut.

'Well, Jones,' said Ruby. 'I guess we're sticking together until we've cancelled the spell. There's no way you can be ordinary if there's a No-Thing popping up randomly now and then. I mean something like that is going to freak normal people out. Of course, there's the spell on the axe to fix too.' Ruby sighed and shook her head as if she'd found out the worst possible news. 'It's a real shame.'

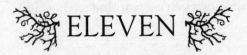

ELEVEN

J ones's brain was whirring as he headed back into the house, trying to come to terms with everything that had just happened and what he was supposed to do now.

'Jones! Listen, will you?' shouted Ruby. But Jones wasn't listening. In fact, he was trying his best to ignore Ruby altogether.

Without realizing it, he'd walked into the kitchen as if in a daydream. Seeing a spot of grease on the window, he leant over the sink and started rubbing the glass with his shirtsleeve. He could see Ruby's reflection as she stood behind him, arms folded, and he knew she wasn't going to leave him alone until she'd had her say. He was beginning to realize Ruby was that kind of person. He wondered if all girls were the same.

'What do *you* want?' he said, checking the glass for any more greasy spots.

'Jones, if we've got to stick together until the spells on Victor Brynn and the axe are sorted out, we need to try and get on. We don't know how long it's going to take.'

'Fine. Stay out of my way and that'll make it easier for me to pretend you're not here.'

'But that's not what I meant—'

'Just because we've got to stick together doesn't mean we have to talk to each other.'

'Jones, I've said I'm sorry. Haven't you been listening?'

'No.'

'So I suppose you didn't hear me asking how you're planning on finding your parents then?'

'No, I didn't. And don't bother asking me again, cos that ain't none of your business.'

'How about you then? It sounded like you know something about his parents. So what—'

It took Jones just a second to realize Ruby wasn't talking to him, and he whirled round to see her looking straight down the barrel of the gun.

The trigger was already moving . . .

. . . the hammer was pulling itself back . . .

Jones grabbed Ruby's wrist, yanking her arm to the side, as the gun fired a shot.

Ruby's bottom lip twitched as plaster dribbled out of the hole in the wall behind her, above the stove. Jones made her put the gun down on the table as it apologized over and over. Then he helped her sit down and gave her a glass of water and waited till she'd drunk it.

'Maitland charmed the gun not to say anything about my parents. He stole me away when I was a baby.'

'Stole you?'

'I've been growing a memory bush in secret and last night I ate the berry off it. Maitland took me to be his apprentice. I wasn't meant to be a Badlander at all: my parents wanted me.'

Ruby studied a spot on the floor and Jones guessed what she must be thinking, knowing what she'd told him about foster families and why some children needed them.

'Well, then,' Ruby said, looking up and managing a smile. 'This memory bush of yours sounds useful. Did you remember where your mum and dad lived?'

'Not exactly. I've worked out what street it was. I don't know if they're still living in the same house, but I'll find them eventually. Maitland taught me how to hunt creatures so I reckon I can track my parents down too.'

'Why don't we go and find them?' said Ruby. 'I'll show you how to be ordinary and fit in, just like I said I would. It's the least I can do.'

Jones shook his head. 'I don't want your help after what's happened. Anyway, what if Victor Brynn appears out of nowhere, or the axe? No. We'll wait here, deal with Victor Brynn when he turns up again, and then I'm leaving. You can have the house and everything in it. The gun. The books. I don't care. But, till then, you're here but you're not here either, just like a tool in a toolbox I'm gonna need at some point.'

'But—'

'If we start talking, pretending to be friends, all you're gonna do is try and get me to do more spells and that ain't gonna happen.'

'I promise I won't.'

'Even if you don't want to, the magic inside you might. I've told you. It's dangerous. It's already tricked you once. We're only gonna use magic three more times.'

'Three?'

'Once when we cancel the spell on the axe and once for Victor Brynn too, but then ...' Jones paused, '... well, I think we've got to do another spell on him.'

'Such as?'

'He told us it's hard to kill a No-Thing, so I figure we don't even try. What we do is cancel the first spell we've done on him and then do a new one. Make it so he comes back in a thousand years, after we're long gone. That way he'll be someone else's problem instead. Does that sound like a good plan to you?'

'Maybe,' said Ruby, trying not to make it sound like she thought it was.

'Good. Then all you need to do is figure out how to cast the spell we need with that magic book you're so keen on and then we'll be set, won't we?'

'I'm not some spanner in a toolbox,' grunted Ruby, as Jones walked out of the kitchen. 'Or even a screwdriver for that matter.' But he chose to ignore her.

Maitland's study was a mess, with papers and books littering the floor. When Jones started tidying up, Ruby decided she had no choice but to stick close and help, in case Victor Brynn returned. It had only taken her a few moments to ask *The Black Book of Magical Instruction* how to cancel the spell on the No-Thing and cast a new one to make him disappear for a thousand years. Grudgingly, she had to admit it was a good plan. But there was no way she was going to tell Jones that.

They worked in silence, refilling the bookshelves, collecting all the papers, and righting furniture. Ruby was given the awful job of peeling the imps off the floor. Their bodies crackled as they came free and left bright, clean patches behind.

She burnt the corpses in an incinerator in the garden, an old metal bin with holes drilled around the bottom. Ruby whispered 'sorry' as the imps burnt and smoke curled up out of the funnel in the centre of the incinerator's lid. But the word sounded useless despite the way she felt. It made her understand why saying 'sorry' to Jones for all she'd done, however much she meant it, wasn't going to make any difference either. She had no way of changing what had happened to him at all. And it made her realize what a terrible thing she had done to him and why he was so upset.

The two children stayed within sight or earshot of each other all day, waiting for a chance to use magic on Victor Brynn or cancel the spell on the axe should they materialize. But, as the hours ticked by, there was no sign of either. The only real excitement came when Ruby opened a door in the hallway, causing a mop to fall out of what was in fact a cupboard. She'd screamed so hard Jones had come running down the hallway from the bottom of the stairs where he'd been fixing a particularly annoying piece of carpet that had been loose for some time.

But he'd stopped as soon as he'd seen Ruby battling with the mop, its smelly white strands whirling round her head, before she threw it to the floor.

'Ruby Jenkins, the great Badlander,' he announced, picking up the mop. 'She sorted you out, didn't she? Ordinary people'll sleep safer in their beds from now on for sure.' Jones propped the mop against the wall inside the cupboard, and walked back to the bottom of the stairs without another word. To Ruby it looked like he was floating on air.

'I'm going to be a Badlander, Jones,' she said, rearranging her hair.

'Yeah? And how's that gonna happen again, exactly?' But Ruby didn't know, so she couldn't say. She banged the cupboard door shut as hard as she could instead. 'I know,' said Jones brightly. 'Maybe the gifts'll help.'

'What gifts?' asked Ruby, still trying to adjust the kinks in her hair.

'Oh, I s'pose you wouldn't know,' said Jones, sounding like he was talking to a little kid. 'There's always gifts for an apprentice after they've Commenced. I could show you how to use them, if you like? If you think that'd be useful?'

Ruby walked down the hallway and stared into his eyes. She was ever so slightly taller than him. She curled the fingers of one hand into her palm until she felt her fingernails and the words she wanted came out.

'You know what, Jones, I'd really love that. Thank you.'

*

When Jones opened the door and showed her into the room with a sweeping bow, Ruby knew he was enjoying making her feel uncomfortable. That he was trying to make it seem as though she was out of her depth in a world she knew very little about. But all the same she wanted to know more about the gifts he'd mentioned so she chose to ignore his manner as best she could.

Jones pointed to the spot below the windowsill where the large oak chest had been. In its place now was another smaller chest, of about half the size. Propped up on top of it was an envelope with Jones's name written on the front. After ripping it open, he read the note and then gave it to Ruby.

'It's pronounced "*weird*", by the way.'

'What is?'

'The word you won't recognize,' said Jones, tapping the page. 'It's Anglo-Saxon for "fate" or "how things are supposed to be".' And Ruby nodded as she started to read . . .

Dear Jones

If this letter has appeared, two things have happened. Firstly, you have carried out your duty to Commence. Secondly, I am no longer in the world and am therefore unable to continue your education. I know you will accept the way the *wyrd* has worked for me, but please know I am truly sorry not to be able to congratulate you on your

Commencement in person. You have been like a son to me and for that I have been truly grateful.

There is so much still to learn. I hope the objects in this chest prove useful as you grow older and become the great Badlander I know you can be. Jones, my boy, of the few apprentices I have tutored you are the only one to have made it to Commencement, and I am sure you will have many apprentices of your own who will carry on both our legacies. Let us hope the *wyrd* is good to you and that you live long, well and successfully. You are a wonderful and talented boy and I foresee a great future for you.

Two words of advice. Always respect the *Ordnung*. And most of all be safe, my boy.

Maitland

'No one's ever written *me* a letter like that,' said Ruby as she folded it up. But Jones didn't seem to hear as he flipped up the lid of the chest. 'Didn't you hear me?' asked Ruby, waggling the letter.

'Yes.'

'Doesn't it make you the least bit upset that Maitland's gone?'

Jones bit the inside of his cheek. 'I was upset till I found out he stole me. But then that changed everything, didn't it?'

Ruby shrugged as she folded the letter. 'If you say so. But it seems like he loved you very much.' Jones stared at her and heard something crackle in his throat as he swallowed and tried not to think about Maitland at all. It was confusing to know exactly what to feel after reading the letter. He coughed and slapped his hands together as if to clear all the thinking inside him, and peered into the chest.

'Right, what have you got in here?' He pulled out a jar with a thin brown worm coiled up asleep inside. 'A Door Wurm. Nice! Do you know what that does?' He beamed at Ruby, but she just stared back at him. 'Oh and look,' he said, picking up a small bottle containing a fine black dust with a cork bung wedged in the top. 'I bet you know how Slap Dust works too. It's very useful if you're in a fix of course. And look! It's good stuff too, from Deschamps & Sons,' and he made a great show of pointing to the name and logo engraved on the front of the bottle. 'Very nice.' Ruby bit her tongue as Jones gave her the bottle so he could pick up a mirror. He whistled and shook his head as he inspected it. The mirror was about the size of a dinner plate, framed in black ivory. 'Blimey, a scrying mirror, and look, polish too!' and he pointed to a tin with words written on it in elaborate font that read:

HEATON'S OLD FAMILIAR
SCRYING POLISH

As Jones clutched the mirror to his chest and reached in for something else, Ruby put the bottle of Slap Dust down and tipped the lid of the chest up and over. It shut with a loud bang, almost trapping Jones's fingers as he whipped back his arm.

'You've made your point, Jones,' said Ruby. 'Thank you.'

And then she turned round and walked out of the room.

Neither of them spoke much after that, not when they ate or washed up afterwards. And not when they took it in turns to go to the loo with the other one standing outside the bathroom, waiting in awkward silence just in case Victor Brynn appeared.

Ruby quickly realized how quiet the house was. There was no television. No hum of a computer screen or the chime of email. In fact, there was nothing to remind her she was in the twenty-first century at all except for the clothes she was wearing. She'd left her mobile phone at her foster parents' house after deciding the police might be able to find her by tracing the phone because she'd seen something like it happen in a movie once. She regretted it now, wishing she could play some music or watch something.

In the end, the quiet was so loud, Ruby resorted to asking the gun questions about how everything worked. Clearly, the house was not wired for electricity given what she'd seen with the lights and the vacuum cleaner, and the stove in the kitchen was wood-fired. But there was running water. So were there bills for that? And what about all the other bills that usually came with houses? Did Badlanders have money? What if someone came to the house? Wouldn't they realize it was all a bit strange and start asking questions? Didn't Badlanders have to go to the doctor? The dentist? Was everything solved with magic and charms?

The revolver didn't seem to know specifics, but assured her everything was covered. 'The Badlander Order's been around for centuries,' it said. 'It'll last for centuries more, whatever happens in the world it's sworn to protect. Badlanders work things out. They use magic. They adapt.'

'Not to girls, apparently,' said Ruby.

Jones listened to all her questions, but didn't say a word. As the day had gone on, he'd become better and better at ignoring Ruby until it seemed to her that Jones had no idea she even existed. And it was then that she decided to slip away to make him at least say something to her even if it was to ask where she was going.

But, as she left him in the kitchen while he was making himself a cup of tea, Jones didn't make a squeak. Nor when she went down the hall. And not even when she went up the stairs.

With each footstep, Ruby hoped Victor Brynn would appear beside Jones, forcing him to scream out her name so she'd have to come running. But that didn't happen and she found herself walking into the room furthest away from the kitchen, which happened to be Jones's bedroom. She sat down on the bed and waited for him to follow her. But there was no sign of Jones.

She sighed and took the gun out of her waistband.

'How long's he going to stay like this?'

'Who knows? He can be a moody boy. Why Maitland kept him on as his apprentice, I'll never know. He didn't Commence any of the others he trained. The two that didn't die in the Badlands had their minds charmed to forget everything, because they had no potential, and were given back to ordinary people to look after. Maitland must have seen something in Jones, though, because it was obvious he wasn't keen on being a Badlander once he started growing up. Just look at the wall, above the bed.'

Ruby looked up and realized it was covered with postcards arranged in neat rows. She hadn't noticed them when she'd sat down, too self-absorbed and angry at Jones. Neither had she clocked them earlier in the frenzy of the Commencement.

'The boy's written on each one. Read the one right at the top, at the start of the first row,' said the gun. 'It's got a picture of a rowing boat on it.'

Ruby stood on the small chair beside the bed, and reached up and just managed to peel the postcard off the wall. Turning it over, she saw a stamp had been drawn in the top right corner where a real one might have been stuck down. It showed a palm tree on a beach, and had been heavily marked with wavy pencil lines to make it appear as though it had been franked. The single line of address read:

To Jones

The message opposite was written in the same clipped and tidy writing.

107

Dear Jones

We told Maitland not to tell you until we wrote our first card but we are your parents. We are on a very long holiday we won in a magazine. We could not take you with us because of the rules in the competition so we decided to leave you with Maitland who we know and trust. We have told him not to tell you about us because we wanted it to be a surprise. Now that we know you are old enough to read we will send you postcards about all the things we are doing and where we are. Take care and do what Maitland tells you. I hope this is all a nice surprise for you!

Lots of love Mum and Dad xx

After Ruby had finished reading she tacked the postcard back on the wall and stepped down off the chair. She reckoned there were about a hundred postcards.

'How long's he been writing them?' she asked.

'Long enough to make up a whole story,' replied the gun. 'Maitland said it wouldn't do any harm. But I told him it would lead to trouble. Jones is a strange boy.'

But Ruby just smiled and shook her head. 'No, he's not. He's just like me.'

'What on earth do you mean?'

'If I pasted all the pages from my diaries around this bedroom, there'd be no wall left at all. Neither of us got the lives we wanted so we had to deal with it somehow. I know exactly why he's done this.'

Hearing a noise behind her, she turned round to see Jones standing there. But, instead of saying something sarcastic or complaining about her being in his bedroom, all he did was nod at her and some of the tension in the room seemed to melt away.

When it was time to go to bed, Jones decided they should stay in the same bedroom and showed Ruby a spare room with two single beds. He sat down in the armchair in the corner, wrapping himself in a blanket, assuring Ruby he would wake her up in a few hours when it was her turn to keep watch.

They'd brought the walnut box for the gun from the study and it lay on the bedside table next to Ruby, just in case. Gentle snores came from within as the gun slept soundly. Ruby took longer to drop off, and Jones listened carefully to her breathing as she tossed and turned, waiting for her to fall asleep.

As soon as Jones heard Ruby sleeping, he got up quietly out of the armchair. After leaving two cushions under the blanket, he crept out of the bedroom and went downstairs to the room where the chest full of Maitland's gifts was still sitting under the window. Picking out the bottle of black Slap Dust, he weighed it in his hand. Ever since he'd shown it to Ruby, the idea of using it had steadily been burning a hole in his head. He pulled out the stopper and sprinkled a little bit of the black powder into the palm of his other hand. Careful not to drop any, he pushed the stopper back into the bottle, and put it in his overcoat pocket.

He licked his lips. His mouth was dry, making it hard to swallow.

'Take me to Chesterford Gardens,' he managed to say. 'It's in Hampstead. London.' And then he slapped his hands together as hard as he could and the Slap Dust crackled and burnt just like he knew it would.

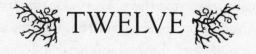

TWELVE

I f anyone had been standing at one end of Chesterford Gardens, at about midnight, they would have seen a boy appear out of thin air and go flying along the pavement on his tiptoes, arms flailing. And they would have probably winced too, as he crashed into a pile of black bags left out for the rubbish collection, bursting one of them, and sending up a cloud of dust that settled on him like dirty snow. But luckily there seemed to be no one around to witness Jones's arrival in London.

His palms felt like they were burning and he blew on them to try and cool them down. He hadn't anticipated quite how generous Maitland had been with the Slap Dust. It was, undoubtedly, the very best and most expensive mixture one could buy from Deschamps & Sons. Jones made a mental note to use much less of it on the return journey after checking the bottle was still intact in his pocket.

He brushed himself down, pulling a potato peeling from his hair, but gave up trying to smooth down all the unruly kinks he could find, reassuring himself it didn't matter how he looked. He was only here to try and locate the house Maitland had taken him from as a starting point to find his parents. If, by some remote chance, his mum and dad were actually still living there, he wouldn't be introducing himself tonight. How could he, until he and Ruby had sorted everything out? Until the spell was fixed and Victor Brynn was banished, all Jones would be able to do would be observe his parents and find out all he could about them. He knew the *fæcce* Maitland had put in the cot to replace him would have died many years ago, but maybe he had brothers or sisters. Jones wasn't sure what to expect. For now, it was just like being on any other Badlander hunt. He needed to be patient, logical and, above all, prepared for anything.

He began walking down the street, assessing one side. A long row of houses were set back from the road, with tiny gardens at the front, most of them full of rubbish, plastic bags and broken glass. Realizing all the houses on this side of the street were abandoned, Jones walked on to the end of the road, where it ended in a junction, and then crossed over and began walking back the other way.

On the other side, the houses were in much better condition, with people clearly still living in them, the curtains drawn and the flicker from televisions dancing madly round their edges. Jones scrutinized each house carefully. And then he stopped. The house in front of him looked vaguely familiar, like a button had been pressed in just the right section of his brain.

He stared at it, taking in the front door, the windows

and the little garden bisected by the concrete path, trying to recall all the details he'd remembered after eating the memory fruit. But it was impossible to remember if it really was the same one Maitland had taken him from. He had no childhood memories to call on either.

Suddenly, the front door opened, as if Jones had disturbed whoever was inside. Embarrassed to be caught watching, Jones walked on quickly, and then glanced back. The woman he saw looked older. Her hair was shorter too. But it was definitely her.

It was his mother.

She was still living here, in the same house, after all this time. Jones felt his heart hammering harder and harder inside his chest as different voices clamoured inside his head, trying to tell him what he should do next.

When Ruby woke up, she saw the dark outline of a body curled up under the blanket in the armchair on the far side of the room.

'Jones?'

She decided he must have fallen asleep and was about to shout louder to wake him up when another thought clicked through the gears in her brain, telling her not to. Instead, she sat up as quietly as she could, then slipped her feet onto the floor.

The gun was fast asleep in its wooden box and Ruby took it out gently so as not to startle it.

'Is it our turn to keep watch?'

'Almost,' replied Ruby.

'So what—'

Ruby shushed it and put it in the pocket of the dressing gown that Jones had lent her, which was grey and woollen and smelt vaguely of boy.

She padded quietly across the floor, careful not to wake the sleeping Jones, and let herself out onto the landing.

After placing the gun on the floor beside her, Ruby knelt down in front of the small chest and opened it. Maitland had stuffed it full of gifts. There was a black dimpled sphere the size of a grapefruit. Next to it was a pink silk bag, full of white cubes the size of sugar lumps with strange-looking red runes inscribed on every face. All sorts of different-sized jars were stacked inside as well, full of either seeds or berries or mushrooms pickled in vibrant red liquids. There was a gnarled stick too, the length of her forearm, which didn't look like anything magical at all.

But Ruby was only interested in one item. When Jones had shown her the scrying mirror, she'd thought it the most beautiful thing she'd ever seen, and had been desperate to wrench it from his grasp. Staring at it again now, she had exactly the same feeling of wanting to hold it.

The black ivory surround felt smooth and comfortable in her hands. But although she'd been desperate to hold the mirror she had no idea what it was supposed to do. All she could see in the glass was her curious face staring back.

'Any idea how to use a scrying mirror?' she asked the gun as she turned the mirror round to inspect the back.

'Not a clue. Maitland tried using one a few times, but gave up because he never got anywhere. A scrying mirror is very difficult to use. It requires great skill and patience.'

'Right,' said Ruby, not believing the gun for a moment.

'It's true. All Maitland did was curse whenever he looked in the mirror and nothing happened.'

'Next you'll be telling me girls can't use them anyway because the *Ordnung* says so.'

'Rules are rul—'

'What if I can do something with it? Just because there aren't any Badlander girls doesn't mean I can't. It feels good to hold it. That must mean something, right?'

The gun muttered something back as Ruby noticed a thin pamphlet tucked inside the chest with the title:

The Beginner's Guide to Scrying

Welcome to this beginner's guide. Scrying as I am sure you know is the art of spying on people and places known to the scryer however far away they might be. In the presence of any scrying object, whether a mirror, a glass ball or even a well-polished tabletop, those with a natural calling will feel a great compulsion to want to hold or touch the item. If you have such a feeling now in the presence of your scrying object then you are ready to begin!

Ruby read on with a great deal of excitement. But the pamphlet gave her very little further encouragement, explaining that successful scrying required many hours of practice to achieve even the basics. Undeterred, she continued reading and learnt three important things:

. . . a scryer may only spy on someone they have already met or a place they have already visited . . .

. . . to see someone or somewhere, the scryer must picture very carefully in their mind's eye exactly what they want to see . . .

. . . the application of a polish (we recommend Heaton's Old Familiar Scrying Polish) will usually improve results, important for a sense of achievement for the beginner. Of course, polish is used by the most adept scryers to turn mirrors into communication devices and, sometimes, large ones can even become portals to visit any location being observed, but this demands years of dedication: see Scrying, Just Spying? *by Thomas Merricoates for the most authoritative work on such advanced practice.*

Eager to try her hand at scrying, Ruby pictured very carefully in her imagination exactly who she wanted to see. As soon as she picked up the mirror, she felt a tingling in her fingertips, as if what she was thinking about was rushing out of her into the mirror, like water disappearing down a plughole or a file being downloaded from an email.

A white dot sparked in the centre of the glass and grew until the mirror was filled with noisy, boiling static.

'Give it up now, girl,' said the gun. 'You're wasting your time.' But Ruby redoubled her efforts instead, holding the two people she was thinking about as clearly as she could in her head until suddenly she blinked and the static disappeared from the glass. The image that replaced it was dark and a little wobbly. But Ruby could see that she was looking down into a dark bedroom, as if she was staring through the ceiling. Below her was a double bed with two adult-sized lumps under the covers. But it was difficult to make out much detail.

Keeping hold of the mirror in one hand, Ruby took the tin of Heaton's Polish out of the chest and prised off the top. She scooped out a pea-sized ball of white polish onto her finger and rubbed it into the glass. The image became instantly clearer, and Ruby could see a man sleeping on the right of the bed and a woman on the left. She discovered she could zoom in and out on what she could see in the mirror just by thinking it, and went in closer on each of the adults in turn, and saw they were both sleeping peacefully.

Proudly, she showed her efforts to the gun. 'See, I must be doing something right,' she announced. 'I must have a chance of being a Badlander if I can do something Maitland couldn't. Look!'

'Well, I'll be,' said the gun. 'It's at times like these I wish I had hands to give a round of applause. Well done, girl! Who on earth are they?'

'My foster parents. The people who look after me,' she

added, remembering that Jones hadn't known what the term meant.

'So they're the ones who should be worrying about where you are?'

'Supposedly,' said Ruby.

'And what about your real parents?'

'Oh, I don't think they'd be too bothered where I am.'

'Why ever not?'

As soon as Ruby started thinking about her real parents, the picture in the mirror changed and she was looking at a messy sitting room in a different house. Empty wine bottles were strewn over a large coffee table. Ashtrays were full to the brim. Fast-food containers and cartons lay scattered over the floor. A man wearing a dirty white T-shirt and tracksuit bottoms was curled up on the sofa, snoring.

'Don't tell me that's your father?' asked the gun. Ruby just nodded.

A woman shuffled into the living room, wearing pink frilly slippers and a nasty green tracksuit. Ruby sighed. 'And that's my mum.' The woman kicked viciously at her husband's feet, almost falling over because she was drunk.

'Gary, wake up! I want you to take me out like a lady. I wanna be treated right.'

The man wafted an arm in the general direction of his wife, as if trying to swat a fly, and then started snoring again.

As Ruby put the mirror down and the image started to fade, the last thing she saw was her mother's angry face popping like a bubble in the glass, and then she was staring at her own reflection.

'Now I see,' said the gun.

'See what?'

'Why you want to be a Badlander.'

And Ruby thought about that. At least, she did for a couple of seconds, until she sensed something behind her and looked back to see a blurry circle appearing at the far end of the room near the door. Before she could stand up, Victor Brynn came hurtling out of the hazy circle and hit the wall beside the door and slid down it, gasping. Ruby froze, too afraid to run past Victor Brynn to get out of the room.

The No-Thing blinked and growled when it saw her. Victor Brynn raised his hands and conjured a wreath of black sparks around his fingers. But before he had time to cast any magic another blurry hole opened to the left of him and the axe came hurtling out of it, spinning end over end towards him, the metal blade winking. The wooden handle caught Victor Brynn on the chin and knocked him out cold, and the axe crashed into a wall and tumbled to the floor.

Ruby was up as fast as she could. 'Jones!' she shouted.

Before she had time to reach the door, the unconscious Victor Brynn was dragged along the floor and sucked back through the blurry hole he'd come through, vanishing into thin air.

Ruby cursed under her breath. 'Jones,' she shouted as loudly as she could. 'Jones! The axe! It's come back!'

The gun fired off a shot at the wall. 'That'll wake him!' it cried.

'Jones!' shouted Ruby. 'We're downstairs!'

When Ruby spotted the axe starting to move across the floor, back towards the blurry circle it had come through, she instinctively grabbed hold of it.

'No way!' she shouted. 'You're staying here.' As she felt the axe begin to judder, she strengthened her grip round the wooden handle. But the axe seemed to have other ideas and started to rise as it pulled towards the hole, the metal head pointing in the direction it wanted to go. It dragged Ruby forward with it. Every muscle in her arms was straining. But she refused to let go as the axe pulled her towards the hole at the far end of the room. She started to wonder what was beyond it and what might happen if she didn't let go.

In fact, there were lots of questions hurtling through Ruby's mind, a big one being *Where on earth is Jones?*

# THIRTEEN

Jones's mother was speaking into a communication device. He knew it was called a 'mobile', a portable alternative to what ordinary people called a telephone that usually sat on a desk or a bureau or could even be stuck to the wall. He had observed different sorts of phones when he'd crept into houses with Maitland and had heard the same mysterious crackle at the other end whenever he'd picked up the receiver.

His mum had plucked the mobile from her handbag as soon as it had rung, before Jones had taken a step instinctively towards her to say something. With the moment lost, he'd stood on the pavement, feeling so awkward and ill-prepared for what was happening he'd turned around and walked on.

'Oh, Mrs Easton, that really is too much,' shrieked his mother, her laugh echoing round the houses as Jones took one slow step after another, the sensible part of his brain reminding him he was only here to observe, not to introduce himself.

As he glanced back towards the house, his mother laughed again. She was standing on the little path that led out through the front garden onto the street.

'Ye-eess, we're leaving now, so say about . . . twenty minutes. Sorry again. We didn't notice the time. Okay. Bye. Bye.' She clicked the phone off as a middle-aged man in a suit and red tie followed her out onto the path. Jones recognized him immediately as his father. He looked older, with more weight in his face and around his throat, and he had less of his blond hair too. But it was him.

'Hurry up,' hissed his wife.

Jones's father grabbed hold of the brass knocker and banged the front door shut. 'We wouldn't be running late if you hadn't taken so long getting ready,' he said, following his wife down the short path towards the open gate at the end, aiming for the street beyond.

'You were the one who insisted on finishing off whatever you were doing.'

'Accounts,' replied the man briskly. 'And I was ready ten minutes ago. I told you.' He slammed the gate hard behind him to make his point.

As Jones kept walking away down the street, he fumbled in the inside pocket of his overcoat for a tiny mirror Maitland had given him for spying purposes. But, instead of using it to watch for a creature creeping up behind him as he would usually, now Jones angled the mirror to see his mother and father walking across the road towards a silver estate car. Its lights blinked. The door locks popped. An engine revved.

For a brief moment, he imagined himself in that car too. Sitting in the back seat and telling a joke, making his parents laugh to stop them worrying about being late for Mrs Easton, the woman his mother had spoken to on the mobile.

The car did a smart U-turn and Jones watched the vehicle pause at the junction at the far end of the street, before turning right and vanishing. Jones dumped the mirror in his pocket and walked on a few paces more, his heart beating fast, then stopped. He hadn't expected things to turn out like this. Now, he was regretting not running up to his parents and telling them precisely who he was. Looking down, he noticed a green weed growing through a crack in the pavement and started kicking at it, cursing Maitland.

Jones was so preoccupied with thinking about his parents, imagining being with them wherever they were going, he didn't notice someone emerging swiftly out of the row of run-down houses on the other side of the street. When a hand landed on his shoulder, he flinched and looked up into the blue eyes of a boy about the same age as him but taller, with his brown hair combed up into an elaborate quiff. With his large protruding nose, he reminded Jones slightly of a crow. The boy was elegantly dressed in a three-quarter-length herringbone coat with a crisp blue shirt and a silk paisley scarf tied loosely, and rather foppishly, round his neck. When Jones tried to step away, a small fairy-like creature with a single big eye in the centre of its forehead flew up out of the other boy's coat pocket and bared a set of sharp teeth. Jones knew what it was immediately. A One Eye. And they were known for being vicious. Something pinged inside his heart as he wondered what to say to this boy. Another Badlander. He knew how the *Ordnung* worked in London.

'You shouldn't be here,' said the other boy. 'Hampstead's my Master's *æhteland*. We're the only ones allowed to hunt on it. Don't you know how the *Ordnung* works in London?'

Jones tried to look blank and shook his head. 'I don't know what you're talking about. What's an *Ord* ... an *Ordnunnn*? And what is *that*?' he said, nodding at the One Eye as it fluttered in front of him. 'What's going on?' he asked, trying to sound scared like an ordinary boy might.

The other boy laughed and shook his head as if seeing straight through Jones's act. 'Move another muscle and my One Eye will bite your nose clean off.' Jones kept quite still, watching the One Eye nervously, as the other boy searched his overcoat pockets. When he found the bottle of black Slap Dust and saw the label, he whistled. 'Deschamps & Sons. Top quality stuff.' He put the bottle in his pocket and crossed his arms. 'We were looking for a *Gást* in the houses on the other side of the road when we saw you arrive. So, instead of lying, why don't you tell me why you're really here?'

'I ain't hunting on your Master's territory.'

The boy gave a little snort that made his elaborate quiff wobble. 'Then why were you so interested in that couple who left in the car?' He smoothed a hand through his hair as if he had all the time in the world to wait for an answer. His well-polished black shoes seemed to be grinning too as the street lights caught them.

124

Jones felt a little knot pulling tighter and tighter inside him. He'd already been away from Ruby for longer than he'd intended. He didn't want to think about what she'd say if she woke up and discovered he'd left the house.

He cleared his throat as he settled on the best lie his brain could come up with, preparing to tell it as well as he could. He knew that if anyone found out that Maitland had died, he'd be punished for not reporting the death immediately. But the situation with Ruby would be far worse. Jones thought there probably wasn't even a punishment for Commencing with a girl because it was so unthinkable. He hung his head in shame. 'I was trying out that Slap Dust. I stole it off my Master and used way too much and ended up here by accident. I only meant to travel a short way. I'm sorry I came onto your Master's *æhteland*. Honest. I'm just a country Badlander and we ain't as good as you townie lot with things like Slap Dust. As for that couple, I was just hoping they didn't notice me like you did, that's all.'

The boy smiled like a fox. 'Do you think I was born yesterday? You're an apprentice like me. Well, not *quite* like me of course,' and he laughed, smoothing a hand through his hair again. 'You didn't come here by accident. You're out hunting to prove to your Master you're good enough to Commence. My Master's desperate to know if I'm ready too. There was something about that couple. I saw the way you were watching them. So, here's the deal. Tell me what you know about them, why you're really here, and we'll hunt them together. That way we can prove ourselves to our Masters and both get to Commence.'

Jones shook his head. 'I ain't got no interest in that couple. Give me my Slap Dust back and I'll get out your hair.' But the One Eye flew right up into his face and perched on his nose and growled.

'Thomas Gabriel's right,' it said in a deeper voice than Jones had expected. 'If you don't tell us the truth, I'll bite your nose clean off if that's what he wants.'

Thomas Gabriel coughed gently. 'It's very obedient.' As if to make his point, he beckoned the One Eye back to him and it perched on his shoulder, from where it continued to glare at Jones. 'Tell you what, let me help you on your hunt, and you can help me find the *Gást* I was looking for over the road. My Master, Simeon, is a sly old dog. He's kept the *Gást* bound in the middle house of that row for years as a test for all ten apprentices he had over the years. I know because I sneaked a look in his private journals. Now, catching a *Gást* would be a rum thing, wouldn't it? That would impress both our Masters. Add that to whatever you're hunting too and we're bound to Commence.'

'You can keep your *Gást*,' said Jones, who was desperate to leave. 'I ain't interested. I just want to get home before my Master finds out I stole his Slap Dust.'

Thomas Gabriel's smile melted away. 'This is your last chance, you little bumpkin. Fill me in on that couple, tell me what you're hunting, or else I'll report you to my Master for coming onto his *æhteland* and breaking the *Ordnung*. And

126

believe me you don't want that. He's a real stickler for doing everything by the book.'

As the other boy stared at him, Jones knew he was serious. So far his lie wasn't working.

'Look,' he sighed. 'Why don't we go into their house so you can see for yourself there's nothing there and I'm telling the truth. If we do that, will you give me my Slap Dust back then?'

Thomas Gabriel smiled, thinking he'd got his way. 'Deal.'

As Jones started walking back towards his parents' house, he was hoping this would all be over quickly so he could get back and ensure Ruby wouldn't know he'd left her on her own. The thought of going into his parents' house as a Badlander made him feel queasy. It didn't seem right at all. This was the place he should have been returning to as an ordinary boy. A place he had already decided he should be calling 'home'.

'Come on, Ruby, don't give up,' shouted the gun in encouragement.

Ruby had been holding on to the axe for what seemed like an eternity. It was pulling so hard towards the blurry hole that her arms were aching as she held on gamely to the wooden handle. Her legs were beginning to tire too. Pretty soon, she knew her body was going to give out. She gritted her teeth, hoping for a miracle.

'Give me a break,' she shouted. 'I'll fix the spell on you if you give me a chance.' But the axe just kept on pulling towards the hole, doing what the spell cast on it was commanding it to do.

Ruby grunted and tried taking a tiny step backwards. She succeeded in moving, taking the axe with her.

'That's right,' whooped the gun. 'And again.'

Ruby took another teeny step, dragging the axe back a little more. It was like pulling an object out of very strong glue.

'I'm going to do this,' she said, willing herself on through gritted teeth.

Her heart was pumping hard. She gulped like a goldfish. Sweat glistened on her arms. And then Ruby realized her hands were starting to slip down the wooden handle. Off came her sweaty right hand and then her left one. The axe's handle spun upwards and crashed into Ruby's chin. Her head jerked back at the impact and she collapsed like a rag doll.

The axe disappeared through the hole, leaving Ruby out cold on the floor.

'Oh,' said the gun quietly. And then it fired off another shot. 'Jones,' it cried. 'Jones! Where are you?'

With a flourish, Thomas Gabriel produced a silver pillbox from the pocket of his herringbone jacket, flipped up the lid and plucked out a brown worm.

'Do you know what this is, country boy?' he asked, holding up the wriggling thing as they stood outside the front door of Jones's parents' house, in the orange glow of the street lights.

'I'd say it looks like your basic Door Wurm,' said Jones,

wondering what Maitland would have made of this boy's theatricality. He grinned when he decided his Master would not have tolerated it one bit.

'And that's funny why, exactly?'

But Jones just shrugged.

Thomas Gabriel tutted and inserted the wriggly tip of the Wurm into the lock of the door. The creature crept inside, leaving only its rear end exposed, and, in a matter of moments, the Wurm had become a key. Thomas Gabriel turned it and there was a *click*. The One Eye had its face pressed against the door as if looking right through it.

'I can't sense any alarm,' it said, fluttering back towards them. 'And there's definitely no one else in the house.'

Thomas Gabriel pushed open the door. 'After you.' Jones looked down the hallway. There was a faint whiff of polish. A red rug lay on the floor. People in photographs he didn't know stared back at him from the walls. Suddenly, he was scared to enter the house.

'Come on!' squeaked the One Eye as it fluttered back and forth down the hallway. Jones willed his legs to work and he stepped through into the hall. Little firecrackers went off in his guts as he looked around. This had been his home once, although he recognized nothing about it, which made him feel curiously empty inside.

Thomas Gabriel shut the door and placed the wriggly Door Wurm back in its pillbox. 'Well? What are we looking for? What's got you interested in the people living here? Are they shapeshifters of some sort? Is that what you're thinking?'

'I told you, I don't know anything about them,' said Jones. 'I made a mistake with my Master's Slap Dust and ended up in the street by accident. That's the only reason I'm here.'

'I'm not stupid. There's something about this couple you're not telling me because you want to hunt them all by yourself,' said Thomas Gabriel, inspecting a photograph of Jones's parents. 'I mean, where were they going at this time of night? It's gone midnight.'

'Beats me.'

'People that age would normally be in bed if they've got work tomorrow. And what about kids? No evidence of that.' Thomas Gabriel gestured with a hand down the hallway. 'Far too tidy.'

Jones opened his mouth to say something then realized he shouldn't. He walked to the nearest doorway instead and stood looking into the living room. 'Look in here if you don't believe me. Everything's normal.' In the grainy dark, Jones noted a large television fixed to the wall and imagined sitting on the white sofa, watching it, snuggled down with his mother and father.

'I'll believe you *when* we've done a thorough search, together.'

Jones hung his head and let out a long breath. 'Fine. Let's get on with it then, shall we?'

Jones had explored many houses, working with Maitland, and knew what ordinary people considered normal. Drifting from the living room to the dining room and then the kitchen, and even the downstairs loo, he reassured himself his mother and father were definitely ordinary, boringly so. And he loved the idea that they were. Thomas Gabriel knew Jones's parents appeared to be normal too, tutting every time they finished searching a room, having found nothing of note like the usual giveaway signs of secret chambers hiding special objects, runes scratched on the floor, and not even when he threw up handfuls of purple Sight Dust, which Jones knew was supposed to reveal any recent psychic disturbances.

'I told you. I'm here by mistake,' said Jones as he watched Thomas Gabriel tapping on the wall as if expecting to find a hidden door or compartment. 'The people living here are just an ordinary couple.'

Thomas Gabriel picked up an unopened letter off the dresser. He looked at the name and address on the envelope. 'So, Mr and Mrs Davison aren't shapeshifters of any sort? They're not keeping a Droll Wurm in the cellar? They haven't been brainwashed by a powerful *Vampyr*?'

'It don't seem like it, does it?' and Jones smiled. He liked the name Davison.

Thomas Gabriel pursed his lips and then pointed a finger skyward. 'Let's check upstairs.' Jones rolled his eyes.

The main bedroom contained a large double bed with a small bedside table on either side. After inspecting the magazines on one of the tables, Thomas Gabriel made a great flourish of deducing that the woman slept on the left of the bed, and Jones gave him a round of silent applause. There was a small bathroom further down the landing, with a white shower curtain pinched together in the middle at one end

131

of the bath. The room smelt of toothpaste and bubble bath. When Jones saw strands of black and blond hair caught in the plughole of the basin, he imagined his own hair getting stuck there too.

Next to the bathroom was a study, where a modest desk sat under a single window. Thomas Gabriel glanced in, uninterested, and then tried the very last door at the end of the landing. When he discovered it was locked, his eyebrows rose quickly, like they were being pulled up on strings.

'A locked door don't mean nothing,' said Jones although deep down something stirred in him. Locked doors in any house were always viewed as suspicious by Badlanders because they were usually hiding things. He'd learnt that during his time with Maitland. Jones watched the other boy take out the Door Wurm from its silver pillbox and feed it into the lock. The door swung open with a creak and both boys looked into the room.

# FOURTEEN

I t was a box room with white walls and bare floorboards. But what caught Jones's eye immediately was the big black pentacle painted in the centre of the floor. Jones put his hand against the door frame to steady himself and breathed as slowly as he could. Finding a pentacle wasn't good. Not good at all.

Thomas Gabriel was tutting and shaking his head. 'You almost had me downstairs. I was about to say *yeah, you're right, there's nothing here, let's go.*' He grinned a big one. 'I've walked past this house hundreds of times with my Master, and not even he's had a hint anything was wrong here. And that must be the reason why,' he said, pointing at the pentacle. 'I bet it's working to conceal whatever's going on here. How did you know?' asked Thomas Gabriel, trying to hide the note of admiration in his voice.

'I didn't,' said Jones. 'I told you, I came to London by accident.'

But Thomas Gabriel just folded his arms. 'Of course you did.'

'What about this?' said the One Eye, fluttering in front of an ornate cabinet on the far side of the room.

Jones heard his heart hammering in his ears. Everything he'd deduced about his parents from walking around the house suddenly didn't seem true any more. They weren't ordinary at all. This house was in the Badlands. 'I want to go,' he said quietly.

'Don't you want to know what's in here?' asked Thomas Gabriel, trying the two doors of the cabinet and discovering they wouldn't open. 'It might tell us what we're dealing with,' he said, feeding his Door Wurm into the lock.

After unlocking the cabinet, Thomas Gabriel folded the doors back, releasing a strong smell into the room. Sandalwood. Roses. Some sort of herb too. Spearmint perhaps. But there was something else beneath it, like the smell of hot metal. It reminded Jones of the camper van's engine after a long journey.

Thomas Gabriel crouched in front of a shelf on which stood two clay figures. They were approximately thirty centimetres tall. A simple face was marked on both of them. One had strands of dark hair glued to its head and the other had blond hair.

The One Eye flew from one figure to the other, scanning them with its big eye. 'They're Witch's Poppets,' it announced. 'This is *Wiccacraeft*,' it said, fluttering back to inspect the pentacle again.

Thomas Gabriel whistled. 'A Witch, eh?' Before he could pick up the Poppet with dark hair, Jones pulled him back.

'Careful.'

Thomas Gabriel shrugged him off and touched the figure anyway.

'It's all right. I know what they do. They're made by Witches to control people, to keep them charmed to do whatever a Witch wants.' He pointed to a little stopper in each of the Poppets' chests. 'I think these are Blood Poppets from what I remember reading somewhere. A person fills the Poppet that represents them with their blood, to show their loyalty to the Witch and her *craeft*.'

Thomas Gabriel opened a slim drawer set below the shelf on which the two clay Poppets were standing. Resting on a red silk inlay were two cut-throat razors. Thomas Gabriel picked up one of the razors and opened it out. The blade looked so sharp it seemed to hum.

'So, it seems the couple living here belong to a Witch.' He gripped the razor a little harder, and his blue eyes narrowed as he looked at Jones. 'You better tell me who you are. What you're really doing here.' He held up the razor to Jones's throat as quick as a flash before Jones could move.

'They're my parents,' blurted out Jones before he could stop himself, the blade of the razor biting cold against his throat, and Thomas Gabriel pressing it tighter and tighter. 'My Master stole me away from 'em. I came to find 'em because I don't want to be a Badlander no more. I want to be an ordinary boy.'

Thomas Gabriel blinked as he tried to understand what he was hearing.

'What do you mean? Who wants that? I don't believe you one bit.'

'It's true.'

But, before Jones could attempt to explain, they both heard a loud hissing sound. It was coming from downstairs. Thomas Gabriel motioned for the One Eye, perched on his shoulder, to go and look, and it came flitting back moments later, panting as it landed on the palm of Thomas Gabriel's outstretched hand.

'It's the Wretch,' it whispered. 'It's downstairs. It must have followed us.'

'What do you mean, followed you?' asked Jones, sounding alarmed, all his disappointment about his parents fading as he began to focus like a Badlander on this new-sounding problem.

Thomas Gabriel just shrugged. 'I visited a graveyard earlier with my One Eye. We found a Wretch, but then we lost it among the graves, so we moved on. It's what Badlanders do, remember? Try and hunt down creatures. Not try and become ordinary boys.' Thomas Gabriel sniggered at the idea of such a thing.

But Jones wasn't laughing. 'Wretches hunt too. Don't you know that? Haven't you studied 'em?' He drew out a small brown notebook from the inside pocket of his overcoat on which was written the title 'Learning Book', and held it up. 'Hasn't your Master made you learn about 'em? If you find one, it has to be pursued and killed or else it comes after you no matter what. It's what they do: turn the hunter into the hunted.'

Thomas Gabriel patted him on the shoulder. 'Well, I know that now.' The One Eye flew straight into one of his jacket pockets and peered up over the edge, its hands shaking.

'Give me my Slap Dust back so I can go home,' said Jones. 'Take a pinch for yourself and go back to your Master. He'll help you set a trap for it. It'll follow you wherever you go until you stop it.'

But Thomas Gabriel shook his head. 'We're not going anywhere. If there's two of us and only one Wretch, the odds are in our favour, don't you think?'

'No, I don't,' said Jones. 'We're apprentices, we're not ready to fight a creature like this on our own.' He flicked through the pages of his Learning Book and stopped when he found the page he was looking for.

'Listen,' said Thomas Gabriel. 'My Master's always giving me a reason why he won't let me Commence. But, if I make a kill myself, he'll have no excuses. We're taking this Wretch on.' He produced two silver knuckledusters from his pocket and slipped them over his fingers.

'But they're very hard to kill without the right weapons,' said Jones grimly, 'it says so right here,' and he stabbed at the page of his Learning Book, hoping to make the other boy stop and think.

But all Thomas Gabriel did was head for the door. 'Then my Master Simeon will be mightily impressed if I pull this off.'

'He'll be getting a new apprentice if you don't.'

Thomas Gabriel stopped when he realized Jones was still rooted to the spot.

'You know what I think? Your Master didn't steal you. He *rescued* you from whatever evil's planted itself here, and raised you as a Badlander. You'll never be an ordinary boy now. The people living here might have been your parents once. But they're not any more. So be the Badlander you are, and help me fight this Wretch.' With that, Thomas Gabriel ran out of the door.

Jones glanced back at the clay Poppets inside the cabinet. All sorts of questions about his parents were humming at the back of his mind, and about Maitland too. Maybe Thomas Gabriel was right, perhaps Maitland had saved him instead of stealing him as he'd thought. And then a mighty inhuman scream made him flinch and he raced out of the room.

Thomas Gabriel was downstairs, one of his knuckledusters smoking. The boy had the Wretch cornered in the hallway and Jones realized Thomas Gabriel must have punched the creature when he saw a bright white mark showing on one of its dark, lithe arms. The Wretch was jet-black, made entirely from what looked like shadow that formed a tall, skeletal figure at least seven feet tall. The arms were long and lean. But the hands were large, out of proportion with the rest of the body, with large talons instead of fingers that curved like sickles and ended in sharp points. The head was a faceless skull, black like the rest of its body, with high cheekbones and a mouth of dark teeth. But the eye sockets were full of bright light that showed there was something alive and intelligent inside.

Thomas Gabriel dropped his right shoulder, feigning a punch, and caught the Wretch with a left hook, the knuckleduster drawing a white-hot mark on its black body, just above its hip.

'Stay clear of its talons,' shouted Jones above the screaming Wretch as it brought an arm swinging round, just missing Thomas Gabriel's chin. 'That's one thing I know from reading the Pocket Book Bestiary.'

'Are you going to actually help me fight this thing or not?' shouted Thomas Gabriel.

Jones found his catapult in his pocket and popped a silver ball bearing in the sling and aimed. But as he did so the Wretch suddenly retreated, vanishing into the wall, and the ball bearing hit the plaster with a loud **POP!** It bounced back hitting Thomas Gabriel in the shin, forcing him to start hopping madly on one leg.

Jones ignored the other boy's cursing, his eyes whipping round the hallway as he looked for the Wretch, trying to spot it, remembering how the creature's physiology allowed it to be either corporeal like a human or non-corporeal at will, making it evasive and difficult to kill.

'*Ssshh*,' he hissed at Thomas Gabriel, who was still moaning about his painful shin, 'I think it's hiding in the wall.'

And then he looked down and realized it wasn't in the walls at all but lurking in the floor near his feet, its black face staring up at him.

'It's in the floor!' shouted Jones as the face vanished. A moment later, a black head popped up, right behind Thomas Gabriel, like a seal breaking the water's surface. 'Look out!' yelled Jones, pointing.

But, as Thomas Gabriel looked round, it was already too late. Two black hands came up either side of him and clamped their sharp talons into his legs. Thomas Gabriel screamed and tried to move, but his legs were pinned. The One Eye flew up out of his pocket, buzzing round the Wretch, snapping its teeth, but the creature took no notice. Jones aimed his catapult again and fired at the Wretch's head, but it ducked down through the floor, keeping its talons speared into Thomas Gabriel's calves. The ball bearing pinged up off the floor and disappeared through a doorway.

A dark leg came up through the floor in front of Jones and kicked out hard, catching him full in the chest. He hit the wall behind with such force that he heard his teeth click before collapsing face first onto the floor. As he shook his head free of the sparks behind his eyes, he felt a weight on his back, pushing him down.

He turned his head to look up and saw the Wretch standing over him, one foot planted on his back, pinning him to the floor. It was holding Thomas Gabriel now in one large hand, its long talons wrapped around the boy's waist, as he kicked and struggled, shouting at it to put him down. But the Wretch just grunted and raised its free hand, the talons curled into the shape of a claw, before

140

reaching into the boy's mouth, stifling his cries. Thomas Gabriel began to tremble as the Wretch pulled out a string of white mist from his mouth. When the creature let go of the end, the white thread began coiling round and round on itself, spinning into the shape of a tiny ball. As Thomas Gabriel went limp, Jones struggled to break free of the foot keeping him stuck to the floor, but it was no use, and he shouted and screamed as the Wretch laid the other boy down. The white floating ball, still attached to Thomas Gabriel, continued to spin round, growing in size as it did.

Jones felt the strength in the Wretch's hands as it picked him up, and then a strange feeling rushed up out of his chest as it reached into his mouth too. Jones saw a white thread being drawn out of him as if the Wretch had found the end of a piece of string inside him. The last thing he saw was the One Eye fluttering near him, frantically whispering something, and then the world went black.

As the two boys lay unconscious on the floor, not a thing stirred except for the strange white translucent balls, spinning and gathering the thread from each boy's mouth, like balls of wool winding larger and larger. The Wretch watched them for a moment more before sinking back down into the floor, apparently satisfied.

Some minutes later, with the white balls bigger now, and floating like balloons attached to the strings coming out of the boys' mouths, a very strange thing happened.

'Jones?' asked a voice that sounded as if it was coming through a tannoy on a railway platform. 'Jones, can you hear me?' If Jones had been awake, he would have realized it was a girl's voice. One he knew very well indeed.

FIFTEEN

'J ones,' said Ruby again. 'Can you hear me?'

She was sitting on the floor beside the chest full of Maitland's gifts, peering into the scrying mirror at Jones. When there was no reaction from him, Ruby purred her disapproval, which made the sore part of her chin throb even more from where the axe had bashed it before knocking her out.

'He can't hear you through the mirror,' said the gun. 'It's for scrying not communicating.'

Ruby pointed at the pamphlet on the floor. '*The Beginner's Guide to Scrying* says scrying mirrors can be used for communication and even as portals.'

'Look, you've got a talent for scrying, no doubt about that. But a portal? Come on! I bet that pamphlet says it takes years of practice.'

'Well, let's see, shall we?' Trying to ignore the dull pain in her chin that was starting to give her a headache, Ruby scooped out a great blob of polish from the Heaton's Old Familiar tin and began rubbing it into the face of the mirror.

*

When Ruby had opened her eyes and blinked up at the ceiling for a second, all she could remember was that one moment she'd been holding the axe, and then the next she was on the floor with her chin throbbing painfully and the gun shouting at her to get up. Gingerly, she'd tried moving her jaw and had found it was still working, which, she told herself as she stood up, was a very good thing. It meant Jones would be able to hear every single word she was getting ready to unload on him for not coming downstairs to help her with the axe or Victor Brynn. But, before going upstairs to find him, she'd felt a fizzing in the tips of her fingers as she'd picked up the scrying mirror to place it safely back in the chest, and then she'd seen Jones in the glass.

Ruby had watched entranced, observing him searching a house with another boy, a Badlander too apparently, who seemed rather arrogant and had the most ridiculously coiffed hair she'd ever seen.

It didn't take Ruby very long to work out where Jones was. His stolen glances at the photos of a couple dotted around the house was the first clue. Ruby had noticed a likeness between Jones and the man in the photo too. The same arrow-shaped nose. A similar mouth with fullish lips and a pronounced Cupid's bow. Even the same colour eyes. So Ruby had guessed Jones had gone to search for his parents even before he'd blurted it out to the other boy after being threatened upstairs with the razor.

But what intrigued Ruby was how Jones had got to the house, a question answered when the two boys began arguing over the Slap Dust. The black dust, it seemed, was a way of travelling from one place to another.

Ruby had clapped her hand to her mouth when she'd seen them defeated by the Wretch. And then her brain had started to pump as she began to work out a plan and reached for *The Beginner's Guide to Scrying*.

With the big lump of polish rubbed in, Ruby took a deep breath and pushed her face into the scrying mirror. She felt her nose bump against the glass, which then softened and gave way as she pressed harder, and pushed her whole face through, as if submerging it into water.

She heard the gun's loud exclamation as her head popped all the way through the mirror.

On the other side, Ruby found herself looking down at Jones from what she judged to be about ceiling height.

'Jones?' Still he didn't stir. The mirror was clearly too small for her to climb through so Ruby ducked back through the glass. Once she was looking at Jones in the mirror again, she asked it to focus on him. The image drew closer to Jones and this time she pushed a hand through the glass, and grabbed hold of his overcoat, trying to shake him into waking up. But it was no good.

She withdrew her hand, deciding on a different tactic, and thought about the other boy lying in the hallway. When his face appeared in the mirror, Ruby pushed an arm through up to the shoulder and her hand felt its way down into the nearest pocket of his herringbone jacket. She had watched the boy's fairy-like creature fly away after whispering something to Jones and hadn't seen it since. But even so she was still wary of what else might be in the boy's pocket as she delved inside. And she was wary of the Wretch too, having no idea if it was still lurking in the house.

The inside of the pocket felt much bigger than it should and Ruby realized it must be charmed to be able to hold a lot of objects. But, as soon as she thought about the bottle of Slap Dust she was trying to find, her hand closed around it.

It didn't take long to work out the address of the house either, after looking at a pile of junk mail lying on the bureau.

Putting the mirror down, she picked up the gun from the floor. 'We need to get going. What do you know about taking on a Wretch?' she asked.

'They're dangerous, make no mistake. Using magic's the most usual way for a Badlander to tackle them.'

'O-kay, any other way?'

'Maitland had a staff made of rowan. As far as I remember, he used it once on a creature like that. It's in the hall with all the others. It has the word "*syrfe*" inscribed around the middle. Maitland marked each staff, stick and cane with their Anglo-Saxon name for Jones to learn,' announced the gun as Ruby ran out of the room.

The rowan staff was wedged into a stand by the front door along with a collection of other staffs and sticks and canes of different shapes and sizes. It was about waist height and as Ruby weighed it in her hand she liked the feel of it.

'There's a special energy in it,' said the gun, watching on

from the dresser where Ruby had put it. 'It's made from flying rowan, a rare type of tree found growing on a mountain or a hillside. Maitland was given the staff on a trip to Norway a long time before he ever had Jones. It's a special piece.'

'I'll look after it.'

'Let's hope it looks after you,' the gun replied. 'Most people start by tackling something a little easier the first time they take on a creature.'

'Well, that's because they've all been boys before,' said Ruby, spinning the staff around and striking a pose like a superhero. But then she remembered this wasn't a game. 'Maybe I should check the Pocket Book Bestiary first on Wretches.'

'No time for that. We need to get going, like you said. The staff cuts through a Wretch like a knife, that's all you need to know.'

'Anything else?' asked Ruby.

'Avoid contact with a Wretch at all costs because it'll sap your energy otherwise. Also, salt and rosemary mixture burns them. There's ready-mixed vials of the stuff in one of the cupboards in the van because it's useful against a lot of creatures. Draw a ring on the ground with it and you'll be protected as long as you stay inside.'

'Thanks,' said Ruby, setting off quickly for the van outside.

The last thing she did before leaving to rescue Jones was change out of her nightclothes and dig out the thick sweater in her backpack. She put it on, together with a stout pair of gloves and a balaclava she'd noticed hanging on a peg in the hall. Ruby looked like a woolly ninja after putting everything on, which made the gun laugh when she returned to fetch it, and the staff, from the hall.

'Forget about the Wretch, you'll cook yourself to death in that get-up,' it said from the dresser.

'I'm not taking any chances; you said a Wretch can sap your energy on contact. I'm not planning on ending up like Jones. I'm rescuing him.'

'Is that so?' replied the gun. 'Well, just remember, however ready you think you are, unexpected things can happen taking on a creature as dangerous as this. You need to be prepared for anything. That's the Badlander motto – BE PREPARED!'

'I am. I've got the right weapon. I've covered up. And I've got you. You're not having doubts now, are you? You're the one who wanted to partner up, remember?'

'No, but—'

'Good, so let's get going, shall we?' After shoving the rowan staff under one arm, and double-checking the vial of rosemary and salt was in the right pocket of her jeans, Ruby took out the small bottle of black Slap Dust from her left pocket and consulted the instructions on the back. Then she tipped out a pile of the dust into her gloved hand.

'I'd go easy on that Slap Dust if I were you,' said the gun as Ruby put the bottle back in her pocket for the return journey. 'We're hardly travelling to another country.'

'I'm just making sure I get there in one piece. I don't want to leave any bits of me behind, do I? There's a warning about it on the bottle. I'm only being prepared like you said.' Ruby picked up the grumbling gun with her free hand and stuffed it into the waistband of her jeans. Then she cleared her throat and addressed the mound of dust in her hand. 'I want to go to Number 17, Chesterford Gardens,' she said clearly. 'In Hampstead, London,' she added. 'Let's make it the living room.'

And with that Ruby slapped her gloved hands together.

# SIXTEEN

She arrived in the living room with such force her trainers left scorch marks on the carpet as she hurtled towards a large armchair. As she landed in it, the whole thing scooted backwards and hit the wall behind with a loud **CRACK!**

Ruby uncurled herself. Someone had lit a small fire in her left shoulder. She gritted her teeth, and listened for anything moving in the house. But it was difficult to hear with the balaclava on. It seemed to be quiet, for a moment at least.

'That went well,' announced the gun, which had fallen out of Ruby's waistband onto the armchair, just before a plasma screen hanging on the wall to the right of them dropped to the floor, breaking with another **CRACK!**

Ruby smelt burning and looked down to see little blue flames dancing over her gloves. Spotting a large vase full of lilies, she tore out the stems and plunged both hands into the water. She left the gloves wet and steaming on the floor, between the two dark furrows she'd ploughed into the carpet.

She took off the balaclava too because everything sounded too muffled with it on.

'Bang goes the element of surprise then,' said the gun as she picked it up. 'I'm astonished the whole street hasn't come knocking.'

'*Shhhh*,' hissed Ruby as she picked up the rowan staff, which thankfully seemed to have survived the journey intact.

'About my offer of us working the Badlands together, I regret to inform you the position's been taken.'

'Yeah, by who?'

'Anyone but you.'

'Let's see about that, shall we?' Ruby made her way carefully to the doorway and peered into the hall. Jones and the other boy were still lying silently.

When Ruby picked up Jones's limp hand, it was cold. His lips had a tinge of blue in them as if he'd been sucking on a blueberry lollipop. But the white globe floating above him was full of bright light and radiating a faint warmth. The thread connecting it to Jones's mouth looked fragile. But, as Ruby tried to break it, she found it was as strong as wire.

Every so often, a little scene played inside the white globe, rather like someone had pressed a secret 'play' button. Ruby saw Maitland holding up what looked like a small dead rat with four eyes and asking a question, and then fading away.

'They're Jones's memories,' whispered the gun. 'The poor boy's had most of his life force drained out of him judging by the state of him. That's what Wretches feed on, Life Balls they're called, which they make from their victims. We've got to kill the Wretch before all of Jones is gone and he's just a corpse. It's the only way to reverse the process, and save him. Looks like his time's almost up.'

A soft creaking noise made Ruby spin round. A dark shadow was moving across the wall. When it stopped, the black skull of the Wretch emerged and stared at her. Ruby began backing away, stuffing the gun in her waistband and then realizing she had left the rowan staff on the floor beside Jones. She cursed because it was too late to go for it now.

The Wretch emerged out of the wall and came quickly towards Ruby, its long arms outstretched and the sharp blade-like fingers swinging and slicing the air. Ruby reached into the right hand pocket of her jeans for the small vial of rosemary and salt. But quickly realized it had broken with the impact of her arrival. Managing to scoop some of the mixture out of her pocket, she flung it at the creature. White spots burnt little holes all over the Wretch's black body and the creature screamed, retreating back. Ruby darted forward and grabbed the staff. There was a sensation of strength and power coming off it now, as if the object had come alive in the presence of the Wretch. Ruby hurriedly backed down the hall, through the doorway at the end into the kitchen where she was out of sight.

Quickly, she took a fistful of the salt and rosemary out of her pocket, crouched down in the middle of the room, and drew a ring of the mixture around her, drizzling it out of her fist, her trainers squeaking on the linoleum floor.

'Is this right?' she asked, drawing the gun out of her waistband to show it what she'd done.

But there was no time for a reply as the Wretch came running into the kitchen and launched itself at Ruby, a black torpedo of outstretched arms and talons. For a terrifying moment, Ruby doubted the mixture would be strong enough to deflect a creature as big and as terrifying as this.

But it worked.

The Wretch was repelled with such force it crashed back into the small table and chairs behind it.

Seizing her chance, Ruby nipped out of the circle and swung the rowan staff one-handed at one of the Wretch's arms as it struggled to stand up. She sliced the hand clean off and it lay twitching on the floor.

Screaming, the Wretch kicked out again. Ruby jumped over its leg – elegantly enough for the gun in her other hand to whistle its approval – and retreated to the safety of the rosemary and salt circle.

'Nice move!' the gun shouted. 'Where'd you learn that?'

'Ballet classes. Mrs Simmons was always telling me I had a nice high *jeté*.'

'She should be training Badlanders,' the gun cried as the Wretch staggered to its feet. 'Now, line me up! Give me a go. I've got a rosemary and salt mix loaded!' Ruby aimed the gun at the creature's head. But, before she could pull the trigger, the Wretch disappeared into the floor, like a black flame suddenly snuffed out, and Ruby was left pointing the gun at the wall. She circled slowly, waiting to see where the creature was going to reappear. And then she suddenly had a thought and took a big step out of the circle.

'What are you doing? Are you ma—'

The gun's voice was snuffed out as the Wretch shot up through the floor inside the salt and rosemary ring with a triumphant scream.

Ruby watched as the creature realized it was trapped inside the circle, unable to step out towards her. Before it had time to sink back down through the floor, Ruby swung the staff as hard as she could, slicing through its neck. The Wretch's head went flying from its shoulders and landed on the wooden counter, rolled down it, then over the drainer, and plopped into the aluminium sink with a thud. The headless corpse collapsed to the floor and lay like a black puddle inside the salt and rosemary circle.

Ruby stood, waiting for something else to happen, until, gradually, she realized the gun was shouting and hollering and whistling. 'You did it! You killed it!' Ruby grinned. She was so proud of herself, her chest felt like a balloon about to burst. 'You need to mark your kill,' said the gun. 'All Badlanders do it to show the creatures they've killed. It's called a *mearcunge*.'

'How do I do that?'

'You just write your name somewhere close to the body.'

But, before Ruby could think about how she might do that, she heard a whooshing sound in the hall and rushed to the doorway to see a tall man appearing from out of nowhere. He was wearing a tweed suit and his long grey hair was pulled back into a ponytail. His face was full of deep creases, suggesting he either laughed a lot or frowned most of the time, and Ruby could not decide which one it might be. He didn't notice her as she watched him, the faint smell of Slap Dust now recognizable to her fading away.

Thomas Gabriel's One Eye fluttered up out of the man's jacket pocket as he inspected the two boys lying on the floor. 'You see!' it cried. 'You see what's happened to your apprentice, Simeon.'

The man grunted and shook his head disapprovingly, observing the white floating Life Balls.

'They're going to be fine,' said Ruby, folding her arms and leaning against the door frame. The man looked up at her. His dark brown eyes were hooded and deep-set. He frowned.

'Who on earth are you?' he growled.

'Ruby Jenkins. And I'm a Badlander. Just like you. Well, I'm starting out at least. Doing it for the sisterhood, you know?'

The man opened his mouth and shook his head. Eventually, he found the word he was looking for. 'Impossible,' he said.

'My name is *definitely* Ruby.' When the man frowned even more, Ruby clicked her fingers. 'Oh, you mean it's impossible because I'm a *girl*? Because of the *Ordnung*-thingy. Well, that's old news. I *am* a Badlander. In fact, *I've* just taken out a Wretch. You know? Big dude. As black as night. I kicked its butt. Took its head clean off in the kitchen with this staff. This gun's charmed to speak. It told me what to do.' As she raised the staff in one hand, and the gun in the other, Ruby cocked her head to one side for effect because that's what she'd seen people in films do when they were making a point.

The man looked like he'd been slapped round the face with a kipper. The One Eye was staring at Ruby too, bobbing in the air, its mouth hanging open and its big teeth showing.

But Ruby ploughed on regardless. 'These boys found something upstairs you should see. A pentacle on the floor and Poppets, I think they're called, in a cabinet. I can show you if you like.' But, when she took a step forward, the man raised his hand, conjuring up a set of white sparks round his fingers.

'Stay right there,' he said in a commanding voice. 'I don't know who or what you are but you're certainly no Badlander.' Ruby watched the white sparks dancing round the man's fingertips and began to sense she'd misjudged the mood and made the wrong impression. Her elation at killing the Wretch was rapidly dwindling.

'But I really am. I'm the first girl Badlander there's ever been. I've even been through Commencement with him,' she said, nodding at Jones, wondering when he might start to come round now the Wretch was dead. The man cursed under his breath, and Ruby remembered what Jones had told her, that no one should know they could do magic together so she decided not to mention it.

When the white sparks around the man's hands began reaching out towards Ruby, she raised the gun, her arm shaking. 'Look, I think we got off on the wrong foot. My mistake. I know it's a lot to take in.' But the man was ignoring her, muttering under his breath, and the white sparks were starting to turn into letters that streamed towards Ruby.

'Stop or I'll shoot,' she warned.

'No, she won't,' shouted the gun. 'I can't fire on another Badlander, sir. Don't worry about that.'

'What? Help me out here,' Ruby muttered to the revolver, not looking away from the man. 'Not even a tranquillizer dart or something else to put him to sleep?'

'No!'

Ruby pulled the trigger anyway and when nothing happened she swore and stuffed the gun back in her waistband. The letters conjured from the man's fingers were closing in on her, but she stood her ground, readying the rowan staff like a baseball bat.

'Stop what you're doing!' she shouted. But the man didn't seem to want to stop. As the first letters reached her, she swung the staff, batting them away. She dodged a letter 'O' as it tried to lasso her round the neck. The curly end of a 'T' caught hold of her ankle and tried to trip her up till she kicked it away.

Dodging this way and that, Ruby hit more letters away, but others kept streaming from the man's fingers until there were too many for her to handle. A jumble of different ones caught hold of the end of the staff and yanked it out of her hands.

In desperation, Ruby pulled out the gun and tried batting more letters away, much to its disgust. 'I'm a gun,' it shouted, 'not a stick!'

Eventually, Ruby gave up and threw the weapon in

frustration at the man before turning to run. But a letter 'T' tripped her up and an 'O' looped round her ankles and slid all the way up to her knees. A letter 'V' turned upside down and landed on the back of her neck, pinning her to the floor.

Ruby could smell something sweet, like melon or apricots, as more and more letters crowded round her. She felt woozy. The letters were at her lips, forcing their way into her mouth. As soon as they were inside her, they dissolved like sugar. The taste was so lovely that she opened her mouth to let more in.

When the man knelt down beside her, Ruby saw him staring at her with his fierce brown eyes.

'My name is Simeon Rowell and I'm Master of the apprentice, Thomas Gabriel. His One Eye found me patrolling my *æhteland* and alerted me to the danger of a Wretch and, judging by the state of my apprentice, it wasn't lying. Now, I need *you* to tell me where the creature is. You can't lie now you're full of a truth spell.'

'I told you. I killed the Wretch before you got here.'

The man stared at her in disbelief.

'It's my first kill,' beamed Ruby.

'Ridiculous,' hissed Simeon. 'No girl could ever manage such a thing. You're lying. What foul thing are you that can lie whilst full of a truth spell? And how dare you ridicule the Badlander Order!'

'I'm not! You Badlanders are so out of date. Why can't girls be Badlanders? What's the problem with that? We can do all sorts of things as well as boys if not better.'

Simeon looked up as the One Eye came flying back out of the kitchen. 'She's telling the truth,' it squeaked. 'The Wretch is in there as dead as a doornail.'

'Told you.' Ruby grinned as Simeon turned to look at her, a look of utter shock spreading across his face. It was the last thing she saw as he flashed another handful of white sparks at her and then she was falling down what seemed to be a very deep dark hole.

SEVENTEEN

I t took two days for Jones and Thomas Gabriel to recover properly. Simeon used magic to relocate them safely back to his house, a four-storey Georgian building set back from the main road. It was hidden behind tall metal gates and surrounded by a lush garden full of large bushes and thick shrubs with green waxy leaves.

The two boys were laid on beds in the same room with their white Life Balls hovering beside them, gradually reducing in size as the life force of each of them returned to reanimate their bodies and minds. Simeon came to check on them from time to time, listening to their hearts and making sure they were kept warm with plenty of blankets and hot-water bottles.

Ruby had never been inside such a grand house but she was kept confined to a bedroom with an ensuite bathroom so didn't know much about the boys except for what the One Eye told her. It would flit in through the large keyhole to check on her every now and then, informing her when a tray of food had been left outside the door and warning her not to try anything stupid. Each time it growled and bared its teeth to make sure she got the point.

Ruby did not see Simeon at all and was only aware of his presence from the arrival and departure of the trays of food and the odd mutterings she heard. The man had also removed the gun, so Ruby was entirely alone. To alleviate her boredom, Ruby started to read the books kept on the one large shelf in the bedroom. She learnt a lot about the life cycle of the Burrowing Troll, the history of Badlanders in France from 1745 to 1750, and about Nathaniel Hewitt, a Badlander who had lived in Hampshire and was famous for accidentally discovering a new species of Wood Sprite after needing to pee behind a tree one night.

So on the third morning of her stay, when a sharp rap of Simeon's knuckles on the door told Ruby she might be getting out, she jumped up quickly off the bed as the man poked his head into the room.

'They've recovered. Come downstairs in five minutes.' He shut the door again without saying anything else.

When Ruby came down the sweeping set of stairs into the grand hallway with a floor like a chessboard, Jones and Thomas Gabriel were waiting for her. The boys looked pale and tired and were standing with their hands behind their backs.

'Go on,' said Simeon as he stood beside them.

'Thanks for saving me,' said Jones. When Thomas Gabriel just nodded, Simeon coughed. Loudly.

'Yeah, thanks,' muttered Thomas Gabriel without looking at her.

'You're welcome,' replied Ruby. 'I'm just pleased you're okay, Jones. To see you again, you know.' When Jones just nodded back curtly, his eyes darting to Simeon, Ruby felt a little deflated inside. But she decided he probably didn't want to appear over-friendly with a girl in front of another Badlander because he was in enough trouble already. So she said nothing else.

'Now the niceties are over, all three of you will come with me. I want to show you something. After which, you, Thomas Gabriel, are to sit down and write out a letter of apology to me for all the aggravation you've caused. Once you've done that, you will learn everything about Wretches there is to know, and I mean *everything*. You will read *every* book, research paper and pamphlet I own on the creatures, and believe me it is an extensive collection, and make your own notes for me to assess.' Thomas Gabriel opened his mouth to protest, but Simeon raised a finger. 'You have maybe one chance left to impress me before I decide whether to let you Commence or wipe your memory and throw you out to survive in the world on your own. Do you understand?'

Thomas Gabriel nodded. 'Yes, sir.'

'Very well.' Simeon straightened his coat. 'Now, let's get on.'

The three children followed Simeon as he led them from the house and through the streets and alleys of Hampstead, walking among ordinary people who didn't seem to notice them as they went about their business, making Ruby wonder if Simeon had done something to make all four of them invisible. But she didn't dare ask.

The Badlander took them to all his favourite places, houses of historical note, pretty streets, pubs, and even up onto Hampstead Heath, where he talked about all the different things that people did there from sunbathing to running and swimming in the ponds. He said not one word about Jones's parents or the Witch's Poppets. As far as Ruby was concerned, it was as dull as any school trip. And she could tell neither Jones nor Thomas Gabriel were enjoying it either. From their glances at each other, nobody was sure why they were being taken to all these places.

By the time they returned to Simeon's house, their feet were sore and they were thirsty and hungry. But Simeon wasn't finished yet. He took them up to the very top of the house and out onto the terrace from where they had a view of Hampstead and beyond.

'I'm sure you'll agree that Hampstead is a beautiful place. It's relatively safe too. Few people die unnaturally or go missing in my *æhteland*. When the *wyrd* decides to take me, I'll leave a legacy fellow Badlanders will admire. They'll say, "Simeon Rowell did a good job for a territory in London; he kept many of the ordinary people he was responsible for safe and well." But what they *won't* know about, what I'll keep secret to my grave, is the presence of a Witch on my territory so powerful not even the most brilliant of Badlanders would dare take her on.'

Simeon glared at all three children, daring them to question him.

'Sir, is that the one whose Poppets we found?' asked Thomas Gabriel.

Simeon nodded gravely. 'This Witch has lived for centuries. Jones, your Master also knew a great deal about her, according to his gun anyway, after I succeeded in breaking the charm Maitland had placed on it.'

'What's it said?' asked Jones.

'Breaking charms can be a messy business,' said Simeon, tutting and shaking his head. 'But I've managed to find out that Maitland had some personal score to settle with this Witch. How exactly he knew of her and tracked her down I don't know, but as soon as Maitland found her in Hampstead it became apparent to him she was far too powerful to take on. It was then he realized that your parents, Jones, were two of the people cursed by this Witch, so he did what he thought was right. He rescued you. Why, Thomas Gabriel, do Witches surround themselves with acolytes like Jones's parents?'

'Because Witches are extremely vain, sir. They like to be worshipped and admired so they curse ordinary people. It's also why they have familiars, so they can tell them how wonderful they are.'

'And?' Thomas Gabriel's forehead furrowed. 'Why else do Witches curse ordinary people?'

Thomas Gabriel clicked his fingers. 'Because Witches like to eat people too sir.'

Simeon nodded and then returned to Jones. 'If Maitland

hadn't taken you when you were a baby then your parents would surely have given you up to the Witch at some point, because, Thomas Gabriel . . .'

'Witches particularly love eating children, sir.'

'Good. Now, the gun told me that Maitland left a *fæcce* in your place, Jones, so maybe she ate that or maybe it died naturally before she could. Whatever happened to it isn't of concern. You were saved and that's what mattered to Maitland because clearly he dedicated his life to raising you as his apprentice. Thomas Gabriel, why are apprentices so important to their Masters?'

'To carry on a Badlander's legacy. To show their Master's good name and standing.'

'Which is something I'm bearing in mind about you, young man.' And Thomas Gabriel nodded. Simeon cleared his throat. 'So, Jones,' he said brightly, 'what to do now? I have a proposition for you, seeing as you have no choice but to forget about your parents and have no Master either . . .'

Jones was looking down at his black boots. Maitland had made him polish them every day and he'd always resented doing it, thinking it a waste of time. Now, all he could think about was how grateful he was to Maitland for rescuing him and bringing him up. The man had been strict, but he'd always been fair too. And then another thought occurred to him.

'Jones?' asked Simeon. 'Are you listening?'

Jones looked up straight at Simeon. 'I may have got

rescued by Maitland and I'm grateful and all cos he was a good Master who didn't do no wrong, but I ain't gonna be a Badlander no more. My parents are still alive and I want 'em back. I'll get rid of this Witch even if you're too scared to, cos that's what it sounds like.'

Simeon's face flickered and his eyes narrowed into slits. Clearly, he was unused to such insolence. 'Listen to what I'm telling you, boy,' he said in a stern voice. 'There's no way to free your parents from this Witch. To break her curse, you'd have to kill her. That's a task beyond my abilities, and believe me I tried in my early days. It was one beyond your Master too. Sometimes, there are occasions when a Badlander must compromise, when he must admit defeat. I've left this Witch alone for years, confronting her only when I have to, and she repays the gesture by not being too greedy in her eating habits. It means I can go on doing my job, protecting the majority of people on my *æhteland*.'

'You're no better than her,' said Jones. 'You shouldn't even be a Badlander. Tell me who she is. Where can I find her?'

'I won't tell you anything, boy! I've already gone to great pains to make sure your night-time visit went undetected, by tidying up all the mess,' and Simeon glared at Ruby too. 'Jones, your parents are the property of this Witch. And they will be till they die. Even if by some miracle she was killed and your parents were freed from the curse, they'd require great care and the use of magic to enable them to recover from its effects.'

'Don't let him tell you what you can't do, Jones,' said Ruby.

'You can go after that Witch and save your parents if you want, just like I can be a Badlander.'

'No, he cannot!' thundered Simeon. 'The Witch is much too formidable a foe. She's created a *Deorcan Flascan*.' Simeon clicked his fingers. 'Thomas Gabriel, translate that for me!'

Thomas Gabriel immediately turned pale because of the unfamiliar Anglo-Saxon word. 'Umm, that's a . . . a . . .'

'What's a Dark Bottle?' asked Jones, and Simeon glanced disapprovingly at Thomas Gabriel before answering.

'It's a Bottle only the most powerful Witches can make. They fill it with all of their greatest fears, and those are the only things that can kill them. Witches bury their Bottle in a special place where it's protected by *Wiccacraeft* or a dangerous creature of some sort and, in most cases, usually both. So even if you know where to look for it then it's almost impossible to steal it. Without her Dark Bottle, this Witch cannot be killed by you, me or anyone else.' Ruby opened her mouth to say something, but Simeon glared at her. 'Not even by a girl who *claims* to be a Badlander!' Simeon stared at Jones down the length of his long nose. 'This Witch is unbeatable. Maitland rescued you, gave you another chance at life. Being a Badlander is your destiny. Well, at least it *was*: you'll never be a proper one now, after the way your Commencement worked out.' He waved a hand at Ruby without even looking at her. 'This *girl* mentioned you Commenced together, but I can only presume nothing came of it, that you weren't given the gift of magic.'

Jones nodded his head. 'Yes, sir, that's right, I can't do magic. Neither of us can.'

Ruby was about to open her mouth to point out that wasn't true, but then remembered Jones's warning that no one should ever know about them being able to do magic. So she just shook her head too.

'Precisely as I expected.' Simeon clicked his fingers. 'Why is that, Thomas Gabriel?'

'Because the Commencement would have been corrupted, sir, when it realized a girl was involved. Magic's never worked for girls,' he sneered in the direction of Ruby, who just managed to hold her tongue.

Simeon smiled for the first time at Ruby. 'Thomas Gabriel's right: the early founders of our Order discovered girls and magic didn't agree. By Commencing together yet failing to receive the gift of magic, you've merely proved an indisputable fact. Magic isn't for girls, it's only for men and boys. So how can you possibly expect to be a proper Badlander if you can't do magic?' Ruby swallowed down what felt like a stone and just nodded. 'I'm sorry, Jones,' continued Simeon. 'This girl has ruined the future Maitland had planned for you. But, on a brighter note, I'd be happy to offer you a place at my side as my Whelp. At least then you'll be able to continue in the Order. I know it's not what Maitland intended but it's the only way to make good of this mess. Whelps can be invaluable to their Masters. In time, after I'm gone, maybe you can serve Thomas Gabriel too, if he goes on to Commence, that is.'

Thomas Gabriel grinned. 'I think you'd make an excellent Whelp, Jones.'

Jones looked at the other boy's smiling face and felt something dark and heavy thud into his stomach as he thought about the future Simeon was proposing for him.

'And what about me?' asked Ruby.

'You're a *girl*,' said Simeon. 'A brave one, admittedly. But nevertheless there's no place for you in the Order. If you're insistent on being around magic, I can put in a word for you at Deschamps & Sons. The store has served Badlanders for centuries. Last week I overheard a clerk saying the stationery department was looking for a junior, to learn how to mix inks. Who knows, you might even work your way up to the shop floor one day if you keep your wits about you. A shop girl! Now that would be something, wouldn't it?' Simeon smiled like an old uncle with no interest at all in children.

'Wouldn't it just?' Ruby managed to say through gritted teeth.

'The alternative is I report both of you to the Order for this abhorrent Commencement of yours. Neither of you would escape punishment and I have no doubt it would be long and very painful.'

'I'll take your generous offer to be your Whelp, sir, thank you,' said Jones, standing up straight and looking Simeon in the eye.

'Jones!' said Ruby. 'Being a Whelp sounds horrible, whatever it is. And what about Thomas Gabriel? Do you really want to be serving him? You'd make a way better Badlander than him.'

Thomas Gabriel opened his mouth, but Simeon held up his hand to silence him. 'Jones, if you can forget about your mother and father and give up on this fanciful idea of being an ordinary boy, I think you'll make a fine Whelp in time. Can you do that?'

'I can, sir, yes.' And Jones ignored whatever Ruby was muttering under her breath.

'Good,' said Simeon. 'Now, I'd like you to return to Maitland's house and remain there until I arrive. Taking you on as my Whelp means the house and all its contents pass to me now, but certain documentation needs to be drawn up and approved by the Order.'

'How long will that take, sir?' asked Jones.

'About a week. Will that be long enough to clean the house properly and organize everything so an inventory can be drawn up ready for when I come to view the house?'

'Yes,' nodded Jones.

'Good.' Simeon smiled at Ruby. 'You can go with him and help. That will give you some time to decide if you want me to put in a good word for you at Deschamps & Sons. If not, then I will return you unharmed to your ordinary life without any recollection of the Badlands at all.'

It was night by the time Simeon allowed Jones and Ruby to leave. He had spent the rest of the day briefing Jones about how he wanted Maitland's house to be meticulously organized. To pass the time, Ruby had been given some old catalogues from Deschamps & Sons and told to study them.

But, instead of reading them, she'd spent most of the afternoon hoping for Victor Brynn to come hurtling out of nowhere. She took great pleasure in imagining over and over again the look on Simeon's face when he realized she and Jones could do magic, just before the No-Thing bit into his neck and started draining his blood.

When it was finally time for them to leave, Simeon opened a plastic container and poured a ring of bright red Slap Dust around them as they stood in his hallway. 'Now, you probably haven't travelled using dust that looks like this before, Jones.'

'No, sir,' replied Jones looking suspiciously at the edge of the circle near his feet.

'That's because it's a special mixture I've created. The base powder is dried beetroot mixed with a sprinkling of other rather more secret ingredients. Not only is it very useful for transporting large objects, it also requires very little actual Slap Dust because of the other things I've added to the mixture, making it cheap to create.' He tapped his nose. 'It's a brilliant and potentially very profitable concoction. But the real advantage it has is that you only need to *think* of where you want to go, making it safer and more convenient than normal dust. The problem of announcing where you want to go has always been an issue of course. I mean just imagine you were fleeing from a creature and it knew where you'd disappeared to? It could come after you. Genius, don't you think?' And Simeon grinned unashamedly as he put the top back on the container. 'Being my Whelp, Jones, means you're going to be trying out all sorts of my rather brilliant inventions. Now, ready to go?'

'Yes, sir.'

Even though he didn't ask her, Ruby put her thumbs up to Simeon and smiled as sweetly as she could. The plastic bag she was holding clinked.

'Don't lose those gun parts,' warned Simeon, pointing at the bag. 'It's a shame I had to split the weapon apart trying to break Maitland's charm, but I'll send over some imps tomorrow to fix it.' He waggled his plastic container of red dust to show how useful his invention could be.

Before Ruby had time to think up something prickly to say in reply, Jones was announcing they were leaving. Simeon opened his mouth to say something, but all Ruby heard was the *whoosh* of the Slap Dust and she closed her eyes.

When she opened them again, she wasn't standing in Maitland's house as she'd expected. Instead, she was standing in the dark, beside Jones, in front of a row of dilapidated houses. There was a faint tang of beetroot around them too, which she put down to Simeon's special Slap Dust.

'This isn't Maitland's house. Where are we?'

Jones walked quickly down the overgrown path towards the middle house in the row. 'Come on,' he said before disappearing through a gap in the front door where a piece of plywood had come loose. He stuck his head back through when he realized she wasn't following. 'I don't care what

172

Simeon says. I'm gonna find this Witch and kill her and get my parents back so I can make 'em better, whatever her curse has done to 'em.' He pointed to the houses across the road and Ruby looked back and realized they must be standing in Chesterford Gardens, the street in which Jones's parents lived. 'I'm gonna be a Badlander for one last hunt and I want you to help me.'

'Why?' hissed Ruby.

'Cos, strange as it is, you're the only friend I got. If it wasn't for you killing that Wretch, I wouldn't be alive. Now, come on, before anyone sees you. I've worked out a plan and we need to get on with it. If you want to learn about being a Badlander, now's your chance.'

Ruby stood there for a moment, wondering what sort of plan Jones had in mind, and then she walked on quickly down the path, excited that, at last, she was going to get to work with Jones and start learning how to be a Badlander.

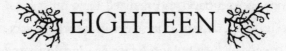

EIGHTEEN

'J ones, what are we doing here? This place doesn't look safe,' announced Ruby as she ducked under a woolly cobweb, the gun parts clinking inside the plastic bag she was holding.

'Looks all right to me,' said Jones.

Ruby pushed at the nearest wall. But nothing creaked or moved, and Jones just shrugged to prove his point.

'Well, it stinks,' said Ruby, wrinkling her nose.

'What do you expect? This whole row of houses has been abandoned. It's the perfect place for a *Gást*. Thomas Gabriel told me Simeon's got one bound in the middle house in the row as a test for his apprentices.'

'What's a *Gást*?'

'A ghost,' said Jones. 'Seeing as this house looks across the street to where my parents live, I'm hoping the *Gást* can tell us something about the Witch who's cursed 'em. If we're lucky, we'll get a clue about how to find her.' He vanished through a doorway into what looked like the living room. When Ruby followed him, she came face to face with a large black spider, as big as a pebble in the centre of its web.

'Well, let's hurry up and find it, Jones. I hate spiders,' she muttered, edging round the web.

Jones was crouched in a corner, inspecting a patch of olive green fungus on the wall, prodding at the rubbery surface.

'Yuck, should you be touching that?' asked Ruby.

'I think it looks right. It's definitely in the book ...'

'What book? What are you talking about?'

'*Clues, Hints and Inklings*. Maitland made me read it. He was always asking me questions to make sure I was learning everything. We were almost at the end.' He shrugged and tore off a hunk of fungus.

'Jones, you're not going to—' Before Ruby could finish, the boy took a big bite and pulled a face as he chewed. But he managed to swallow. 'That is so gross. Are you sure it's safe?'

'Long as it's in the book.' Jones patted his tummy as if congratulating it and it gurgled back. '*Gásts* live on a different plane of existence to us which is why you usually don't see 'em. But most types of *swamm* record traces of 'em. *Swamm* capture little moments that you can hear or watch back if you eat a bit. I need to know what sort of *Gást* we're dealing with before we try and catch it.'

'Why's that?'

'Hopefully it's human cos if it's something like an Ogre or a Troll then it's going to be trickier to catch.' He offered Ruby what was left of the fungus, but she shook her head. 'Townies like Simeon and Thomas Gabriel wouldn't dream of eating

175

it either, that's why country Badlanders are better. We don't mind getting dirty.' He popped the last bit of fungus into his mouth and grinned as he chewed. He imagined Maitland being proud of him, using the knowledge he'd been taught. It meant not thinking about how disapproving his Master would have been about why he was doing it, to give up on being a Badlander.

'So what happens now?' asked Ruby.

'We wait, and hope the *swamm*'ll show me something—' and all Jones managed after that was a strange throaty sound as the fungus began to take effect.

He felt all the hair on his head stand up. His body convulsed with such force, his chin dropped onto his chest and bounced up again. As he blinked, he felt a tingling all over his body.

'Jones? Are you all right?'

He nodded as he started to hear the mutterings and whispers of someone. It sounded like a man's voice. He tried picking out words and phrases, but they ran away from him too fast, as if someone was tuning a radio backwards and forwards.

'Jones?' asked Ruby again just as urgently.

'I can hear something. It sounds like a man, but I ain't totally sure. I need to get a look in a—'

A man in a grey suit came striding out of nowhere towards him and Jones's heart jumped. The man walked straight through him and disappeared into the wall behind.

Jones gave Ruby a big thumbs up. 'Thomas Gabriel was

right. Simeon's definitely put a *Gást* here. And it's human. A man. I saw him. He's about forty years old, with black hair combed in a parting.'

Next Jones saw other glimpses of the *Gást* from the past: a grey-suited trouser leg and a smart black shoe disappearing through a wall, then the thing looking out of a window onto the street, muttering to itself, its hair as black as boot polish. In another instant, Jones witnessed the *Gást's* head floating past like a balloon.

As the fungus wore off, the tingling sensation in Jones vanished. And, after a nutty-smelling burp that seemed to last for an eternity, he felt perfectly normal again. 'All we need to do now is perform a ghosting, a *betreppende*,' he said to Ruby.

'And that means?'

'Catching it.' Jones felt a cold breeze slick over his neck. The rotten door behind him slammed shut, making both him and Ruby jump. 'Doesn't sound like he's planning on making it easy, though,' said Jones, his breath turning frosty.

The dust on the floor began to swirl and as it settled they could make out a message in the dirt:

'We'll see,' announced Jones, scrubbing out the words with his black boot. He started picking various things out of his overcoat pockets, laying them on the floor, as the dust swirled again, rising in little thunderclouds that scrunched together and flew at the boy like dirty snowballs. He ignored them, raising the collar of his coat for some protection. When one of them caught him full in the face, leaving him spitting and coughing, the faint sound of laughter rang around the room. As Ruby watched Jones rubbing the dust out of his eyes she glanced around warily, wondering what else the *Gást* might have in store for them.

She studied the various things laid out on the floor. A piece of chalk. A small white candle. A box of matches. A blue biro. An empty jam jar complete with a lid. And, beside these items, three white envelopes.

'This is what you need to capture a *Gást*?' she asked, with concern given the specialized weapons she'd needed to take on the Wretch.

Jones nodded. 'Nicked it all from Simeon's house. These are for later, though,' and he put the envelopes and the blue biro back in his pocket. He drew out a small brown notebook from the inside of his coat and began flicking through the pages. 'As long as we follow the instructions I've got written down in my Learning Book, we should be fine.' A cold draught blew across the room, trying to disturb Jones as he found the page he wanted, but he ignored it and then snapped the notebook shut. 'Right, let's get to work. I ain't tried this on my own before.'

Jones drew two large circles on the floor a few metres apart, facing each other. Around the edge of each one he wrote various symbols, copying them out of his Learning Book, which Ruby held open for him.

'Each one's got to be perfect,' he said, rubbing out one symbol and starting again. The whole exercise wasn't made any easier with the cold draught blowing through the house and the doors constantly slamming and the dust swirling. Spiderwebs broke free too and flew around the room. But Jones battled on until he was left with a stub of chalk and symbols he was happy with. It had taken him over an hour.

In the centre of both circles, he drew a small intricate shape that looked rather like a snowflake. There was only a tiny nub of chalk left in his fingers when he'd finished.

'Almost there.' He tried to light the candle, only for the cold draught to blow out the match. 'Candlelight draws out *Gásts*,' he informed Ruby. 'They hate that.' Jones used his overcoat as a shield, holding up one arm like a bird inspecting its wing, and successfully lit the candle with Ruby helping to protect it too. He let it burn enough to be able to drip some of the hot wax into the bottom of the jar and then stood the candle in it until he could let go. Satisfied, he then placed the jar containing the flickering candle in the centre of the room between the two chalk circles and stepped inside the first one he'd drawn.

'Get in your circle,' he said. 'Quickly. The light'll start to draw the *Gást* out onto our plane of existence. Then he'll be just like us, able to touch and feel things, meaning we can catch him. But it's dangerous,' continued Jones. 'The slightest touch from one'll poison you, and make your body die, turning you into a *Gást* too, stuck between this world and the next one.' Ruby picked up the plastic bag of gun parts and stepped quickly into her circle, for once not feeling the need to ask any questions of Jones. 'Stand on the symbol in the middle,' he instructed. 'Make sure your feet are completely covering it.' As Ruby did so, Jones adjusted his feet too. 'Now, don't panic.'

Before Ruby could ask why she might, she felt an odd sensation in the air around her. It seemed to be vibrating. And then a piece of something that looked like armour materialized in front of her with a slightly green tinge to it. Sections were being conjured quicker and quicker out of the air all around her, fitting together to create a metal dome. In a matter of moments, she was entirely contained within it.

There was enough space for Ruby to hold out her arms and touch the sides, after she'd put the bag of gun parts down. Through the grille in front of her face she could see Jones had been surrounded by a similar shell. It looked like he was trapped inside a small green igloo covered in sharp, lethal-looking spikes.

'How are we supposed to catch a *Gást* stuck inside these things?' shouted Ruby.

But Jones just pointed towards something in the far corner of the room. Putting her face close to the grille, Ruby twisted to see what it was. She saw a shimmering patch of air, which looked rather like a puddle hung up to dry. A nose was poking out of it, sniffing the air nervously.

'He's coming!' shouted Jones. 'They're shy at first. But he won't be able to resist the light.' Ruby saw a man's face appear from the puddle of air. He was middle-aged with a large nose and a chin marked by a pronounced cleft in the middle. A prominent forehead jutted out over a pair of eyes, deeply set into dark cups that made the whites stand out. His skin was greyish like soggy cardboard. The man had a haunted look about him, like an animal on the verge of being hunted down. As he leant further forward, exposing more of his body, Ruby gasped when she saw a large gaping wound in his neck.

'Someone must have slit his throat,' said Jones. 'A lot of murder victims end up as *Gásts*, trapped between worlds. It sends 'em mad. Makes 'em more and more dangerous too.'

By now the *Gást* had emerged fully into the room. He wore a grey suit made from thick material paired with old-fashioned brown brogues, and had dark, oily-looking hair, neatly combed. He reminded Ruby of someone she'd seen in a film about the Second World War, where everyone had smoked and smiled and stuck together against 'Jerry'.

The *Gást* walked between Jones and Ruby and stood over the candle. He seemed fascinated by the flickering flame. The deep slit across his throat glistened black. When he looked up at Ruby with his haunted-looking eyes, she started to feel sorry for him, imagining how lonely it must feel not to be fully dead or alive. She swayed up onto her tiptoes, pressing her mouth against the grille, wanting to tell the man how sad she felt for him. But as soon as her feet came up off the chalk symbol, written on the floor, little pieces of the armour around her started to disappear.

'No!' cried Jones, as soon as he saw what was happening. 'Ruby! Don't! It's trying to make you forget about staying safe.' The sharp sound of Jones's voice brought Ruby to her senses and she planted her feet firmly back on the floor, and the armour healed up around her.

The *Gást* smiled and winked at her before walking towards Jones, stopping in front of the boy's grille and peering in.

'I saw you the other night in the street with Simeon's boy, the funny-looking one with the silly hair. Simeon's done that before, pitting two apprentices against each other to see who's best. I've seen lots of boys like you come and go over the years. I'm Simeon's little secret, you see. He keeps me here to help weed out the good apprentices from the bad ones. That other one's come in here a good few times and never even got a sniff of me.' When the *Gást* grinned, the wound in its neck smiled too. 'But if you're Simeon's apprentice what's with the girl? Is she your girlfriend?'

'I'm not Simeon's apprentice,' said Jones.

'No?'

'And I'm not his girlfriend,' said Ruby. 'We're partners.'

The *Gást* turned to look at Ruby, genuinely surprised for a moment, and then laughed. 'You mean you're a Badlander?'

'That's right.'

'Well, are you willing to risk coming out of that shell of yours to save your *partner*? A *Gást* like me can open up this tin can of his anytime I like.'

182

'Rubbish!' shouted Jones. 'It's trying to trick you again, Ruby. It can't get in. As long as I keep my feet over the symbol, I'll be fine.'

'But what if you don't?' hissed the *Gást*. 'What if you fall off your perch, little birdie?' The man stuck a long finger through the grille and tried to touch Jones. The boy lurched back, but managed to keep his feet firmly rooted on the symbol.

The *Gást* hissed in disgust, pushing its hand in further through the grille. When it accidentally touched the bars, blue sparks erupted, causing it to cry out in pain and pull back its arm.

Enraged, the *Gást* walked smartly across the room towards Ruby.

'What about you? Can you manage to stand still too?' The *Gást* stuck a long finger through the grille and tried to touch her. Ruby wobbled back, just managing to keep her feet stuck to the floor. 'If you're planning on catching me, you're going to have to crawl out of those shells at some point. Then I'll get you for certain. So why prolong the wait?' It reached in its arm further, forcing Ruby to lurch back. And this time when the creature touched the grille there were no blue sparks. No cries of pain.

The *Gást* looked shocked for a moment before withdrawing its arm and testing again by touching a finger lightly to Ruby's armour. Still no blue sparks. It peered at Ruby and tutted loudly, before turning round and winking at Jones. 'Someone must have written a symbol wrong. They're so hard to get right, aren't they?'

The *Gást* turned its gaze back to Ruby and laid both hands flat on the armoured shell, moving them around as if feeling for something.

'There must be a fault somewhere. A little spot I can—' It stopped as it felt something to its liking and dug the tip of a fingernail into the armour and cut a tiny slit into the metal. 'Well, well, well,' it said, and then launched both hands at the hole it had made, tearing at it with its nails.

Ruby screamed as the creature ripped out a small chunk of the armoured shell and flung it to the floor. The *Gást* bent down and put one eye against the newly made hole to look in.

'Hello, my pretty. I'm coming to get you. Once I touch you, you're going to die slowly. But that's the easy part. It's the bit after that that's hard, being stuck between two worlds. You'll have plenty of time to realize that.' It stepped back and stuck a sharp nail into the hole, beginning to slice through the armour casing as if it was using a paperknife to slit open an envelope.

Ruby screamed again.

'I've got a better idea,' shouted Jones, and the *Gást* wheeled round to see the boy standing right behind it, holding out the jam jar with the candle still burning inside. 'How about you get inside this jar instead?' Jones joined his thumb and forefinger on his free hand together to make a small circle over the top of the jar. Written on his skin, in blue biro, were a series of symbols. They started to spin round, faster and faster, until they were just a blue ring humming round the top of Jones's hand.

The *Gást* shrieked as its head stretched towards the mouth of the jar, like a piece of chewing gum being pulled. And then in one quick **THLUMPF!** the *Gást* was sucked down through the circle of Jones's thumb and forefinger and into the jam jar. The boy slammed down the lid, screwed it on tightly, and held up the jar to have a look. Without any air, the candle's flame faded and died out. Through the smoke trapped inside, Ruby saw little red sparks fizzing and bouncing against the glass, and then she stepped off her symbol to make the damaged armour surrounding her disappear.

'Got 'im,' grinned Jones like a little boy who'd just caught a beetle. Ruby stared at him for a moment and then whacked him hard on the arm. 'Ow! What's that for?'

'You know exactly.'

'I had to trick him somehow.'

'By writing a symbol wrong so I'd be a decoy?'

'I'd never have let you come to any harm. Never.' Jones held up the jam jar. 'He's a beauty, Ruby, and you helped catch him. A Wretch and a *Gást* in just a few days. That's going some.' Ruby folded her arms and puffed out her cheeks. But when she pulled her best angry face it came out in a weird smile, because she couldn't help being pleased. Jones was beaming as he peered into the jar. 'We're a step closer to finding out more about this Witch now, thanks to you.'

R uby was sitting on the dirty floor, watching the little red sparks collide against the inside of the jar.

'You're sure it can't escape?'

'Yep.' Jones took the three white envelopes out of his pocket and laid them on the floor. 'As soon as it passed through the portal I made with my hand, it's stuck in the jar till I release it. It's an old curse. Maitland told me it was used to put genies in lamps a long time ago.'

Ruby tapped the jar and the red sparks fizzed angrily. 'What's happened to the *Gást*?'

'It's changed into a safer form. One we can work with. Open the lid and I'll show you.'

'Are you sure?' Jones nodded and Ruby picked up the jar, which felt very cold, and unscrewed the lid, not at all sure she was doing something safe. As soon as she twisted it off, the remnants of the candle smoke wafted free. And all the red sparks floated to the top too, but none of them drifted out of the mouth of the jar, much to her relief.

Jones took the jar from Ruby and turned it upside down,

giving it a smart tap so the candle dropped out onto the floor. Still none of the red sparks came free as they fizzed inside it.

'So how do we ask it about the Witch?' asked Ruby.

'Everything in the world, living or dead, is made of energy,' replied Jones, setting the jar upright on the floor, 'even a *Gást*. When it passed through the portal, all that happened was its energy changed into a different form.' Jones picked up one of the white envelopes and lifted the flap. 'Now, if you know there's energy in everything, you can put that knowledge to good use. All you need is to combine the right items together and you can make things happen the way you want.'

Tiny black seeds tumbled from the envelope into the jar and fizzed as they burnt up and disappeared. 'Ragwort seeds go first.' Jones paused to consult his Learning Book. 'Then it's rattle grass pods and after that the dried oak leaves.' Jones emptied the contents of the other two envelopes into the jar. As soon as they were absorbed, a ball of blue mist formed at the bottom of the jar, swelling steadily until it was full of a milky blue light.

The light drifted up to the neck of the jar, collecting the red sparks as it did, and stopped just below the rim. It hardened rapidly into a transparent gelatinous skin across the top of the jar.

'Nature's a special thing,' said Jones. 'Maitland told me you should treat it with respect. But most people don't and that's their loss cos it means they can't do things Badlanders can.'

'It seems like Maitland taught you lots of useful things,' said Ruby.

Jones nodded. 'I s'pose he did,' and he smiled as the *Gást*'s face appeared in miniature on the jelly-like screen in the neck of the jar. 'Maitland was a good man,' he said, looking up at Ruby, and she nodded back.

'It's tight in here,' said the *Gást* in a shrill voice. 'I can hardly breathe. Can't you put me somewhere bigger?'

'You're a *Gást*,' said Jones. 'I know you don't need to breathe. There's no point trying to trick me.'

'When I get out of here, I'll poison you very slowly and painfully.'

'You mean, *if* you ever get out of there,' replied Jones.

The face in the jelly-like screen grinned. 'Glass cracks pretty easily. If this jar breaks, I'll be out before you even hear the smash. Only someone very inexperienced would have put me in here. Or someone very stupid.'

Jones picked up the jar and threw it at the wall before Ruby could tell him to STOP! It bounced off harmlessly like a rubber ball, pinging off into a dark corner.

'It's a Bouncy Jar,' grinned Jones. 'Charmed not to break. I nicked it from Simeon's house, remember? Most Badlanders have them lying around for work like this.'

The *Gást* was still cursing when Jones picked up the jar and set it down in the middle of the floor again. 'Now, you're going to tell me what I want to know or else I'll bury this jar somewhere it'll never be found.' A string of rude words came out of the jar which Jones and Ruby ignored.

'Go on then,' groaned the *Gást* after calming down.

'The couple living across the road at number seventeen. What do you know about them?'

'Been there for years. Quiet as mice.'

'No one suspicious coming and going?'

'Not that I've seen.'

'Not even a Witch?'

'I wouldn't know a Witch from a whistle. Broomsticks are a bit last millennium if you know what I mean. They hardly go around in cloaks and hats either these days. It's not a good look if you want a quiet life.'

'A woman then?'

'That doesn't really narrow it down, does it?'

Jones tapped his lips as he recalled everything he could remember about the night Maitland had taken him, after eating the memory fruit. He saw his parents. And then he remembered there'd been an older woman with them too, bending down to look at him in his cot. 'I heard a name once,' he said, 'a long time ago, when I was a baby. Does Angela mean anything to you?'

'Never heard it.'

Jones frowned. 'What about Mrs Easton? The woman who lives in the house opposite said that name the other night when she was on her phone.'

'Nope, not heard that either.'

Jones sighed in frustration.

'But I've seen it,' the *Gást* continued with a smirk.

'What do you mean? How can you *see* a name?' Jones asked.

'Say please or I won't tell you.'

'You'll tell me everything or I'll bury this jar after I've put another *Gást* in there with you. Or how about a Drudge? You'd have a real party then, listening to it describe everything that's bad about the world. That would really help the centuries fly right by.'

'All right. No need for threats. It's best if I show you what I've seen. This is the most recent. A couple of weeks ago.'

The *Gást*'s face disappeared and in its place appeared a view from the window of the room they were in, overlooking the street and the houses opposite. It was daytime. After a few moments, a white van drew up and parked on the other side of the road. On the side panel was written:

A. EASTON
ARTISAN BAKER & PÂTISSIÉR
EST. 1965

When the driver's door opened, a rather plump lady struggled to haul herself out of the front seat. When she finally managed it, the van rose up a good few centimetres. She was matronly-looking, about fifty years old, and wore a tweed skirt with sensible brown shoes and a beige V-neck sweater with a white shirt. A pair of glasses dangled around her neck on a chain and her brown hair was pulled back into a bun. Jones recognized her immediately.

'That's her! That's the woman called Angela I was asking about.' Jones turned to Ruby. 'She was with my parents the night Maitland stole me! I saw her with 'em after I ate the memory fruit. She looks exactly the same.'

They both stared into the jar and watched as Mrs Easton walked to the back of the van and opened the rear doors and lifted out a large cake. Jones's parents were already coming out of their house and down the little garden path to greet her. They all kissed each other on the cheek like old friends before vanishing inside the house.

The vision faded and in its place the *Gást*'s stony face was back, staring up again from the jar.

'What else have you seen?' asked Jones.

'That woman comes to see them a couple of times a month. Brings a big cake sometimes. Don't ask me what flavour.'

'Does that sound normal to you?' Jones asked Ruby.

Ruby shrugged. 'Everyone likes cake, I suppose.' Jones tapped his fingers against the jar to try and help him think. 'Look,' Ruby continued, 'if they were normal people then I'd say yeah, fine. Cake-*shmake*. But given your parents are cursed by a Witch and it looks like this woman has been visiting a lot then I think it could be fair to say that maybe it's weird. Mrs Easton could be the Witch we're after, but how can we know for sure?'

'I reckon it's her. She doesn't look like she's aged at all, like normal people do.' Jones tapped the jar again. 'What else have you seen?'

'Like I said, she comes and goes,' said the *Gást*.

'Show us all the other times you've seen her.'

Jones and Ruby watched more moments play out. They

were mostly the same, with Mrs Easton arriving in her van and delivering a cake during the day. And then a visit occurred at night. It was much the same as the others Mrs Easton drove up in her van, got out and went to the door and rang the bell. But something about it made Jones uneasy.

'There!' he said suddenly.

'What?' Ruby peered closer.

'In the van! Looking out of the window.'

Ruby looked harder and she saw it. A small clay Poppet just like the ones in the cabinet in Jones's parents' house. It was standing up on the seat, peering out of the passenger window as Mrs Easton waited on the front doorstep. It watched her being welcomed into the house by Jones's parents and then it sat down and disappeared from view.

'It's her, Jones,' said Ruby. 'Mrs Easton's the Witch.'

'Now all we've got to do is track her down so we can find out about this Dark Bottle Simeon told us about. '

'Not a problem.' Jones looked at Ruby, somewhat surprised. 'Jones, I'm going to show you the wonders of the Internet.'

Jones frowned. 'I've heard people talking about that, but I ain't never seen it. What is it?'

'A secret world only ordinary people know about. It can tell you anything you want in an instant.'

'Where is it?' asked Jones, his eyes growing wide.

Ruby held up her hands. 'All around us. You just have to connect to it.'

'How?'

'With a computer or a phone or a tablet. The Internet is

192

a lot easier to use than magic and far less dangerous. If you really want to be an ordinary boy, you're going to have to learn how to use it. You've shown me how to catch a *Gást*. Now I'm going to show you something you don't know about.' Jones was looking at her with his head cocked to one side, a slightly surprised look on his face. Ruby just shrugged and folded her arms. 'Look, I like working together, but I know it's not what you want, so I'm going to do what you asked me the first night we met. I'll help you learn how to fit into the ordinary world as long as you teach me more about being a Badlander. Even if I can't do magic I don't want to go back to being an ordinary girl. Not now. There's nothing about my old life I miss.'

'Okay' and Jones nodded and screwed the lid back on the jam jar, despite the *Gást*'s protestations, and put it in his pocket. 'But we have to tidy up first: we don't want Simeon knowing we've been here,' he said, standing up and brushing down the dirt and dust from his trousers. 'We need to remove all the symbols on the floor.'

'What about making a mark, for capturing the *Gást*?'

'We ain't doing that,' said Jones and Ruby pulled a face. 'I don't want to make a mark. I'm not planning on staying a Badlander, remember.'

'But I am, and I didn't get a chance to make my mark for killing the Wretch. The *Gást* counts, Jones. You said you wouldn't have managed without me.'

'No mark,' said Jones firmly. 'I don't want anyone knowing we were here. What if Thomas Gabriel finds it, or Simeon?

Besides, you don't make a mark on someone else's territory in London. That's what the *Ordnung* says.'

'Well, the *Ordnung* says lots of stupid things as we know,' said Ruby pointedly. 'That's two creatures for me now and nothing to show for it,' she muttered as she stood up, picking up the plastic bag full of gun parts.

But Jones wasn't paying attention any more as he started rubbing out the symbols around one of the circles on the floor with the sleeve of his overcoat.

And then Ruby saw the tiny nub of chalk on the floor and heard a little voice in her head, telling her to grab it, without Jones seeing. So she did.

Without her phone, Ruby wasn't sure how to get onto the Internet so she was relieved when they found an Internet café on the main road about a ten-minute walk from Chesterford Gardens, sandwiched between a McDonald's and a travel agency.

'We're lucky, there aren't many of these types of places left,' she informed Jones as they went inside.

'Why's that?'

'Because people usually just go onto the Internet at home or on their phone if they're out.'

Jones watched Ruby's fingers tapping away on the keyboard and he was in awe of her knowing what to do. She found Easton's Bakery & Patisserie very quickly. The shop was in Hampstead on a street called South End Road. Jones was amazed when Ruby made the computer show them exactly where the shop was on a map. It gave them a bird's eye view and it seemed that the shop backed onto part of Hampstead Heath with a mass of trees behind it.

'What else can the Internet do?' asked Jones, patting the warm plastic edge around the monitor of the computer.

'All sorts of things,' Ruby replied. 'Ask me anything, and I'll make it give us the answer.'

'Will we kill the Witch?'

'I don't mean questions like that. It can't tell you the future, only facts.' He frowned at her. 'It's like your Pocket Book Bestiary,' she explained. 'That holds lots of information about monsters, right? Like their history, what weapons to use and stuff like that. But it can't tell you the future, can it? It can't tell you if you'll actually kill a Wretch or an Ogre or whatever creature you're looking up. Just how to do it.'

'And the Internet's the same?' Jones sounded a little disappointed.

'Well, no, it can do other stuff.'

'Like what?'

'Like entertain you for a start.' Ruby clicked on the YouTube link and brought up a clip from an old cartoon called *Tom and Jerry* which she knew her grandparents had always found funny when they'd been alive and her life had been happier.

Jones's eyes lit up as he watched the cartoon cat chasing the cartoon mouse around the kitchen. When it was over, Ruby searched for a clip from an old black-and-white Charlie

Chaplin film because she and her grandfather had roared with laughter whenever they'd watched it.

'More,' whispered Jones as the clip finished.

But there was no time to watch anything else because it was late and the Internet café was closing, so Jones sighed and slid off the chair. After leaving, Ruby led Jones towards the McDonald's next door, but he pulled back, afraid of the bright lights and big windows.

'We can't go in there.'

'Why not? It's where people go when they're hungry, especially kids like us.'

'I know, but . . .' Jones tried straightening his overcoat and smoothing down his hair. 'I ain't never been in one.'

'You'll be fine.' Ruby beckoned him in as she held open the door for him.

She showed him how to choose from the big menu above the counter, answering all his questions about the differences between nuggets and burgers, and shakes and ice cream. When she made him order, pushing the boy forward, he recited nervously what they were going to have. He watched in amazement as the server, in her beige outfit, listened to him intently, tapping the order into the till. When it came to paying, he produced a small leather purse from an overcoat pocket.

'Maitland gave me an emergency fund for when we were out hunting,' he whispered as he unzipped the purse and handed over a ten-pound note.

'Thank you, Jones,' said Ruby.

'Thank you, Ruby,' he replied.

They sat eating their burgers and drinking their milkshakes. The only thing Jones was unsure about was the slice of green gherkin in his bun. But he loved the fries, dipping them one after the other into the white frilly cup of ketchup sitting on his tray, and chomping them down to his fingertips.

'Good?' said Ruby.

'Yeah.'

Ruby toasted him with her Coke. 'To your first ever burger.' Jones grinned like a hamster, his cheeks stuffed full of bun and burger and fries.

But when he noticed a man sitting in the corner, watching them, a white cup of something steaming in front of him, Jones felt goosebumps bubbling up all over his body. The man's skin was very pale. His face was drawn, almost gaunt, and he had long, spindly fingers. Jones couldn't help glancing at him after that.

'What're you looking at,' whispered Ruby, leaning forward.

'Nothing,' mumbled Jones.

Ruby balled up her paper napkin and dropped it onto the floor. 'Oooops,' she announced, crouching down and picking it up, giving her time to glance at the man.

'What about him?' she whispered as she sat down opposite Jones again.

Jones started organizing the things on his tray. When Ruby touched his arm, he looked up at her. 'All this is so nice,' he said quietly. 'I like burgers and fries and sitting here

197

talking, and I never believed I'd ever do anything like it. But it's hard to forget everything Maitland taught me, like how to tell when people ain't people at all.' He shifted nervously in his chair. 'What if I can't turn off being a Badlander? What if I kill the Witch to rescue my parents and they end up being okay, but then one day we come to a place like this and I can't be ordinary?'

Ruby dumped her tray on top of Jones's and stood up. 'Then you need to start practising being ordinary, at letting go of what you've been taught. Come on.'

She walked to the nearest bin and cleared the trays and then stacked them. Then she put her arm through Jones's and walked him out through the glass doors. As the pale man watched them leave, Jones could feel a fizzing in his chest.

When he came out onto the street, Jones started looking for a dark alley or a deep shopfront in which he could hide and wait for the man in order to follow him. It was part of his instinct and a feeling difficult to shake.

'Maitland's not here any more,' whispered Ruby, sensing how uncomfortable Jones was. Keeping her arm hooked into his, she started walking briskly down the street, taking him with her.

She felt him start to relax the further they went along the pavement.

'See. It's just going to take practice. That's all.'

'Okay,' said Jones. But then he stopped so suddenly he nearly pulled Ruby's arm out of its socket.

'What the—'

But Jones just pointed at the bank of television screens in the shop window of the electrical store beside them. They were all tuned to the same news channel and an identical newscaster was mouthing at them from every screen. Above the right shoulders of all of them was a headshot of Ruby and a headline beside it read 'Missing Girl'. Ruby watched the screens change to footage of her foster parents' house. When a policeman appeared on camera, she turned away and started striding down the street, the gun parts clinking in the plastic bag she was still holding. By the time Jones had caught up with her, he was almost out of breath.

'I just thought people would forget about me,' said Ruby, looking around nervously. 'No one's ever really bothered about me before except my grandparents and they're both gone. Simeon was right. Running away and becoming a Badlander is probably the most stupid idea I've ever had.'

'No, it's not,' said Jones. 'You killed a Wretch, remember? And helped me catch a *Gást*.'

'All I own are a few clothes stuffed into a rucksack. I've got eighty-five pounds and seventy-three pence, saved up from pocket money and a paper round. When I ran away the other night, it felt like a million pounds.'

'Maitland had money. You can have that. You won't have to go back to being an ordinary girl if you don't want to.'

Without saying anything else, Jones grabbed Ruby's hand and led her down the street until he spotted an alley where they would be out of sight from prying eyes. He took out the bottle of black Slap Dust which Simeon had returned to him in case of any emergency now he'd agreed to be his Whelp, and poured a tiny amount into his left hand and a little into Ruby's right hand, before putting the bottle away.

'You're already a Badlander, Ruby. You just need to keep practising.' He winked at her. 'So are you ready?'

Ruby smiled and then, locking arms, they slapped their hands together, and vanished, leaving nothing but loose sheets of newspaper blowing across the alley as evidence of them ever being there.

TWENTY

J ones stepped back from Ruby and scrutinized her in the early morning sunshine coming through the bathroom window. He frowned. Clicked the pair of scissors he was holding in frustration.

'You still look like you.'

'Cut it any shorter and I'll look like a boy.' Ruby smoothed a hand over her head. Her hair barely reached over the tops of her fingers now. She sighed at the sight of all her black curls lying in the sink like giant commas. One of the things she most liked about herself was her rich dark hair.

'You're the one who said you spent all last night worrying about being on the television.' Jones picked up Maitland's old cut-throat razor and prised open the blade. 'Let me go over your head with this and no one'll recognize you. I know how to use it. Maitland taught me. You'll still be the same on the inside. You'll still be a girl, however you look.'

Ruby stared at the sharp edge of the razor catching the sunlight, and then shook her head. 'I've got a better idea. Go and look out any clothes you've got that'll fit me. I'll come

201

and find you,' and she walked out of the bathroom before Jones could say any more.

When she arrived in the bedroom a few minutes later, Jones had laid out most of his clothes on the bed. Ruby had found one of Maitland's old baseball caps and, wearing it pulled right down over her eyes, it was difficult to recognize her.

'Looks all right, I suppose,' said Jones grudgingly.

After looking through Jones's clothes, Ruby picked out a grey cashmere sweater, with a small hole in the neck, because it looked like the softest thing he owned. The wool smelt of boy. So did the pair of beige trousers she put on. She completed her outfit with a pair of tatty white plimsolls, and a battered brown belt with a small silver buckle. But when she stared at herself in the mirror she shook her head.

'I need a coat. You wear one and so did Maitland, and Simeon and Thomas Gabriel do too. All the Badlanders I've met seem to have one.'

'It's cos of the pockets. They're usually charmed to hold more than you think. You never know what you might need in a fix.'

'How about that one?' and Ruby pointed at an army camouflage jacket hanging in the wardrobe.

'Go ahead. I wore it a few times, but preferred my overcoat.'

There was a label inside with a name written on it in black marker pen that said 'Private Owens'. Ruby tried the jacket on and plunged her hands into the deep pockets, imagining all the things she could fit in there as she admired herself in the mirror. And then something occurred to her when she saw a battered old leather backpack in the bottom of the wardrobe. 'Since I'm not like other Badlanders,' she said, slipping the pack onto her shoulders, 'I think I should be different.' She checked herself in the mirror. 'Perfect for my scrying mirror. And no one'll recognize me now,' she said, nodding.

'It's not just about how you look. It's about being confident too when you're a Badlander. Knowing what you're doing.'

Ruby pulled the baseball cap back down over her eyes and spoke in a different, deeper voice. 'Jones,' she announced dramatically, 'I will do my best.'

They spent the rest of the morning in Maitland's study looking at books about Witches. Ruby and Jones both agreed that going anywhere near a Witch meant taking every precaution possible. So they were keen to read up on how to stay safe, in preparation for a trip back to Hampstead that night to find out what they could about Mrs Easton's Dark Bottle.

Maitland had a whole section on the creatures and Jones worked his way through it, making notes as he skimmed through the pages of each book.

The Pocket Book Bestiary was full of information too. It didn't take Ruby long to realize there were different grades of Witch, and sub-grades within each one of those. Every kind of Witch was defined by a dizzying array of different characteristics ranging from things like their age, the size of their nose, the colour of their eyes, to how many warts there were on their body and even what they ate.

The book made it very clear that although Witches could perform magic it was nothing like Badlander Magic. The book called it *Wiccacraeft* and there were different theories as to how Witches came by it. What the books all agreed on though was that a single bite from a Witch could poison any Badlander who'd Commenced, turning the magic inside them bad.

'Jones, we've got magic in us. What if we get bitten by Mrs Easton? Simeon and Thomas Gabriel said Witches love munching down children. Who says Mrs Easton won't try and take a bite if she catches a whiff of us. They've got noses like bloodhounds apparently, can sniff out an apprentice up to a mile away.'

Jones turned a page in the book he was reading. 'It says here rye drops turn Witches right off eating children. Maitland's got a jar in the van; we can chew some before we go looking for her.'

Ruby tapped the page she was on. 'But this one says rye drops only work with *certain* types of Witches. We need to know what sort Mrs Easton is. Three-Toed. Dimple-Skinned. Blob-Warted. Bluebell Syrup works most of the time with a Flared Hair Witch but White Rose Petal powder is best with a Goggle-Eyed one.'

Jones sighed as he looked at all the books piled around

him. 'This is hopeless. We need to know more about what sort of Witch Mrs Easton is before we can get close and spy on her safely. Can't you use your scrying mirror?'

Ruby shook her head. 'It only works on people I've met or places I've been.'

Jones slapped his book shut and stood up. 'Come on, maybe there's another way to find out more about her.'

Simeon had sent over some imps that morning to fix the gun as he'd promised. And he'd sent them very early indeed. An old brass tin had appeared out of thin air in the kitchen with an alarm clock stuck on top which had gone off a minute later at exactly 6 a.m.

Ruby and Jones had come down the stairs, rubbing their eyes, to investigate the noise and found a note fixed to the tin wishing them a 'Good Morning'. Written beneath had been an instruction that now they were awake they should start preparing the house immediately. Neither Ruby nor Jones had felt that was a good idea at all. So it wasn't until after breakfast that they opened the tin, and a group of tiny grey imps had popped out and lined themselves up, ready and waiting to work on the gun. After being given the plastic bag containing the weapon's parts, they'd set to work immediately.

When Jones and Ruby returned to the kitchen, having spent most of the morning in Maitland's study, they discovered the gun was fully repaired, and it was very happy about it too. It was lying on sheets of newspaper on the table, shouting at the grey imps to clean it in all the right places.

The creatures were using rags in their tiny, clawed hands, cooing as if they'd found a gun made of gold.

'Ahhh, Jones, my boy!' roared the revolver when it saw him. 'I'm back. Better than ever. I gather you're to become a Whelp according to what these good little imps have told me.'

'That ain't happening,' replied Jones.

'What?'

'I've got other plans than what Simeon thinks. We're gonna kill this Witch what's cursed my parents as soon as we've found her Dark Bottle.'

All the imps breathed in together and started chattering among themselves.

'But you can't go back on your word. Not to someone like Simeon.'

'I can too. Now you need to tell us everything you know about—'

'I'll warn you now, Jones, Simeon hasn't erased Maitland's charm completely, he's just changed it so I can tell him things. So I still can't tell you anything about the Witch.' Ruby and Jones stepped back immediately in case it fired.

'Bloomin' Simeon,' said Jones. 'All he wants is that Witch kept secr—' He paused as something occurred to him. 'He only sent you back to keep an eye on us, didn't he?'

'No.'

Jones glowered at it. 'I'll dig a hole for me and Ruby to put you in and forget about you,' he threatened.

'All right, all right. Yes, Simeon asked me to keep an eye

on you and I agreed. I'm to send these imps back if you do anything to disobey him. Turn out your pockets, boys, we've been rumbled.' All the imps sighed and threw down little grains of Slap Dust on the table, which Jones scooped away.

'What's in it for you?' asked Ruby, picking up the gun.

'I'm to be Thomas Gabriel's gun if he Commences. My legacy will go on.'

Ruby laughed. 'What, with that numbskull!' She aimed the gun at an imaginary Mrs Easton. 'Look, me and Jones have got a Witch problem. Up for helping even if you can't tell us anything about her?'

'Work with you again? Never.'

'I thought you wanted to be partners.'

'You *threw* me at Simeon, another Badlander! I'm sorry, but I have to think of my reputation. I've worked with some of the best Badlanders around, including Maitland, may he sleep peacefully according to the *wyrd*. So I expect my new owner to be of similar calibre, not come over all hysterical and use me like a rudimentary missile. I'm not a rock. I'm a Webley Mark 1 Service Revolver from 1897 and need to be treated with respect!'

There was a round of applause from the imps, who cheered and waved their little rags as they stood on the table.

'I'm sorry about what happened,' said Ruby, eager to convince the gun she meant it. 'Honest. I didn't mean to hurt your feelings. I just panicked. I didn't know what else to do.'

The gun merely sniffed and said nothing as Jones plucked

two tins of baked beans from a cupboard and peeled off the lids using the ring pulls.

Ruby cleared her throat. 'I'm very sorry I threw you. I won't do it again. Ever.' The gun remained silent as Jones clattered about with a pot, pouring in the tins of beans before selecting a wooden spoon. He hit the clicker on the gas stove and a blue flame sprang up round one of the rings.

'Help us take on this Witch and you could be famous,' continued Ruby. 'We're going to try and do something not even a great Badlander like Maitland dared to do.'

'Which is precisely why you shouldn't try it,' the gun retorted. 'You're just kids. You wouldn't even know where to start.'

'Well, we already know who she is.'

'Of course you do,' said the gun.

'Her name's Mrs Easton. Bakes cakes apparently.'

Jones smiled to himself as he heard the gun grumbling. As the beans warmed, he cut some slices from a home-made loaf of bread and put them under the grill.

'If I was to ever think about working together again,' said the gun, 'I'd expect you to look after me. Polish me. Clean me.' Ruby rolled her eyes. 'Looking after me instils discipline. And that's vital for any Badlander. Even a girl one.'

'Fine.'

'And I expect you to listen to my stories too.'

'About what?'

'My great adventures. They're educational.'

208

'Is that right?'

'Of course. What other reason could there be?' Ruby bit her tongue as various answers came to mind. 'Wait till you see a thirty-foot Spiny Ogre rampaging towards you or a gaggle of Brute Trolls coming at you from all angles. Their breath alone can turn a sunny day into a pea-souper in a matter of seconds, and then you really need your wits about you. It'll be at times like that when you'll remember my stories and won't be afraid, because you'll know I've been there and done it and survived.' The imps cheered again. Ruby tried to shush them, but it was too late. The gun was in its stride now. 'I remember I was up in Scotland once, on the moor with Maitland. On one of those warm summer evenings when the midges are as thick as mist.'

'Is this going to take long?' asked Jones as he pulled out the toast and started to butter it. 'We're about to eat.'

'You eat, I'll tell stories. I've got three in mind.'

Ruby shook her head as Jones raised his eyebrows and put down a plate of hot beans on toast in front of her. He shooed the imps away as they all leant forward to smell the food. Keeping an eye on them as they climbed back into their tin and pulled on the lid, he put down his own plate of beans and started to eat.

The gun cleared its throat and began to speak in an overly theatrical voice. Something about Scottish mist and moorland and one of Maitland's earliest hunts which he'd written up in his journal as 'The Case of the Cave *Ents*'. But Jones had already switched off. He'd heard it all before. And then something occurred to him and he put his knife and fork down and stood up.

'There might be another way we can find out more about Mrs Easton without asking the gun.'

'How?' asked Ruby as the gun complained about being interrupted.

But Jones was already walking out of the kitchen.

The memory bush was still in the hallway by the front door where Jones had left it a few days before. The soil in the pot was dry. But even so the bush seemed to have thrived in its indoor environment. The leaves were still a rich, dark, waxy green.

Jones checked carefully for a fruit and when he found one his face lit up, but he didn't take it straightaway.

'I'm sorry I ain't been around to look after you,' said the boy, wiping a thin sheen of dust off the leaves. 'Everything you showed me last time was brilliant. It's helped me find out loads of things. So can I take the new berry? It's really gonna help.' The bush seemed to think about it for a moment and then it parted its branches to allow him to take the fruit.

Before Jones ate the small purple fruit, he announced very clearly, as he had done the first time, what he wanted to see. 'I want to watch the best memory I have that's to do with Angela Easton. One that can tell me most about her and what sort of Witch she is.'

Jones popped the fruit in his mouth and bit down and chewed and swallowed. As his eyes started to feel heavy and

210

began to close, he fully expected to see his parents with Mrs Easton. But that is not what he saw at all . . .

He was lying in a cradle on Maitland's desk and he could tell immediately that he was remembering a time from when he was just a baby again. To his right was Maitland, sitting behind his desk, and he was speaking to someone standing in front of him. It was Victor Brynn, not a skull this time but fully formed, pale and drawn, his teeth still as black and sharp as pencil points. His arms were clamped by their sides and it was clear that he was bound by some sort of charm that rendered it impossible for him to move as white sparks flickered round him.

'I may have been your apprentice once, Victor, but now I make my own decisions.'

Victor Brynn made a tutting sound. 'Indeed. You've become everything I'd hoped. A true Badlander.' *The No-Thing's tongue slicked between his teeth like a lizard testing the air as he spoke.*

'I tried my best,' *said Maitland.* 'I hunted down this Witch according to what little you told me about her and found her on Simeon Rowell's æhteland in Hampstead. She's a nasty one, like you said. Six-Toed and Goggle-Eyed too. Extremely rare. And the very embodiment of something evil.'

'Well, you need only look at me to know that,' *hissed Victor Brynn.*

'You were a great Badlander, Victor, and a special Master to me too. I wanted nothing more than to kill this Witch and rid you of the infection she's given you that's poisoned the magic inside. What better way would there have been for me than*

211

to pay back everything my Master did for me?' Maitland leant forward. Shook his head. 'But you hunted her a long time ago. She's grown far more powerful since she bit you and made you a No-Thing. There's no way I can kill her. She's made a Deorcan Flascan. She can't be defeated.'

'So, you're giving up?' Maitland's jaw tightened as Victor Brynn's tongue flashed between his black teeth. The angry No-Thing tried to move, but the white sparks around him flashed brighter and he cried out in pain. 'You're giving up on me! Your own Master! Me, who raised you from a tiny thing. A Deorcan Flascan can be found. I know a way. Go to St Crosse College in Oxford. Seek out the Lich, Du Clement, who the Order keeps locked up in the chapel crypt. Du Clement is the Order's secret, an encyclopaedia of knowledge on all things and the greatest authority on Witches there's ever been. If anyone can help you, he can. He'll know how to find a Dark Bottle.'

'Do you think the Witch won't have her Dark Bottle well protected?' said Maitland. 'Even if I can find it, stealing it will be nearly impossible.' Maitland shook his head again. 'I haven't trained one apprentice successfully so far. Who'll carry on my name if I die trying to save you? I'm sorry, but I've made my choice. I've chosen this boy over you, my friend.'

'You chose that thing over me!' hissed Victor Brynn. 'A child! The magic within me can still be mended. The Witch's infection can be removed if you find the Dark Bottle and kill her.'

'I need a future, Victor. That's what this boy is. There's something special about him. I'm sure of it and I've learnt from my mistakes with other apprentices. He'll make us both proud.

Carry on my legacy and yours. I'll make sure of it. Everyone in the Order in years to come will know that the great Badlander, Jones, was taught by Maitland, who was himself taught by Victor Brynn. Our names will live on through this boy. We must be resigned to our wyrd. Me, as a teacher, and you as a No-Thing. There is nothing I can do to help you now except keep you charmed in the hope that, one day, this curse might be lifted one way or another if the wyrd allows. It's either that or death and I don't have the courage to kill the Master who brought me up. Who loved me like a son.'

Jones watched as whites sparks of magic shot out of Maitland's free hand and wound themselves tighter and tighter around Victor Brynn, making him cry out in pain. Victor Brynn cursed, snapping his teeth as he shrank away into just a skull with sharp black teeth that floated down onto the desk and settled on a pile of papers.

When Jones opened his eyes, Ruby was hopping about ,waiting to see what he knew. 'Well?' she asked.

TWENTY-ONE

I t was mid-afternoon the same day, as Jones and Ruby were sitting at the small drop-down table in the camper van, when Thomas Gabriel appeared from out of nowhere. He went flying down the central aisle of the van and slammed into the back of the vehicle before plopping down on his backside. He stood up quickly, rearranging his hair and snapping his herringbone coat around him.

Not even Ruby could think of anything to say. Jones was just staring too.

'Compact spaces like this van can be difficult to materialize into with Slap Dust,' announced Thomas Gabriel, trying hard to regain his composure.

'As you've so clearly demonstrated,' said Ruby, raising her eyebrows at Jones.

'Which is why it's good to practise. And what on earth is this?' asked Thomas Gabriel, looking about, trying to move the conversation on from his embarrassing arrival.

'A van, like you just said,' replied Jones, and Ruby stifled a laugh.

'I *meant*, what are you doing here? I went round most of the house looking for you until I found the gun in the kitchen and it told me you were cooped up in here.'

Ruby shut the book that was open in front of her on the small drop-down table, without saying a word. The embossed silver title on the front read *The Badlander Encyclopaedia*. Next to it sat an open road atlas. Thomas Gabriel squinted at the page before Jones shut that too.

'What's in Oxford?'

'Lots of things, probably,' said Ruby. 'Houses. Pigeons. Dogs.' She shrugged. 'So I guess dog po—'

Thomas Gabriel looked at her down his very large nose. 'Bang goes your job at Deschamps & Sons once I tell Simeon you're slacking off. You're supposed to be busy cleaning the house.'

Ruby's face puckered up and it looked like she was going to cry. 'Oh, please don't tell him, Thomas Gabriel. I'd ... Well, I'd be ...' Thomas Gabriel actually thought she was about to burst into tears. Ruby looked him straight in the eye. 'I'd be devastated,' she said with a smirk. Jones tried not to laugh as Ruby smiled.

Thomas Gabriel's ears turned pink. 'You should be treating me with a little more respect.'

'What, cos you're Simeon's boy?' asked Jones.

'Because I came here to tell you something about the Witch in Hampstead. I've found out her name for starters.'

'Oh, you mean Mrs Easton?' said Ruby.

Thomas Gabriel opened his mouth, but nothing came out.

'Jones, help him out before his brain explodes,' she said and pointed to the jam jar sitting on the counter beside the sink. Jones picked up the jar, unscrewed the lid, and thrust it under Thomas Gabriel's nose.

The *Gást*'s face appeared in the thick translucent jelly in the neck of the jar and laughed when it saw Thomas Gabriel peering down. 'So! The idiot with the stupid hair, we meet at last. But only because someone else passed Simeon's test before you did.' The *Gást* smiled. 'Loser. Looks like someone else found Simeon's *Gást* before you did.'

Thomas Gabriel looked up at Jones, his bottom lip wobbling ever so slightly. 'You ... you captured the *Gást* I told you about.'

'I thought it might be useful.' Jones grinned. 'It's seen Mrs Easton coming and going to my parents' house. I'm gonna kill that Witch and free my parents.' He slapped on the lid and handed the jam jar to Thomas Gabriel. 'I was gonna hide it in one of the van's cupboards so you and Simeon wouldn't know. But it's yours if you want it. Just tell your Master you caught it and he'll Commence you. That's what you want, ain't it?'

'I can't give it to him now, can I? The *Gást* will tell him the truth.'

'Then tell it not to.'

Thomas Gabriel looked at the jam jar, weighing it up. 'I've got a better idea. I'll help you kill the Witch. Simeon'll have to Commence me then.'

'No thanks,' said Ruby.

'You're going to need all the help you can get. Especially as you haven't got much time.'

'What do you mean?' asked Jones.

Thomas Gabriel paused, enjoying the fact that for once he knew something the others didn't, and then he reached into his pocket and brought out what looked like a small tube of glue with a white cap screwed on.

'I copied something from Simeon's journal on to this Imitator. I'd say it's pretty useful.' Thomas Gabriel pointed the tube like a finger at Jones. 'Simeon hasn't been telling you everything. Your parents haven't got long to live.'

Thomas Gabriel unscrewed the lid and squeezed the bottom of the tube. Lines of words shot out of the nozzle and arranged themselves in rows in the air, and Jones and Ruby started to read.

Journal Entry 18th June

*I have encountered many strange things, but now my eyes have truly been opened. Maitland is dead, cut down a few days ago by the abomination of a **Wédorcnéus**. His apprentice, Jones, survived and has Commenced but not of his own accord. Now, through circumstances I can still barely comprehend, Jones Commenced with a girl he rescued on the night of Maitland's demise. Of course, the Magic rejected them both, given the girl's involvement.*

But there is more.

Maitland, it seems, had told the boy he was an orphan

217

with no clues as to the whereabouts of his parents. But, after discovering his Master had lied, Jones went looking for them. His search led him here, to Hampstead, where he discovered far more than he expected. That his mother and father are cursed by the witch Mrs Easton and beholden to her.

I have found out some of why Jones ended up as Maitland's apprentice by forcing Maitland's gun to tell me the barest of facts. It seems Maitland hunted down the Witch some twelve years ago with a view to killing her, although I failed to uncover exactly why he sought Mrs Easton out. Yet, when he discovered the extent of her powers (she is virtually impossible to defeat as I well know), he took a different course of action. According to the gun, Maitland stole Jones, who was then just an infant, as an act of mercy. He has done a decent job of raising the boy as far as I can tell. There's certainly more about him than Thomas Gabriel who, I fear, will surely go the way of other failed apprentices and end up as a gift to Mrs Easton, given her taste for children.

Such, then, is the past, but what now of the present?

I will organize for the girl to work at Deschamps & Sons where she will be whipped into shape, and learn for herself that girls have no place in the Badlander order except to serve men. But it is Jones who presents the biggest problem. It had been in his mind to free his mother and father from the Witch to fulfil his vain hope of becoming a normal boy. A ridiculous idea of course

218

and fortunately, through my powers of persuasion, he saw
reason and agreed to be my Whelp. It means I will take
ownership of Maitland's house and possessions according
*to the Ordnung, which is a **most** satisfactory outcome!*

In time, I expect Jones to forget about his parents and
become a loyal Whelp if treated well. I have despatched
him back to Maitland's house for a week to clean and
tidy. But it serves another purpose too. He will be busily
engaged for the night of St John's Eve which falls in less
than a week's time. His parents, being now her longest-
serving and most devoted followers, are due to be eaten
this year by Mrs Easton, such is the Witch's custom.
Once his mother and father are gone, LIFE WILL GO ON
*AS NORMAL, all this mess will be forgotten, **and** I will*
have Maitland's house and all his possessions!

Jones said nothing for a moment and then swiped angrily at the shimmering words, sending them spinning into the air.

'I can help you, Jones,' said Thomas Gabriel as he squeezed the tube again and the words were swallowed back into it. 'I'll help you kill this Witch.' Jones and Ruby glanced at each other. 'Didn't you read what it said? If I don't Commence, Simeon will give me to the Witch like his other failed apprentices. This is my last chance to prove I'm really ready for Commencement. Jones, St John's Eve is on the twenty-third of June,' continued Thomas Gabriel. 'It's the nineteenth today. That means you've only got four days to save your parents. So let me help you.'

Jones was quiet as he weighed up the options. 'Okay, then,' he said eventually and tapped the cover of the road atlas. 'We're going to Oxford tonight. To St Crosse College.'

'What on earth for?' asked Thomas Gabriel.

'Because we've got to find the Witch's Dark Bottle if we're gonna kill her.'

Thomas Gabriel's face lit up. 'Is that where it is, in Oxford?'

'No. But there's a *Lich* in Oxford who might be able to tell us where it is.'

Ruby cleared her throat. 'Jones, I've been meaning to ask. What exactly is a *Lich*?'

'Something that's usually a bit mad,' replied Jones.

'And dangerous,' added Thomas Gabriel. 'All types of *Lich* are very dangerous, at least if you get on the wrong side of them.'

'Right,' said Ruby. 'Of course they are. I mean, why wouldn't they be?' She slapped her forehead as if such a thing had never even occurred to her.

TWENTY-TWO

The interior of the chapel of St Crosse College, Oxford, looked gloomy in the moonlight. Ruby felt as if she was standing in a shipwreck at the bottom of the sea. Her hands were still tingling from the Slap Dust and she rubbed them, before turning her attention back to Jones and Thomas Gabriel, who were busy inspecting a large stone wall.

'You've been looking for ages,' said Ruby with a degree of annoyance. 'Are you sure there's a secret door?'

'Yes,' replied Thomas Gabriel. 'If my One Eye says there is then there is,' and he pointed at the creature flitting back and forth across the wall, scanning the brickwork with its one big eye. 'I already told you. They can sense things like secret doors.'

'So where is it then?'

Jones wasn't listening. He was standing on his tiptoes, peering at a coat of arms carved into the wall above him. Two small dragons sat, either side of a shield, gazing out into the chapel. There was something carved into the centre of the shield too, but it was difficult to see it clearly in the moonlight and it was taking a great deal of squinting to work out what it was. Tilting his head this way and that, Jones's eyes lit up when he saw the image of a door. The cogs started turning in his head about what it might mean, but, before he had time to say anything to the others, the latch on the main door of the chapel clicked up, sending a loud noise echoing round the walls. Someone was coming. Ruby and the two boys scattered for cover. She and Jones ended up behind a tall plinth on which stood a large marble sculpture of an important-looking gentleman, while Thomas Gabriel flashed into the nearest pew and ducked down, the One Eye flitting after him.

A tall, bony-looking man, whose dark, rumpled suit looked a little too big, closed the door behind him.

He stood, listening for a while. When he seemed satisfied he was alone, he walked halfway up the nave of the chapel and then cut left through the pews to arrive at the section of wall opposite the main door which the One Eye and the others had been inspecting. Standing below the coat of arms, he rummaged through his trouser pockets and took out a small globe illuminated from within by a pale creamy light. Jones and Ruby had a perfect view from where they were hiding and they watched him lob it into the air where it remained suspended above him, casting a ghostly light over the wall.

Jones watched carefully as the door engraved on the shield he'd found reacted instantly to the light and started to move. It drifted free onto a bare patch of wall, from where the door began to grow, its bottom edge reaching down towards the floor, until it was easily large enough for a man to step through. Having reached an appropriate size, the stone engraving transformed noiselessly into a real wooden door.

Jones shot a look at Thomas Gabriel when he saw the boy straining every sinew to see over the top of the pew he was hiding in to watch what the man was doing. Jones flapped a silent hand at him to try and tell him to crouch back down out of sight, but Thomas Gabriel didn't seem to notice, or to Jones's mind didn't want to.

When Jones looked back to see what the man in the suit was doing, he saw that the globe full of creamy light had drifted down and fitted itself against the door. The light within it was almost gone and Jones realized it had transformed into a simple doorknob.

The man turned it and opened the door, revealing a set of stone steps disappearing down into the dark.

'Du Clement!' he shouted down the stairs. 'I'm coming down. It's time for your bedding to be changed, worst luck.'

But, before he could take a step, a large **BANG!** went off like a thunderclap and he whipped round like a cat as the noise echoed round the chapel.

Jones could see instantly what had happened. Thomas Gabriel had been so eager to see what the man was doing that he'd leant too far forward, dislodging a hymn book left on the shelf of the pew.

'Who's there?' shouted the man, as the noise died away, one hand raised and white sparks fizzing round his fingertips. 'Come on out,' he said. 'Show yourselves.'

Jones motioned at Thomas Gabriel, who nodded because he knew what Jones was asking him to do, and took a deep breath before standing up to reveal himself to the obvious surprise of the man.

'Don't hurt me, sir,' whimpered Thomas Gabriel. 'I didn't mean any harm.'

'Who are you?'

'Aloysius, sir. I'm a Badlander like you, well, just an apprentice.'

'Are you indeed?'

'Yes, sir, I knew you must be a Badlander too after you used that Moon Globe,' said Thomas Gabriel, pointing at the doorknob. 'I've heard how rare they are. Only very special Badlanders would own such a thing, I know that.'

The man in the dark suit fired a set of white sparks at the doorknob and it floated off the oak door and became a Moon Globe again. He held it up, casting its pearly light around the pews to see who else might be lurking in them.

'What are you doing here? Are you on your own?'

'Yes, sir.' Thomas Gabriel emerged from the pew into the nave and held up his hands. 'Just me, sir. I was out on a hunt. Practising. My Master and I are passing through Oxford and he sent me off on an exercise to locate a One Eye he'd hidden as a test.' Thomas Gabriel plucked his One Eye from his pocket and held it up by its wings for the man to see. 'I was just on my way back to my Master,' continued Thomas Gabriel, 'but when I saw this college and the chapel I couldn't resist a peek. I've read about the research fellows at this place pretending to be ordinary people so they can study. I'd love to be one when I grow up. When you came in, I was scared and didn't know what to do. That's why I hid. But then I saw your Moon Globe and well, to be frank, sir, my excitement got the better of me.'

'And who is your Master?'

'Thackery, sir. Thackery of Dartington,' lied Thomas Gabriel without missing a beat.

The man seemed to be considering this until a loud murmuring rose up the stairs that led down into the crypt.

Thomas Gabriel cast a glance at the doorway. 'I suppose there must be something very important down there if you can only open the door with a Moon Globe.'

'Just dusty old books,' smiled the man. 'Nothing of interest to a boy like you.' He pushed the door to, leaving it just ajar. 'So, Aloysius, you want to be a research fellow, you say?' He walked towards Thomas Gabriel, checking the pews as he passed them, to be sure no one else was hiding, as the boy nodded. 'Well, luckily for you, I'm Elgin Pindlebury, the resident research fellow here. Ever since the foundation of the college, a Badlander research fellowship has always existed. We research rare creatures, studying the combat techniques, weapons and magic most effective against them. Ordinary people don't know of our studies of course. There are other secrets too and I'll let you into one of them. The clock tower in the college quadrangle isn't exactly what it seems. Let me show you, before I set you on your way,' He put his arm around Thomas Gabriel's shoulder and guided him towards the main door.

Jones and Ruby moved away from the statue. With Pindlebury talking, and Thomas Gabriel doing his best to keep him occupied by asking questions, they hurried towards the oak door in the wall and pulled it open. Ruby darted down the stairs into the dark. But, when Jones tried to follow, he couldn't, bumping against an invisible barrier. He tried again. But he was unable to pass through the doorway and didn't know why.

Jones crouched down, wary of being seen, and when Ruby peered back round the corner to see where he was, he waved her on.

'I can't get through!' he hissed. 'Just go on your own. See what you can find.'

As soon as Ruby had gone, Jones shuffled low to the end of the nearest pew and risked a peek towards the main door. Thomas Gabriel seemed to be engaged in a particularly animated discussion with Pindlebury, obviously doing his best to buy them some time.

But, as the other boy's voice rose in a panic, Jones began to realize something was going wrong. Pindlebury was casting a spell, firing white sparks from his hands that were wrapping themselves tight around Thomas Gabriel, pinning his arms by his sides. With Thomas Gabriel bound tight, the man held out his hand flat as if about to feed a sugar lump to a horse.

In the man's palm was a black, wriggly thing and Jones wasn't entirely sure what it was. He scuttled silently down the far side of the pews to try and see more, stopping when he had a better vantage point. His hand curled around the catapult in his pocket, just in case.

'I told you I didn't mean any harm,' whimpered Thomas Gabriel. 'I won't say anything about that door if that's what you're worried about.'

'I'm not worried about it in the slightest,' said Pindlebury, and smiled. He pointed at the wriggly creature in his hand. 'This is a Memory Leech. I've been studying them on and off for a while. Now, of course, I could use magic and wipe away your memory of what you've seen here because that door isn't something you should know anything about. But this seems a most opportune moment to watch the Leech at work, don't you think? A research fellow is always looking for a chance to do some practical research. Willing subjects can be hard to find.'

'Please, sir, I don't want that thing anywhere near—'

'Stop whining, boy. This isn't your run-of-the-mill Memory Leech. It's a rare subspecies, a penetrating worm or *smeawyrm* of the slimy variety, what we call a *slipigne smeawyrm*. It's very precise. All I do is tell it how many minutes to take out and it'll eat them up from your memory. It won't hurt. Just tickle a bit. At least, that's what all the research says. But I'm intrigued to see it for myself.' Thomas Gabriel whimpered as

227

the black Leech reared up in Pindlebury's hand as if already sensing it was about to go to work. 'Look on the bright side. I get to do some research and won't need to speak to your Master about you trespassing, meaning you won't get into trouble with him. We both win.'

Jones was busy trying to work out what he should do as Pindlebury placed the head of the Leech close to Thomas Gabriel's ear. He could see the slimy thing desperately trying to get a hold with its toothy mouth, and Pindlebury was struggling to control it.

'Interesting,' announced Pindlebury, 'I never realized quite how strong they were when so close to a host.'

Jones could see the One Eye desperately trying to get out of Thomas Gabriel's coat pocket, but the boy's arms were bound so tight by his sides it was trapped. He raised his catapult, his mind fizzing, still unsure about what was the right thing to do.

Pindlebury leant forward and spoke clearly to the Leech. 'I'd like five minutes extracted from this boy's he—'

A scream erupted and echoed through the chapel.

Pindlebury looked around at the secret door in the wall. So did Jones, cursing. He heard the rapid clatter of feet coming up the stone steps and then the oak door was flung open to reveal a skeleton looking somewhat confused. But when it saw Pindlebury it seemed to know exactly what to say.

'*Mon Dieu*, Pinndlebairry,' it announced. 'Knnooowww theeesss, you iigggnorrraaamus. You wheell beee the lassst fellowww of St Crosse to keeep me, Charles Du Clement, 'ere.'

228

Jones knew what a *Lich* looked like from his studies and he recognized the name Victor Brynn had mentioned to Maitland. So Jones knew this was the *Lich* they'd come to find. He watched the creature scuttle rapidly towards the main door where Pindlebury was standing. The man looked horrified. Thomas Gabriel didn't look particularly happy either.

'Wait!' shouted Jones, standing up. 'Mr Du Clement, I need to ask you something. How do I find a Witch's Dark Bottle?' But the skeleton kept going.

Jones saw Pindlebury glance over at him, clearly wondering who he was, judging by the increased look of confusion on his face. And then Jones saw what was going to happen next before the man did. A strange shrill sound started up as Du Clement sailed through the air towards Pindlebury, air whistling through the gaps in his jaw.

The skeleton hit the man full in the chest and they both landed in a heap, Pindlebury's head hitting the stone floor with a nasty crack and knocking him out cold.

As Du Clement struggled to stand up, Jones could see that some of the skeleton's ribs had sprung loose in the impact. He took careful aim with his catapult. A silver ball hissed through the air and hit Du Clement in the left thigh, sending the skeleton's whole leg flying, splitting apart into its various bones. The *Lich* tottered, but managed to stay upright, and lifted the latch on the door, heaving it open. Another ball bearing hit its hand, splitting all the bones apart, but then Du Clement was gone, hopping into the night.

Jones rushed towards Thomas Gabriel, yelling at him to help, pointing out that Pindlebury's spell had disappeared, meaning he could move again. Thomas Gabriel raised a foot ready to squash the wriggly black Memory Leech on the floor.

'No!' shouted Jones. 'We might need it,' and he pointed at Pindlebury as he ran past. 'Now come on!'

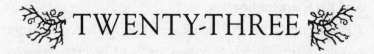

TWENTY-THREE

When Pindlebury opened his eyes, Jones stepped forward and stood over him.

'Are you all right? Your head's got a nasty bump on it.'

The man blinked up at him from the cold, stone floor and swore, then muttered a few dark words at Ruby and Thomas Gabriel too.

When Pindlebury tried to stand up, he found that his jacket had been pulled down over his shoulders, trapping his arms in the sleeves. His belt, which had been around his waist, was now tied around the tops of his knees. Before he could say anything, Jones pointed to a pile of bones heaped on the floor. Du Clement's skull was sitting on top, muttering to itself in snippets of French.

'He fell apart when we got hold of him,' said Jones. 'He was trying to climb up the ivy and escape over the college wall when we grabbed his leg. He's all there.'

To the three children standing over him, Pindlebury

seemed to breathe a huge sigh of relief, and then his face turned serious. 'You need to let me go,' he snarled.

'We will,' said Jones. 'We just want to find out something from Du Clement first.'

Pindlebury scowled, addressing all three children. 'You are in *a lot* of trouble, whoever you are,' and he gave Thomas Gabriel a particularly cold stare.

'Don't worry, the *Lich* isn't broken,' said Jones. 'He says he can put himself back together. That he falls apart a lot.'

'Do you know who I am?' asked Pindlebury.

'*Un* nincompoop,' cackled Du Clement.

'I'm the Badlander research fellow of this college. Appointed by the Order to look after this *Lich*, and to whom you're going to answer for all of this. You're making it worse for yourselves every moment you make me lie here!'

'We're just here to ask Du Clement a question,' said Jones.

Pindlebury snorted with derision. 'Go ahead! He's as mad as a hatter. Du Clement may have been a scholar once, but after he was bitten by a *Lich* the Order placed him in the chapel's crypt as a means of preserving his vast knowledge. The process of turning into a *Lich*, combined with being imprisoned in the crypt for over two hundred years, has turned his mind to mush. As the resident fellow, I'm the only one who can get any sense out of him.'

'With this you mean?' Jones held up the bottle he'd found in Pindlebury's pocket which had 'Thinking Stimulant' written on the label and the Deschamps & Sons logo above it. Jones popped off the lid. 'Smells like sage and a few other things.' He pointed to the label on the back of the bottle. 'We burn it apparently.'

Thomas Gabriel shook a yellow box of matches like it was a kid's toy.

'Luckily, we found these in your pockets too.'

'This is outrageous,' hissed Pindlebury. 'Du Clement is an abomination. A *Lich*. He's also a secret. Who told you about him? I demand to know at once.'

'No point really,' said Thomas Gabriel, and held up the wriggling black Leech. 'You won't remember if we do tell you.' Pindlebury struggled to get up as soon as he saw the Leech, but all he succeeded in doing was rolling around on the stone floor. Eventually, he stopped and started to conjure some magic, but before he could finish the spell he was intoning, Thomas Gabriel's One Eye landed on his chest and bared its teeth at him.

'No magic,' it hissed. 'Or else I'll bite that tongue clean out.'

Pindlebury took one look at the creature's teeth and decided not to finish the spell.

With the man watching, Jones tipped out a small amount of powder from the bottle onto the floor in front of the pile of bones. Thomas Gabriel struck a match and as soon as the powder was lit it began to smoulder. Du Clement stopped his muttering as a sweet-smelling smoke wound up through the holes that passed for his nose.

Jones cleared his throat. 'Monsieur Du Clement? Can you hear me?'

'*Oui.*'

233

'I think you might be able to tell us how to find something we need.'

'*Oui*. I afffvvve mucccch knowleddge ov lots of zings. Whoo tollld youuuuu about me-ee. Ze Order keeps me locked awaaayyyy. I ammm zere duurrty leeetttle sea-kret.'

'I remembered hearing it from someone called Victor Brynn.'

'Ahhh, Viii-ctorrrr. *Mon Dieu*. He was a goooood reee-seeeaarchhh felllowww, *un bon* studenttt. Bet-ter zan Pindlebairy. Not fiiit to wipe Viiii-ctorrrr's behhhind.' Pindlebury muttered something loudly under his breath. 'Zzzzo, whaat eees eeet u vant to knowwwww.'

'How to find a Dark Bottle. A *Deorcan Flascan*.'

'Ahhh, for a Wee-tch. To keeel ehhhhrrrr.'

'Yes. I want to know how to find the Dark Bottle for a Witch called Mrs Easton.'

Pindlebury laughed. 'Good luck with that.'

'Can you tell me, Monsieur Du Clement?' asked Jones, ignoring Pindlebury. 'Can you tell me how to find a Dark Bottle?'

'Oh, yessss. But fiiirrrst you mussst tell me somezing too. Somezing I do not know. C'*est* fair, *oui*? How you say een Eenglish? Teeet forrr Taaat. Zat is ze priii-ce of knowww-leddge. You zink zat's fair, Pindellberry?'

Pindlebury laughed. 'What can a boy know that the great Du Clement does not?'

Jones stared into the black empty eyes of the skull, thinking about everything Maitland had ever taught him.

And then he thought of something else that his Master would never have known, let alone believed. When he looked at Ruby, she nodded and he knew she must have already had the same idea. 'I know girls can do magic,' he said.

'Like a Wee-tch uuu meeen? Using her *Wiccacraeft*. But evvverywone knows zis.'

'No. Not like Witches. I mean girls can Commence just like boys and use Badlander magic. They can be Badlanders too. Magic works for girls.'

'I zzeee. And can you prove eeet?'

Pindlebury laughed. 'Of course he can't because it's simply not true.'

'Yes, it is,' said Ruby, taking off her baseball cap. She did a little bow in front of Du Clement. 'Monsieur Du Clement, my name's Ruby. I'm a girl. Me and Jones here Commenced together by accident and it means we can do magic together now too. We got *The Black Book of Magical Instruction* and both of us can read it.'

'Rrrruuubbbeee. *Oh, très jolie, ma fille.* Showwww me uuur magic.'

'We only know one spell.'

'Zen show me zat.'

Thomas Gabriel and Pindlebury were both staring, mouths wide open, as Ruby plucked one of Du Clement's bones from the pile and laid it in front of her on the floor.

'How long would you like me to make it disappear for?'

'Fiiive seccondsss, *s'il vous plaît.*'

'Right.' Ruby cleared her throat. 'And how do you say that in Anglo-Saxon exactly?'

'*Fif brachwíla*,' said Pindlebury quietly, who seemed as much intrigued as amazed at the prospect of a girl using magic.

Ruby grabbed Jones's hand and pointed at the bone on the floor, speaking as clearly as she could. '*Andweardnes áflíeheþ fif brachwíla.*'

When a white spark shot out of her fingers and the bone vanished through a blurry circle which had appeared, Pindlebury gasped and Thomas Gabriel cursed. But Du Clement just counted . . .

'. . . *Un* . . .

. . . *deux* . . .

. . . *trois* . . .

. . . *quatre* . . .

. . . *cinq* . . .'

. . . the bone flew back through the blurry circle and landed on the floor, making Du Clement cackle a scratchy laugh.

'*Voilà*,' said Ruby, placing the bone back on the pile, followed by a curtsey.

'Bravo!' shouted Du Clement. 'Bravo! So, girrrls are juste as gooood as boyyze.'

'That's what I keep telling everyone. The *Ordnung*'s all wrong,' said Ruby.

'It's a trick,' shouted Pindlebury. 'The boy did it on his own somehow. Must have done.'

'No, I didn't,' said Jones and he raised his hand and pointed at another bone and tried exactly the same spell. But this time nothing happened. Not even a spark from his fingers.

'Yezzz,' announced Du Clement. 'Eeet mussst beee truuu. Yuuuu 'ave proved eet. But I would keeep it zeeecret, no? Ze Orrderrr eees not so-oo inter-essted in such thingzzzz as you knowww.'

'But why?' asked Ruby.

'Beeeecccauuuse sometimesss people don't want to belieffff somefing if it scares zem. Zey must understand it feeersssst so zey are not so scared. But zis takes time. And for ze Order it will take a long time I zink. Noowwww I ammm to tell yuuuu somefing, no?'

'About the Dark Bottle, yes,' said Jones.

'All Daark Bottelles arrre eeedden in a speshial place. A cerrtaine graveyard. Where ze earth is verrry powerful and draws creeetures to eeet. Very few people know zis place. And only ze mo-ssst braaave Badlanderrrs would ever go zere.'

'Or possibly the most stupid,' mocked Pindlebury.

'Ahhh, yesss, Pindelberry, youuuu are saying you woold like to go zere, *non*?' And Du Clement grinned as the research fellow tutted. 'Nowwww, to find ze Daark Bottelle youuu want, youuuu must go to eeeach graaaave and do a speshial theeng. You must get ze gravestones toooo tell you what iz beeerrried below. You know zis skill?'

'No,' said Jones.

'Well, to make a graaavestone talk eess not so 'ard, no, Pindel-berry?'

'You want me to tell this little tyke how to do it?'

'Yesss, I want to know if youuu know. Uu are ze ree-search felllowww, no? And I beleeeeve I am ze one who hasss a say in whezzzer you earn your theees-is at ze end of your stay heeeere in ze coll-edge.'

Pindlebury sighed and looked up at Jones. 'Louis Greizmann, born 1763, died 1845, discovered how to make gravestones whisper. It was considered a major breakthrough at the time because it meant being able to hunt through graveyards and burial sites much more easily. No unnecessary digging, you see? Just make the stones tell you what's lurking below ground.'

'Greizmann whhas a drinkerrr,' laughed Du Clement. 'We gotttt in trubbbble in Paris wun night. *Mon Dieu!*'

'How do we make the gravestones speak to us?' Jones asked Pindlebury.

'A certain symbol inscribed on each stone will make it tell you what's buried there. Greizmann was an artist—'

'Eeee always liked to draw. He doodled somefingg on a gravestone one night when 'e was drunnnk and got ze shock of hisss life when eet whispered to 'im!' Du Clement cackled. 'Eeeee showed me. Eeeee said listen to zis, Charlie! Now I show you. Give me one off migh 'ands, *si'l vous plaît. La droite.* Annd a pen and *papier.*'

Jones searched in the pile of bones for a hand and found the right-handed one. When he noticed a pen clipped to the front pocket of Pindlebury's jacket, he plucked it free and took a chapel service sheet from the one of the pews.

'Nowww, hold ze *papier, s'il vous plaît.*' Jones held up the paper and the skeleton's hand scratched a symbol on the paper. 'On-ly a few peeeple in ze world kno-ww of what I am tellingg youuuu nex-t. Ze Daark Bottelles of Eeenglish Weeetches are heeden in ze graveyarrd of zee church in the village called Ingoldsby in ze county of Hereforrdshire. Go zere and youuuu vill find ze Daark Bottelle you waaannnt, ze one zat beeelongs to ze Witch youuu know. But eeet weel be gurd-ed. Ze gravestone will tell you what else lurks zere, with ze Bottelle. Be careful, *mes petits.* Be verrrry careful. Zere weel be dangerous foe protecting eeet for sure. A Wee-tch will not give up her Bottelle easileee.'

'Thank you,' said Jones.

'No, zank uuu,' laughed Du Clement. 'A girl who can doo *magique. Mon Dieu!* I zought I kneeew everyzing.'

Du Clement asked for all his bones to be taken back down into the crypt, saying he would put himself back together. When Pindlebury informed them a carefully wrought piece of magic prevented any Badlander except him, the fellow, into the crypt, Ruby simply sauntered through the doorway with a handful of Du Clement's bones in her arms.

'You mean any *male* Badlander?' she announced without looking back.

Ruby returned all of Du Clement to the crypt, locking him back into his small cell which she'd opened with the key hanging on the wall that she'd spied when first going down there. Meanwhile, Thomas Gabriel and Jones spoke together in hushed voices, as they studied the Memory Leech, with Thomas Gabriel rifling through a copy of the Pocket Book Bestiary.

'You don't need to use that on me,' said Pindlebury. 'I won't say a word. Not even about the girl.' But it seemed the two boys had made a different decision as they shut the book and came towards him, the Leech wriggling in Thomas Gabriel's fingers.

'It's all right,' he said as Pindlebury whimpered. 'We've read up how to do it.'

Pindlebury looked into Jones's eyes as the Leech snapped its tiny teeth. 'I could show you and the girl how to use magic. No one need know.'

'I ain't doing magic.'

'Why on earth not?'

'Cos I just want to be an ordinary boy.'

Pindlebury tutted. 'Impossible. Not after Commencing. You'll never be an ordinary boy now.'

'I will too,' and Jones nodded at Thomas Gabriel to use the Leech on Pindlebury to shut him up. Thomas Gabriel whispered to the creature how many minutes it was to extract from the man's memory and then fed it into Pindlebury's ear

240

as the Pocket Book had instructed, making him cry out. When the Leech had vanished, the man quietened down and went still. His eyes closed, but Jones could see them moving beneath their lids.

Thomas Gabriel consulted the Pocket Book. 'Once the Leech is done, it'll wriggle back out.'

'What do we do with it then?'

'I'm going to keep it. It's a rare one. A *slipigne smeawyrm*. It'll be really useful in London for anyone who sees things they shouldn't.' Thomas Gabriel nodded at the unconscious Pindlebury. 'He'll wake up after we're gone and think he slipped and fell and knocked himself out. The Leech is a clever creature, being able to create a story like that. It even gives its host a headache to back it up. Pindlebury won't remember a thing. Not even that you and Ruby can do magic.'

Jones looked warily at Thomas Gabriel. 'You can't tell no one about me and Ruby doing magic together,' he said.

'You think anyone would believe me? Simeon would think I was mad and then I'd never Commence.' Thomas Gabriel held out his hand and they shook silently. But, when Jones tried to let go, Thomas Gabriel held on. 'Graveyards are dangerous places, you know.'

'So?'

'So what if you need to use magic in the one where the Dark Bottle's hidden?'

'There's ways of staying safe without casting spells,' and Jones pulled his hand away.

'But why, if the magic's in you?'

'Maitland always said magic was dangerous unless you can learn to control it. He told me, if you can't, it ends up controlling you, and I don't want it ever doing that. I'll only ever use the magic inside me if there's no other way.'

TWENTY-FOUR

The following morning Jones was up early. He knew it would take a couple of hours to get the camper van ready for the journey to the graveyard to look for Mrs Easton's Dark Bottle. He and Maitland would always check over the vehicle ahead of any long trip to ensure it would not let them down, so he wanted to make sure it was ready for the journey.

He inspected the oil level, topped up the window-washer fluid, and then made sure each tyre was pumped up to the correct pressure. He also checked all the lights were working too.

The petrol tank was half full, but there were three jerry cans full of fuel stored in the shed. Jones poured the contents of one into the tank and stowed the other two securely in the van. Using the road atlas, he'd already worked out there was more than enough fuel to complete the 250-mile trip to Ingoldsby and back again. Which meant that he wouldn't have to face any difficult questions at petrol stations along the way.

*

As Jones prepared the van, Ruby packed all the things he'd written down on a list for her. It consisted largely of basic provisions they might need to cook with, such as eggs, butter and cheese, along with home-made bread, biscuits and various tins of beans, all of which were stored in cupboards in the kitchen. The items that needed to be kept chilled, like milk, butter and bacon, were in a very cold pantry and Ruby presumed it must have been charmed as she stood shivering, picking everything out.

'Yep, no 'frigerators; the *Ordnung* doesn't allow it,' said Jones when she asked about it, after dumping the bags of food in the van and then stowing everything away in the cupboards under the boy's direction. 'Badlanders ain't allowed to use certain things ordinary people do, cos of the *Ordnung*. They have to get round it using magic instead. It's just the Rules.' Jones shrugged because he didn't know what else to add.

'How come you're allowed the van?'

'The *Ordnung* lets Badlanders use vehicles. They're a way of getting around without using things like Slap Dust, which some books say is bad for you if it's used a lot. I ain't sure that's true but Slap Dust definitely ain't practical during the daytime, that's for sure. But what's really useful about a vehicle, especially a van, is you can take everything you need with you.' Jones opened a cupboard jammed full of jars and pots filled with all manner of things from pickled blue beetles to multicoloured beans. 'Hunts can take days, weeks sometimes, so you need to have somewhere you can live with all your essentials. The van'll be our home while we're looking for the Dark Bottle and we can take everything with us we might need. Graveyards are dangerous places,' he said. 'Lots of creatures live there,' he added, 'so who knows what weapons we might need,' and Ruby thought about that.

When Jones opened a cupboard at knee height, Ruby felt a blast of cold air and she figured it must have been charmed.

'Where does all your food come from?' she asked as they started to put away all the things that needed to be kept chilled.

'Maitland had an arrangement with the local farmer. He delivers a box every week with cuts of meat and milk. As for everything else, we grow it ourselves, fruit, vegetables, we even have bees for honey.'

'Isn't that hard work, growing lots of things?'

'Things grow by themselves. You don't need magic for that.' Jones looked out of the window at the sun and reckoned it was about midday. 'We should leave soon so we've got all tonight for looking round the graveyard. There's a couple of things we need to do first, though.'

Before leaving, they checked on the tiny black *Scucca* pup which had bitten Ruby on the finger. After opening the black metal box in which it had been placed, they peeked inside. The tiny *Scucca* was curled up on a bed of shredded paper. A caul covered its head, and a jelly-like membrane was growing over the rest of the creature too.

'If a pup hatches too early,' said Jones, 'and they don't eat, the ægg grows back round 'em, protecting 'em to give 'em another chance.' After closing the lid, and making sure the clasp was secure, he locked the box and placed it back under his bed. And then he gave Ruby the key.

'What should I do with it?'

'Keep it. The *Scucca* belongs to you now. He's your hound. If we make it back and you still really want to be a Badlander then you can grow 'im up like me and Maitland were going to try and do.'

'But Jones—'

'*Scucca* pups are very difficult to find. Me and Maitland spent ages looking for 'im. Proper Badlanders would give their thumbs to have that one. The Pocket Book'll tell you about *Scuccan*. And there's a special book on Maitland's shelves called *The Training Manual for Scucca Hounds* by Severin Lafour.' As Jones blinked, waiting for her to say something, Ruby realized he was giving her a present, a big one.

'Thanks, Jones,' she said.

Jones grinned and his cheeks turned red as if someone had lit a tiny fire in his mouth. 'Thanks for being my friend. And for showing me the Internet, and for saving my life an' all. I ain't really had a chance to say too much about it before.'

The final thing they did before leaving was to carry the chest full of Maitland's Commencement gifts out of the house and place it in the van because Jones wanted anything that might be helpful with them for their trip to the graveyard.

Ten minutes later, he watched the cottage growing smaller and smaller in the rear-view mirror. He glanced at Ruby to tell her he was glad he wasn't alone, especially since Thomas Gabriel would only be turning up in the graveyard if he could sneak away from Simeon without making him suspicious. But Ruby was concentrating hard on the Pocket Book Bestiary, reading up on all the creatures he'd warned her they might encounter in the graveyard. The gun was in her lap as well, telling her all sorts of useful bits of information too. As Jones steered the van in silence, it dawned on him that if they did find the Dark Bottle and manage to defeat the Witch then he and Ruby wouldn't be together for much longer, working as a team. And, the more he considered that possibility, the stronger an odd feeling in his stomach became, until he wasn't quite sure what to make of it. Instead of trying, Jones hid all his thoughts deep down inside him and focused on the road, listening to the clink of jars and bottles in their cupboards, reassured that Maitland had been diligent in making sure the van was well stocked with all sorts of useful things.

Ruby's head was full of facts about Ghouls, Wraiths, Demons and all manner of other creatures by the time they arrived in Ingoldsby. It was early evening as they drove into the village and the sun was turning the rooftops golden. Ruby placed the Pocket Book into the black backpack beside her feet, which contained the scrying mirror, and looked out of the window.

Cars were parked on either side of the narrow street with two wheels up on the pavement. Jones drove on and the road widened before they found themselves puttering through a square with a pub on one side. People were sitting outside on wooden benches, drinking and smoking. Ruby and Jones heard snatches of drunken laughter. As the VW engine gurgled and popped, the odd person looked up as they passed.

They followed the high street out of the square. There were gift shops and antique dealers as well as a delicatessen. Jones kept driving, on out of the village for about a mile, until they saw the graveyard. It was large, very old and pretty. A white gravel path ran from the lychgate to the wooden door of the small church, winding between the gravestones. Wild flowers grew in purple, red and yellow patches.

Jones pulled the van over and Ruby wound down her window. The grass had been cut during the afternoon and there was still a sweet green smell lingering in the air.

'Looks quiet enough,' said Ruby.

'Now maybe, but there's a Badlander rhyme about graveyards and cemeteries . . .

> The *Scucca* is a vicious hound,
> In deadland is it often found,
> So on a hunt in blackest night
> Expect a growl, and then a fight.'

It's to remind you to be careful. Most graveyards have a *Scucca* and it'll always defend its territory to the death. That pup at the house ain't nothing compared to a full-grown one.

It'll bite off your head in a flash and chew it down, skull and teeth and skin an' all.'

'So how do we deal with an adult?'

'Let's find somewhere to park up and I'll show you.'

It was a still, clear night when they returned to the graveyard. They walked down the lane with their shoes clicking and the stars burning bright above them, having parked the van in a side track a little way down the road, rested and eaten (Ruby had noted that beans on toast seemed to be Jones's speciality). They lowered their voices as the church came into view and by the time they reached the lychgate and stood underneath its tiny roof on the flagstones they were silent. Even the gun which Ruby was holding had stopped talking about one of its greatest adventures in a graveyard with Maitland.

Jones nodded to Ruby and she nodded back, then he held up the Y-shaped hazel stick he'd brought from the van. He held the forked ends lightly, in the 'V' of each hand, keeping them in place with his thumbs, and walked forward slowly into the graveyard. His feet crunching on the gravel path sounded too loud in the still of the night so he stepped onto the grass. As soon as he did, he felt the stick twitch and steer him slightly to the left.

He let the stick guide him between the gravestones, with Ruby and the gun following him, keeping an eye out for anything moving in the shadows. Eventually, Jones was led to a clear patch of ground where a large memorial stone lay on the grass. The inscription on it was worn by the wind and rain and difficult to read.

The stick tugged downwards and Jones let his arms drop until the end of the stick tapped the stone, and then it went dead in his hands.

'It's the *Scucca*'s lair,' hissed Jones and Ruby nodded, crouching down as if wary of disturbing what was lurking below ground.

Carefully, she handed Jones the long metal tube she'd been carrying which was as light as a bamboo cane. Jones stuck the sharp pointed end of the tube into the ground beside the memorial stone and then pushed it into the earth. He kept on shoving until just over a metre of the tube had disappeared into the ground, and then he leant over and put an ear to the cupped end sticking out, and listened. When he stood up, Jones shook his head at Ruby.

'It's not there. We need to wait till it comes back and then we can seal it in.'

He withdrew the metal tube from the ground and pointed to a hedge across the road from the graveyard. 'We'll hide there.'

'In the brambles?'

'Yes! We don't want to be out in the open when it comes back.'

Before Ruby could say anything else, Jones put his fingers to his lips and pointed behind her. She looked round to see a dark blob moving fast down the hill about a mile away.

'We need to go. Now!' shouted Jones, setting off at a run.

'Go!' shouted the gun and Ruby followed Jones, sprinting so fast the air whizzed in her ears.

They hid in the hedge, thorns digging into them at all angles, as the *Scucca* slunk between the gravestones, its two shoulders working like big pistons. It stopped and sniffed the air and growled in their direction and Ruby felt the noise rattle her teeth.

'*Scuccan* don't like being outside their deadland for long,' said Jones, squeezing Ruby's arm reassuringly. 'So even though it can probably smell us we're safe here cos it's already been out of the graveyard tonight.'

'They get so big, don't they?' said Ruby, watching the *Scucca* lose interest in what it could smell outside the boundary of the graveyard and start sniffing a gravestone instead, the top of which was brushing its chest.

'He's a large one,' agreed Jones. 'Your pup could grow up to be that size one day.' Ruby wasn't sure what to think about that but Jones was pointing before she could say anything. 'Look! It's going to ground.'

The *Scucca* stopped beside the large memorial stone, where they'd stood moments before, and started to paw it. A fissure appeared down the centre of the stone and then it split apart, the two parts opening up and folding back until they were lying flat on the grass. The *Scucca* padded down a set of stone steps and disappeared. When it was gone, the two parts of the memorial stone folded back into place and became a single slab again.

'Come on,' said Jones.

'Where's it gone?' asked Ruby as they ran across the road back to the graveyard.

'The deadland makes a burrow for the *Scucca*. The hound and the earth have a special relationship. It'll sleep there. Now's our chance to trap it in its burrow.'

When they reached the memorial stone, Jones plunged the hollow metal tube back into the ground and put his ear into the cupped end and listened. When he beckoned Ruby to listen too, she placed her ear into the cup and heard a deep rumbling underground and realized the *Scucca* was snoring.

Jones rummaged in the charmed pockets of his overcoat and drew out four silver pegs that tapered to sharp points and looked like huge silver fangs in the starlight. He pushed one into the ground beside every corner of the memorial stone until their tops were level with the grass.

'The silver stops the door from opening. But it's best the *Scucca* stays asleep cos he's so big he could bash his way out, so I've got these too.' Jones drew out a collection of black glass balls that looked like Christmas tree baubles and laid them out on the ground.

The gun in Ruby's hand chuckled when it saw them. 'Clever boy,' it said. 'Maitland would approve.'

After making sure the hollow metal tube was stuck fast in the ground beside the memorial stone, Jones picked up one of the glass balls and tapped it against the rim of the cup. It was like cracking open an egg and he dripped a dark ball into the tube. As Ruby watched the black substance unravel, she realized it was a collection of musical notes bound together in a tight ball, separating as they tumbled down the tube. A couple of them drifted free and she heard a beautiful, relaxing sound before Jones plucked them out of the air and shoved them down the tube after the rest.

'They're called Sing-Songs. They're sleeping charms. Strong ones, enough to keep an Ogre asleep, so hopefully they'll work on the *Scucca*.'

He placed a charm into the ground at intervals all around the memorial stone, eight in all, with three down each side and one at either end.

When he'd finished, he handed Ruby a piece of chalk and took one for himself and they started in one corner of the graveyard, taking the gravestones two at a time, writing on each one the symbol Du Clement had shown them and then listening to what each gravestone told them was lurking beneath the ground.

They each made a list as they went, recording anything of note hidden in the ground. Most of the time it was just bones in coffins and ashes in pots, but Ruby discovered a *Vampyr* lurking hidden undisturbed for centuries in one grave, a small Ghoul in another and a Wraith trapped in a tomb. She had to tell the gun to be quiet more than once as it became increasingly excited about all the creatures they were uncovering.

Jones discovered a pot of money that was over 200 years old. He also found a Dark Bottle buried in a grave beneath a simple-looking stone, but it did not belong to Mrs Easton. The stone whispered it had been put there by a Witch called Agnes O'Riordan over fifty years ago and that it was protected by a *Gyldenne Wurm*. When Ruby asked what sort of creature it was, Jones told her that a Golden Worm was a lithe, winged serpent that breathed fire and as far as he knew could only be killed by very select weapons about which he knew very little.

He made a note of the Golden Worm and then shook his head and sighed. 'Who knows what we're going to find guarding Mrs Easton's Dark Bottle,' he said, moving on to the next stone.

When Ruby walked on from one stone, having heard it whisper that all the ground contained was the corpse of a young man who'd died from tuberculosis, she heard a noise and looked round. She caught sight of something dropping off the outside of the church, from high up. It was a small figure that landed on the ground with a deep thud and then stood up with its pointed tail swishing angrily.

'Gargoyle,' warned Jones and Ruby aimed the gun, remembering what she had read about them in the Pocket Book. She waited for as long as the gun told her to as the Gargoyle ran at them, its stone body creaking, and the ground shaking, and then she fired at the weapon's command. The bullet caught the creature on the shoulder, taking out a chunk of masonry in a spray of dust. A second bullet caught it square in the chest and detonated, causing the creature to blow apart, and Ruby and Jones had to duck as different-sized pieces of stone rained down around them. After landing in the grass, some of them crawled a little way until they shuddered and gave up. Jones kicked at one, pinging it off the end of his boot into a nearby bush. He grinned at Ruby.

'Good shot.'

The gun was less complimentary. 'Whatever's next goes down in one clean shot. It might be the difference between living and dying, Ruby.'

They continued to work, moving methodically among the gravestones until the early morning light began to seep into the sky. There was still a lot of the graveyard to cover in their search, but they decided they should stop rather than risk being seen. Jones kept looking back over his shoulder as they left, trying to weigh up how many more nights it might take to discover where the Dark Bottle was hidden.

'We'll find it before St John's Eve,' said Ruby, patting him on the shoulder, and Jones nodded. 'We've got three more days.' But Jones just carried on walking, deep in thought, wondering whether that would be enough time.

When the small number of people turned up for the morning service, none of the congregation noticed that a stone gargoyle was missing from the outside of the church. And no one noticed a tiny inscription, a *mearcunge*, scratched on a post of the lychgate that read: *Gargoyle (Ruby Jenkins)*.

TWENTY-FIVE

The next night, as they continued their search, the temperature dropped lower than they expected and they found they were cold and tired by the time the birds began singing and there was too much daylight for them to continue without being seen by ordinary people. Ruby had dispatched another Gargoyle as well as a small Grey Gobbling which had crept into the graveyard and watched them for some time as they moved between the gravestones. Jones had eventually spotted it digging down into a grave. He'd informed Ruby that Gobblings had extremely sensitive noses and were attracted to graves by the smell of gold and silver buried with their dead owners. The Gobbling had shrieked upon being discovered and sprinted at Ruby with its mouth full of sharp yellow teeth, and its clawed hands outstretched, but she hadn't panicked and had taken only one shot to put it down this time, which the gun had been pleased about.

The Gobbling was a filthy, foul-smelling creature and Ruby was glad when she'd melted the body away. Jones warned her there might be a nest nearby since Gobblings weren't usually solitary animals. It meant they kept looking up warily whenever they heard a noise. But no more of the creatures appeared.

By the time they left the graveyard in the morning, they had found the location of three more Dark Bottles. But none of them belonged to Mrs Easton. Jones trudged back to the van in silence, and didn't seem to be listening to Ruby as she reassured him they would find the Dark Bottle they were looking for the next night. They were both tired and hungry and, by the time Thomas Gabriel appeared later that morning, he found them lying on blankets, fast asleep in the sunshine, and he woke them gently.

'We've found Dark Bottles, but not the right one,' said Jones, rubbing the sleep out of his eyes.

'I'll come and help tonight,' Thomas Gabriel told them, 'as long as I can get away from Simeon.'

'Is he asking about us?' Ruby asked as she sat up and stretched out her legs and made her knees click.

'No, as far as he's concerned, he thinks you're doing what you're told and getting Maitland's house ready for him. He's heard nothing from the gun or the imps he sent to you and I've told him I've dropped in a couple of times to check on you. He seems happy with that.'

'Thank you, Thomas Gabriel,' said Jones.

That evening, Ruby and Jones returned to the graveyard as early as they dared, in the twilight. They were optimistic about finding the Dark Bottle with Thomas Gabriel's help.

And they were proved right. Only half an hour after turning up, Thomas Gabriel discovered it, listening to a small gravestone covered in chewing gum-coloured spots of lichen. The name inscribed on it was '*Jonathan Pryor*' but the stone whispered to him the coffin containing the bones of the dead man had been removed and replaced with a Dark Bottle belonging to a Witch called Mrs Easton. Thomas Gabriel waved the others over.

'Is it here?' asked Jones, breathing hard as he arrived, a smile lighting up his face.

'Yes. But the gravestone said the creature guarding it is a horrible one.' Thomas Gabriel lowered his voice. 'Mrs Easton buried an *Ent* with her Dark Bottle.'

Jones lost his smile immediately. 'What sort?'

'*Græge fýste.*'

'A Grey-Fisted *Ent*? You're sure?'

Thomas Gabriel nodded.

'What's an *Ent*?' asked Ruby.

'A problem,' muttered Jones as he lay down and put his ear to the ground. After standing up and brushing the dirt from his trouser legs, he started to discuss how best to proceed with Thomas Gabriel, while Ruby consulted the Pocket Book to find out more. She barely noticed Thomas Gabriel vanishing silently with a pinch of Slap Dust.

By the time Ruby had got the general picture and flipped the Pocket Book shut, Jones was already pushing silver spikes into the ground marking out four corners of a big square around the gravestone.

'So an *Ent* is basically like a Giant?' asked Ruby.

'If you say so.'

'Okay, maybe not technically but near enough, right?'

Jones just motioned to her to pick up the hollow metal tube as he took out some more Sing-Songs from his overcoat pocket.

Ruby clicked her tongue against her teeth and shook her head. 'Actually, the Pocket Book doesn't mention those as being any good for *Ents*. Not Grey-Fisted ones anyway.'

'I'm improvising,' said Jones, cracking open the first Sing-Song and dripping it down the hollow centre of the metal rod stuck in the ground. 'The book doesn't say they *don't* work. Are you an expert on everything *Ent* suddenly?'

Clearly, Jones was very anxious about whatever was in the ground beneath them and Ruby decided it was best not to argue in a graveyard in the middle of the night. 'So what's the plan?' she asked eventually, 'or are you and Thomas Gabriel best friends now?' which she regretted saying immediately.

Jones looked up at her. 'We're gonna dig the Dark Bottle out. Slowly. Thomas Gabriel's gone to get help.'

Thomas Gabriel reappeared a few minutes later, holding a large canvas bag and a battered old tin with a label stuck on the top. When he opened the lid, six imps popped out like gymnasts and landed on the grass, lining up in a row. Despite their entrance, the imps looked quite old, with knock-knees and grey hair, and Jones was not impressed.

'How long have they been in there?'

'A few years.'

Jones peered down at the nearest imp, which had a wizened face like an old plum. When it smiled, it revealed only two top teeth. Jones looked straight up at Thomas Gabriel in disgust.

'Okay, they've been in their tin for about fifty years,' Thomas Gabriel admitted. 'But they're good workers. Simeon made a note about them on the label. I couldn't take any of the jars or tins of younger imps he uses now in case he noticed they were missing.'

Jones sighed as he looked along the line of little creatures. 'They look like they'll struggle to lift a pebble, let alone dig.'

'It's the best I could do.' Thomas Gabriel snapped his herringbone coat around him and reached into the canvas bag which was full of lanterns, their candles waiting to be lit. 'Let's get them digging, shall we?'

The imps worked more quickly and efficiently than Jones thought they would, their sharp nails cutting away the turf in long strips which they rolled up and laid neatly on the ground. Then they spaced themselves out evenly around the grave, one at either end and two down each side, and began to dig through the loose soil, using their hands, a brown spray going backwards, out between their legs. The little piles of dirt grew larger and larger, hissing as the earth landed. No one said a word. When a barn owl glided over the grass and passed them, Ruby was spooked at first and put her hand over her mouth to stifle her cry. She watched the bird disappear down the lane, as her heart pounded in her ears.

The imps stopped digging when one of them saw something poking up out of the earth. Jones lay on his front and peered down into the deep hole the imps had dug. He inspected the protruding thing carefully. It was not a bone or a tree root, and it took him a few seconds to work out what it was in the orange light the lanterns were giving out.

'It looks like the hilt of a dagger,' he whispered. Carefully, he reached down and just managed to touch the handle of whatever was sticking out of the earth. It was cold and he felt a tiny vibration, the *beat . . . beat . . . beat* of something.

He motioned for the imps to get to work again. 'But go slower this time,' he advised quietly.

The imps did as they were told, working carefully with their fingers to scrape away the earth. Slowly, they revealed the long, slim neck of a bottle poking up, which Jones and Thomas Gabriel crouched down to inspect.

'That must be it,' said Jones. 'That must be the top of the Dark Bottle,' and Thomas Gabriel nodded in agreement.

It was fashioned from black glass, making it impossible to see through. But it was obvious that something was lodged securely in the top and could only be pulled out using the hilt that Jones had touched.

The imps kept digging slowly. But they all froze when a clod of earth came away from below the neck of the Bottle revealing part of a very large finger. It was covered in tough grey skin, and ended in a big yellow fingernail, pointed and sharp.

'Looks like a Grey-Fisted *Ent*, all right,' said Thomas Gabriel. He held his breath as the imps brushed away the earth until everyone could see more of the finger. It was big. Covered with coarse black hair. A knuckle like a knot tied in rope under the skin.

Jones motioned to the imps to carry on digging. They went even more slowly now, but nobody complained as a very large hand was revealed, the slim neck of the Dark Bottle poking up through two fingers like the stem of a flower. As the other hand was uncovered, everyone could see they were clamped together around the body of the Dark Bottle, covering it completely.

Jones whispered to the imps to climb up out of the hole and they hauled themselves out and stood in a line, looking down at their work so far, the candles in the lanterns flickering around them.

Jones lay down and reached out a hand to try and move the fingers from the Bottle, but they were too far away. He had to shuffle forward until he was almost in danger of toppling into the hole. When he felt strong hands round his ankles, he looked back to see a couple of the imps holding on to him, giving him the thumbs up, and he shuffled forward more until he was tipped up like a wheelbarrow. Jones waved at Thomas Gabriel to lie down next to him.

'Touch the hilt sticking out of the top of the Bottle.' Thomas Gabriel reached out an arm and just about touched it, and felt the vibration as Jones had done. 'Can you feel its heartbeat?' asked Jones. Thomas Gabriel nodded. 'I'll move the fingers. Tell me if the beat changes and I'll know to stop.'

With the imps making sure he didn't topple in, Jones peeled back one finger at a time, but they kept curling back into the same position around the Bottle so, in the end, he dug out more earth and then grabbed hold of the big grey wrist and pulled it. It was heavy, but the whole hand slid away and Jones saw the Bottle for the first time. It was bulbous below the long slim neck, rounded like a large glass onion. It was too black to see what was inside.

Ruby was down on her front too, on the other side of Thomas Gabriel, and, with imps holding on to her ankles too, she reached down and started to dig out more of the earth around the other big hand that was still around the Bottle. She paused when Thomas Gabriel motioned that the heart was beating faster, and they all lay still, until it was safe to go on again. Slowly and surely, Ruby moved the other hand until they could see the whole Bottle sitting on a section of the sleeping *Ent*'s stomach, rising up and down as the rest of the creature lay buried in the ground. The Dark Bottle reminded Jones a little of a long-necked decanter of port that Maitland had kept on a sideboard.

'Can you lift it?' asked Jones and Thomas Gabriel licked his lips before nodding and shuffling forward. When he felt imps holding on to his ankles too, he moved even further to reach into the hole. He watched the *Ent*'s breathing and as the Bottle rose he reached out and cupped both hands

263

around the main body of the Bottle. He took a deep breath, and tried to lift it. But it was much heavier than he expected and difficult to get the leverage he needed, so he had to let go. He shuffled even further forward on his front, to find more strength in his arms, and then reached out again for the Bottle. This time he managed to lift it, teetering on the edge of the hole, with the imps puffing as they held his ankles.

But, as Thomas Gabriel lifted the Bottle higher, the imps started shrieking and his One Eye began yelling too and fluttering around his head. Even the candles in the lanterns seemed to be flickering madly. A sudden fear gripped Thomas Gabriel's heart and he struggled to breathe as he wondered what was happening behind him. When a hand grabbed his shoulder, he flinched, dropping the Bottle back onto the *Ent*'s stomach, before he was hauled up to his feet.

Simeon was staring at him with a face like a thundercloud, and Thomas Gabriel could barely breathe, as Jones and Ruby looked on in grim silence.

'I went . . .' The man paused because the anger inside him was so strong. 'Tonight, I visited a house where I keep a *Gást* as a test for boys like you, to find out how close you'd come to finding it. To decide whether to Commence you. And what did I find?' Simeon glared at Ruby. 'I found a *mearcunge* written by you! You, girl!' Ruby glanced at Jones, not sure what to say when she heard him mutter something. 'And then,' continued Simeon, 'one look in my scrying glass tells me you're all he—'

The rest was lost in a great rumbling sound.

And then the *Ent*'s head burst up through the earth ten metres away, great clods of earth falling from its lumpen ears. A huge arm came up through the ground, sending gravestones flying, and a coffin soared through the air like a brown torpedo and opened as it landed, a mummified corpse tumbling free.

Simeon's brain changed gear from red-hot anger to cold-brained thinking as everyone backed away.

'Do exactly as I say,' he shouted, 'and maybe we'll all live to see the morning.' The huge creature continued to emerge from the ground, rather as if it was clambering out of a bath. 'Without thorough planning and preparation, we're going to need to be lucky to beat this.' Simeon glared at the children for a moment. 'But then perhaps dying is preferable to what I can promise will happen to you all after this is over.'

'But I've already planned for the *Ent*,' said Thomas Gabriel, puffing out his chest. 'I'm prepared just like a good Badlander should be.' He took out a wizened yellow fruit from his pocket. 'You'll be proud of me, I promise.'

Before Simeon could swipe the fruit from his hand, Thomas Gabriel bit down and swallowed a mouthful of the bitter fruit. And then he stuffed the rest of it in his mouth and chewed and chewed, juice dribbling down his chin.

'Have you lost your wits, boy?' cried Simeon, shaking his head. 'What have you done?'

'Exactly what I need to do, to show you I'm ready to Commence,' said Thomas Gabriel.

TWENTY-SIX

When Jones had seen the fruit in Thomas Gabriel's hand, he'd grabbed Ruby's wrist immediately and dragged her away before the other boy had even taken a bite. The imps had backed off too, scattering into the dark and disappearing among the gravestones, where they cowered and squeaked and then went silent. Even the One Eye flew like an arrow into Jones's overcoat pocket to hide.

'What's he eating?' asked Ruby as Thomas Gabriel polished off the fruit.

'A *wuduæppel*. One way to take on a Grey-Fisted *Ent* is to transform into something bigger. But it's only for Badlanders who know what they're doing. It takes great skill choosing a creature, to get it right.'

'It didn't mention it in the Pocket Book.'

'Most Badlanders consider it an act of treachery, changing into a monster to fight another. You need special permission from the Order to do it. Thomas Gabriel must have known his Master had the *wuduæppel*.'

266

Ruby was about to ask more, but stopped at the sound of the *Ent* standing up in the graveyard, the lanterns scattered around it, the odd candle in some of them still lit. The creature was about twenty metres tall, with a pot belly and dark bristly hair sprouting on the backs of its arms and chest. A dewlap of loose hanging grey skin wobbled as it shook its body free of earth and roots.

'There,' Jones shouted, and Ruby got a glimpse of the Dark Bottle before the *Ent* closed one huge fist around it and roared, its red tongue flapping against a mouth of rotten teeth. Clearly, the creature was not going to give up the Dark Bottle without a fight.

Ruby and Jones could see Thomas Gabriel crouched on his haunches with Simeon down beside him and they could hear the man telling his apprentice to throw up the *wuduæppel*.

'No,' shouted Thomas Gabriel. 'I'm a good Badlander. I'm going to show you I can take on this *Ent* so I can Commence.'

'It's too late for that now,' roared Simeon. 'You're not right for Commencement. You're a stupid boy and a liar. You're no apprentice of mine any more.' All Thomas Gabriel could manage in response was to cry out and clutch at his stomach. 'I'll clear up this mess,' Simeon shouted at Ruby and Jones, 'and then I'll deal with you, Thomas Gabriel. I'll cut you down, whatever foul creature you've chosen to become. I'll take great pleasure in marking two *mearcunga* here tonight, for both the beasts I'm going to kill.'

Simeon strode purposefully towards the Grey-Fisted *Ent*, which licked its lips and smiled a ragged grin when it saw him.

Simeon raised his hands.

'*Gebíed mé lígetslieht*,' he shouted. Ruby and Jones watched his fists glow light blue and then he banged them together three times. 'In the name of the Order, I despatch this foul *Ent*, to protect the world, using the gift of magic that I, Simeon Rowell, possess and control.' Ruby could see that his fists were glowing golden now and then Simeon took one arm back and hurled something out of his hand. A golden missile flashed towards the *Ent*, but the creature held up the Dark Bottle and the projectile fizzled out like a firework and dropped to the ground before hitting its mark.

Simeon stared at the *Ent*, watching its belly shake as it howled with laughter.

Then the *Ent* roared as it came stomping forward and the sound seemed to stir Simeon. In a panic, he flung back his other golden fist and threw it forward, releasing a second missile at the oncoming creature. But that fizzled out too and the *Ent* snarled as it drew back its free arm and swung a fist at Simeon. It was too big to dodge and it hit the man like a train. Simeon went flying through the air, his coat billowing round him, and landed near Ruby and Jones with a horrible thud that made them gasp.

The Grey-Fisted *Ent* waited for the man to get up, but there was no sign of life. When the creature sniffed the air, Jones pulled Ruby back into the dark shadows beside the church.

The *Ent* sniffed again and took a lumbering stride towards them, then stopped again and scanned the ground ahead, peering into the dark for them.

'What are we going to do, Jones?' whispered Ruby.

'It all depends on Thomas Gabriel now. On what sort of creature he's going to become,' and he pointed as Thomas Gabriel rushed to his Master's side, in full view of the *Ent*, which began watching in fascination at this new entertainment.

Ruby and Jones could see that Simeon was badly hurt, that his breathing was blood and spit. And with Thomas Gabriel closer now too they could see the boy's right eye had turned yellow. In fact, everything on his right-hand side was starting to look very different. His foppish chestnut hair was already a dark grey. His right arm was rapidly growing and, as his hand swelled, the fingers ballooned to the size of rolling pins.

'I wiii-llll Commm-mence,' he said, his voice sounding warped and strange because the right half of his face was becoming much larger than the opposite side. 'An-thnd I'll be-ee a gwreat Baddd-looonderrrr too-ooo.'

Simeon was breathing fast, but he managed to find the words he wanted. 'You'll die tonight like me,' he wheezed. 'You're not skilled enough to use a *wuduæppel* ...' Simeon choked a laugh. 'Typical of you ... No ... no ... good at anything ...' He laughed again and coughed before his

269

breathing became laboured and his head dropped to one side. Ruby gripped Jones's hand as the man died and she looked away.

Jones was busy watching Thomas Gabriel. As the other boy grunted at his dead Master, and stood up, Jones gasped as the whole right side of his body swelled so quickly the clothes covering it shredded in an instant, and fell away. Thomas Gabriel grew rapidly taller as his right leg lengthened, and the bare foot beneath it broadened into a grey, bony, clawed thing, the size of a small family car. In a matter of moments, half of the boy's body had become *Ent*-like. But the left-hand side of Thomas Gabriel remained boy-sized and it flailed like a small flag atop a huge, thick mast as the half-formed *Ent* wobbled on one gigantic leg. Thomas Gabriel put his massive right hand down on the earth to steady himself. The fist was huge and it was black. The *Ent* half of his body was much larger than the Grey-Fisted one that had been woken from the earth.

'Oh, Jones, what's happened to him?' asked Ruby.

'He ain't changed properly. I said it was hard. He's only changed to half an *Ent*. A Black-Fisted one by the look of it,' and they watched the Grey-Fisted *Ent* try to make sense of what new creature was standing in front of it.

The half boy, half *Ent* gave a reasonably sized roar, which ended with a high-pitched squeak, rounded off by the part that was still very much Thomas Gabriel. The Grey-Fisted *Ent* cocked its head at such an odd noise and then decided it was worth investigating and loped towards Thomas Gabriel, who was managing to walk, using his massive black hand like a crutch. The ground shook as both *Ents* lumbered towards each other.

'Black-Fisted *Ents* hate Grey-Fisted ones and vice versa,' said Jones. 'They're natural enemies. So at least Thomas Gabriel tried to change into something half decent.'

'Do you think he's changed enough?'

'I don't know. Black-Fisted *Ents* do pack a bigger punch cos they're much larger. So, if he lands a blow just right, he might be okay. As long as he doesn't break the Dark Bottle. He's got to remember that's why we're here.'

Jones licked his lips in nervous anticipation as he watched Thomas Gabriel try to lift his huge arm off the ground and balance on his one massive leg at the same time. Wobbling, Thomas Gabriel swung a punch at the Grey-Fisted *Ent* and completely missed, spinning round in a circle before crashing to the ground.

'We're going to have to help him,' said Ruby. But as she got ready to run, pulling the gun out of her waistband, Jones held her back. He put his finger to his lips before she could say anything and nodded across the graveyard at the huge crater from which the Grey-Fisted *Ent* had emerged.

The *Scucca* was crawling from out of the same place in the ground, planting its two front paws on the grass and then hopping its back legs up too. It sniffed the air as it watched the Grey-Fisted *Ent* slam a big fist into the *Ent* side of Thomas Gabriel, making the strange hybrid creature groan as it lay on the ground.

271

The *Scucca* turned to face the church, and it seemed to be aware of Jones and Ruby right away. It growled and padded in their direction.

'Time to move,' said Jones. 'The Sing-Songs and the silver spikes must have got dislodged in all the ruckus.'

Ruby and Jones kept out of sight in the shadows as they crept quietly beside the church, aware of the *Scucca* stopping periodically and sniffing the air as it attempted to locate them. Jones kept glancing at the two *Ents*, watching what was going on, nervous about what might happen to the Dark Bottle.

He could see Thomas Gabriel lying on his back as the Grey-Fisted *Ent* came at him again, its large arm raised. But this time Thomas Gabriel was quicker. He launched his huge arm, swinging it up and round before the other *Ent* could hit him.

Jones heard the large black fist make a satisfying thud as it hit the other *Ent*'s head before the creature tottered away. Ruby kept hissing at Jones to keep up as the *Scucca* followed them, but Jones was too worried about the Dark Bottle, and looked back again to see the Grey-Fisted *Ent* pull up a couple of gravestones and hurl them at Thomas Gabriel, who punched them away, splintering them over the grass. But the stones were only a distraction as the Grey-Fisted *Ent* came at Thomas Gabriel and landed a blow on the *Ent* half of his body. But this time the Grey-Fisted *Ent* didn't back away, staring instead at the pint-sized part of the creature lying in front of it. And then it raised its fist.

Jones ran on after Ruby, with the *Scucca* quickening its pace behind them. When Ruby crouched down out of breath behind a large gravestone, deep in conversation with the gun, Jones stopped and looked back again.

To his relief, Thomas Gabriel had grabbed the Grey-Fisted *Ent* by its throat with his giant hand, and he was using the creature as a crutch with which to stand up on his one massive leg. Thomas Gabriel's black fist was clamped tight like a vice. He was choking the Grey-Fisted *Ent*, which was clawing at the huge black fist with one hand as it held the Dark Bottle safe in the other. But Thomas Gabriel held on tight, squeezing harder and harder.

Suddenly, there sounded a great crack as the neck of the Grey-Fisted *Ent* broke and Thomas Gabriel snapped the creature's head clean off. The headless body slumped to its knees and the hand holding the Dark Bottle opened as the corpse fell to the ground.

Jones watched as Thomas Gabriel lunged and reached out his boy-sized hand to catch the falling Dark Bottle, which he did safely before it could crash to the ground. Jones pumped his fist and then heard a deep growl close by.

The *Scucca* was facing him. For a moment, time seemed to stand still and then the creature charged, and, in that second, Jones thought of how short his life had been and of all the things he wished he'd done.

A loud bang from behind made him flinch and the *Scucca* crumpled instantly to the ground. With his ears still ringing and his hands shaking, Jones looked back at Ruby, who was standing in a triangular stance, holding the gun with both hands.

'You're as good as any Badlander I ever met,' he said quietly, his voice all shaky, and Ruby smiled back as the gun started hollering about what she'd just done.

By the time the *wuduæppel* had worn off, Jones had disposed of the bodies of the *Scucca* and the Grey-Fisted *Ent*, melting them away into great lines of white foamy bubbles that popped as they disappeared. But the graveyard was a mess and nothing could be done about that. Gravestones lay scattered and broken over the grass. Great furrows were ploughed into the earth. Coffins were splintered apart and strewn like driftwood. Old bones glinted in the moonlight.

Jones and Ruby skirted round it on their way to Thomas Gabriel who, now restored to his normal body and with his clothes in rags, was standing over the body of Simeon with his One Eye perched on his shoulder. The old grey imps were beside him, standing in a line, sniffling and wiping their eyes as Thomas Gabriel tipped up the little pot of dust he was holding. The brown dust sparkled as it fell and Thomas Gabriel watched the body of his Master dissolve.

'Do not be afear'd
It is only the *wyrd*
That says you must go
From this world that you know.

Do not be afear'd
It is only the *wyrd*
That wants you to leave
Which means I won't grieve.

Do not be afear'd
It is only the *wyrd*
That rules all our lives
And always decides

The length of one's life
All its joy, all its strife,
So do not be afear'd
It is only the *wyrd*.'

Jones and Ruby kept a respectful distance until the body of
Simeon was gone.

When Thomas Gabriel was ready, he turned round and
came towards them. He was smiling as he opened his fist and
out dropped a silver key bobbing on its chain.

The gun in Ruby's hand piped up instantly. 'It's against
the *Ordnung* for an apprentice to take a key without their
Master's blessing. It can affect their Commencement. You
need to tell the Order what's happened. That Simeon's dead.'

Thomas Gabriel smiled innocently. 'I think I deserved
the key, don't you?'

'Tell him, Jones,' said the gun. 'Warn him what he's doing.'

Jones stared at the key and shrugged. 'It ain't my business.

Besides, I don't think the *Ordnung*'s worth talking about, do you?' and he looked at Ruby, who shook her head.

'So, we're all agreed then,' said Thomas Gabriel and he swung the silver key in front of the gun as if to taunt it. 'Anyway, my Commencement's got to be a good thing,' he announced. 'If Jones wants to get his parents back before that Witch can eat them tonight, he's going to need someone who can use magic.' He stopped swinging the key and looked at Ruby and Jones. 'You're going to need all the help you can get to kill Mrs Easton and I'm more than happy to help because I want that Witch off my *æhteland*.'

TWENTY-SEVEN

Jones and Ruby decided to drive to London rather than use Slap Dust like Thomas Gabriel, who was eager to get home and Commence. They didn't want to leave the van in the field where it might draw attention to itself and Jones wanted to take everything with them too, given the task ahead of them in Hampstead.

They drove through what was left of the night, Jones blinking through his tired eyes as he focused on the road and Ruby keeping him company by reading up all she could on Witches in the Pocket Book, the gun snoring in the backpack by her feet. At one point, Jones pulled over and they both drank a yellow, bitter-tasting tonic poured out of a bottle into a spoon, which he assured Ruby would reinvigorate her. He was right, and Ruby soon felt the tiredness melting away from her eyes and the stiffness in her bones disappearing.

They arrived at Simeon's house in the sharp, early daylight, with the traffic already building for the morning rush hour into London. The tall gates had been left open by Thomas Gabriel allowing them to pull into the semi-circular driveway in front of the house. After Jones had turned off the engine, Ruby slammed the Pocket Book shut.

'Well?' asked Jones.

'Witches eat their longest-serving acolytes every year on St John's Eve during what's called the Witching Hour, the hour after midnight. There's a well-known book all about it called *The Power of the Hour* apparently. The meal's supposed to help boost a Witch's *Wiccacraeft* for the year ahead.'

'Does it say how to use the Dark Bottle?'

Ruby delved into the old battered backpack beside her feet and took out the Bottle. Grabbing the stopper, she pulled it out very slightly. 'There's a dagger pushed down into the neck. Do you see?' Jones nodded as he saw a sharp blade being drawn out, as black as night. 'A Witch puts all her greatest fears in a Bottle like this, and I reckon the dagger's infected with it somehow. Put your ear close to it.' Jones heard the faint whispering of voices and pulled away, spooked by the talking blade. Ruby slid the knife carefully back into the neck of the Bottle, and made sure the hilt was pushed in tight before putting it away. 'Stab Mrs Easton with the knife and she'll die. Her greatest fears will kill her.'

'Simple as that?'

'As simple as that.' Ruby managed a smile that Jones couldn't quite match. He wanted to tell Ruby how scared he was, not of the Witch, or even of dying, but of never becoming the ordinary boy he so desperately wanted to be. Even though Simeon had told him his parents could recover from Mrs Easton's curse if the Witch was killed, he wondered

278

how long it might take and how hard it would be. It scared Jones to think that killing the Witch might mean nothing if his parents took years to become normal again. What if he was all grown up before they were better?

Thomas Gabriel banged on the van window and made them both jump. He grinned at them and held up a copy of *The Black Book of Magical Instruction*. His One Eye was fluttering round it excitedly.

'Think we can trust him?' whispered Ruby as she took off her seat belt.

'The way I see it, three of us is better than two,' said Jones, taking off his belt as well. He leant forward towards Ruby. 'And if he can do magic then I'm gonna need him to help my parents get better, once the Witch is dead, after being cursed for so long.'

Thomas Gabriel was still smiling after they opened the doors and stepped out onto the gravel drive.

'Commenced as soon as I got back. I've already started learning how to use magic. I think I'm a natural.' He flicked his fingers and muttered the word '*Æppel*' and a small set of white sparks circled his fingers. They spun and whirled and vanished to reveal an apple in his hand. When he offered it to Ruby, she shook her head and he bit down hard into the waxy red skin to prove it was real. He grinned at Jones as he chewed.

'See, nothing went wrong with my Commencement like your gun said it would. The magic works fine, just like it should.' And he took another bite to prove it. 'Do you have a plan for the Witch? I read up on Dark Bottles. For the dagger inside the Bottle to work the best it can, it needs to be plunged straight through a Witch's heart.'

'We knew that,' said Ruby, glancing at Jones to reassure him.

'First of all, I want to observe the Witch's shop,' said Jones. 'Find out exactly what we're dealing with. After that, we can work out a plan.'

'There's not much time, Jones,' said Thomas Gabriel, taking another bite of the apple.

'Be prepared, remember, that's how Badlanders work. Maitland used to say there's always a way to get something done if you look hard enough.'

'What if Mrs Easton knows we've taken the Bottle? She must have some connection to it. She might be waiting for someone to turn up. Or she might even be trying to find it now.'

Ruby cleared her throat. Held up the Pocket Book. 'Once a Dark Bottle's been hidden, a Witch feels no attachment to it. All her fears placed inside it must be renounced completely.'

'Fine, I know where the shop is,' said Thomas Gabriel, tossing away his apple core.

Jones shook his head. 'Just me and Ruby'll go. The Witch might get suspicious if Simeon's apprentice is snooping around. Besides, Ruby's a girl. The Witch won't suspect anything.'

Thomas Gabriel whirled his fingers and muttered a word or two and fired a shot of white sparks at a bush, which set fire to some of the leaves. 'I'll just keep practising then. And, by the way, I'm *not* an apprentice any more. This is my house now. My *æhteland*. That's why I'm helping you. And remember I own Maitland's house as well, given that everything Simeon owned will pass to me. But I suppose if you're nice I might give it back to you,' and he shrugged at them.

Jones and Ruby bought coffees in a small café and sat in the window seats, drinking out of white mugs, watching Mrs Easton's shop, which was positioned a little further down the street. They had spotted it from a distance as they walked along the road. The sunlight had been bouncing off a large glass window, making it difficult to see in, but there was a white wooden board above the shop with black lettering that read: Easton's Bakery & Pâtisserie. There was a large house attached to the shop. As they studied the comings and goings of customers, they saw nothing out of the ordinary.

When a ginger cat appeared out of the dark mouth of an alleyway and started walking towards the shop, Jones watched it with interest.

'Cats are very sensitive to certain creatures. It might give us a clue about what's in that shop or the house behind it.'

'We know what's in there, Jones. A bloody great Witch,' said Ruby, under her breath. 'I'm not sure sitting here's going to tell us much we don't know already.'

'Witches have familiars, creatures they like to have around. We ain't just taking on a Witch, Ruby. There's other things in there with her. It would be good to know what they are.' He leant forward in his chair, eager to watch the cat. 'Cats are very sensitive to Demons and Wights.'

But his face fell as the cat padded straight past the shop door and hopped up onto the sill of the large window beside it, where it sat down and started washing its ears.

'So what else do Badlanders look out for?' asked Ruby.

'Dogs'll show you things. They're sensitive to most types of Trolls and *Ents* and will pull their owners away from a particular building if they sense something they don't like about it. Or sometimes you'll notice there aren't any birds on a roof when there's others perched on the tops of buildings around it. That'll tell you there's a *Gást* there.' He nodded at a mother wheeling a pram, walking towards the shop. 'Babies are sensitive to little creatures. They can start bawling and then shut up as soon as they've gone past a place with an *Ælf* in it.' Ruby watched the mum go straight past the shop, but there was no sound from the baby. When a couple of pigeons landed on the shop's roof and began cooing gently, Jones cursed under his breath. He knew time was ticking on and they hadn't learnt anything useful so far. 'Is it really true what you told me 'bout your scrying mirror, that you can only spy on someone if you've met them before or places you've been?'

'Yes.'

Jones drummed his fingers on the table as his brain whirred. 'You've seen Mrs Easton when the *Gást* showed her to us. Does that count?'

282

Seeing they were the only customers in the café, Ruby unzipped the battered black backpack by her feet and took out the mirror. She looked into the glass, focusing hard on trying to see Mrs Easton. But nothing materialized. Eventually, she shook her head. 'I need to go into the shop if I want to see anything in the mirror.'

Jones grunted. 'That could be dangerous.'

'So? Isn't that the business we're in?' Ruby took out the Dark Bottle and gave it to Jones for safekeeping, and he put it in one of his charmed overcoat pockets as she zipped up the mirror inside the backpack. 'All I need to do is go in, buy something, and come out again, then I'll be able to spy on the shop and the house behind it too.' She stood up, hefting the backpack onto her shoulders. 'Jones, there's no other way of knowing what's in there. You're just not used to working with anyone else except Maitland.'

'It's not that. You're the only friend I've got. Who else is gonna show me stuff on how to be an ordinary boy?' He blushed a little round the edges.

'I'll be fine. I've got this,' she said, inching the gun out of her jacket pocket so Jones could see it but no one else. 'And Mrs Easton'll never suspect I'm a Badlander. And another thing: I read up on Witches that are Six-Toed and Goggle-Eyed last night. Mrs Easton might be a rare kind of Witch, but her type only eats *boys*, not girls. So she won't be interested in me, will she? While I go into the shop, why don't you go round the back? Find out if there's a way in. We need to know everything we can, don't we?'

Jones grabbed her hand before she turned round and handed her the bottle of black Slap Dust. 'Just in case,' he said. 'We meet back here as soon as we're done.'

'Any last advice?'

'If you see anything strange, get out as fast as you can.'

The pink cake boxes in the shop window were stacked like bricks to make a semi-circular wall too high to allow anyone to see into the shop. Laid out in front of it were cakes of various shapes and sizes on stands, with some under glass domes. The icing on them looked so elegant and pristine, Ruby wondered if they were made of plastic. Heaped all around the stands were colourful tins of sweets – sherbet lemons, pear drops and wine gums – elegant white cartons of chocolates tied round with red ribbons and wooden bowls full of green, pink and white sugar mice with black dots for eyes and long tails made from white string. Loaves of bread were arranged down each side of the window display and beautiful jam tarts were sitting on top of them.

Ruby heard her stomach gurgle and then remembered she had a job to do.

When she opened the door, a little silver bell tinkled. A young woman was sitting behind a long rectangular counter made from glass at the far end of the shop. She looked up from her newspaper and studied Ruby briefly before returning to her reading again, turning the page and blowing a pink bubble of gum that popped. Inside the glass counter in front of her was beautiful patisserie arranged in rows. There were chocolate eclairs as long as her foot. Beautiful tarts, large and small, full of fruit and made with rich butter pastry bases. Huge gingerbread men lay on trays with big iced smiles, and elegant cupcakes covered with different-coloured icing were arranged in rows. There was a line of chocolate cakes, some topped with shavings of dark chocolate, one with elaborate white and dark chocolate roses, and others topped with cream and meringue with icing piped around the edges.

Behind the counter, slatted wooden shelves were full of freshly baked loaves of bread of all shapes and sizes. A doorway to the right of it was blocked off with a curtain made from long strands of multicoloured beads that reached to the floor.

As Ruby walked towards the counter, she kept glancing at the bead curtain, wondering what was behind it. But her curiosity disappeared as soon as she saw a picture on the front of the newspaper the shop girl was reading. It was her. It was a picture of her face.

Ruby tugged her baseball cap further down over her eyes as the girl put the paper down and smiled.

'What can I get you?'

'Chocolate eclair, please.'

'We got large or small,' said the shop girl, gesturing at the cakes inside the glass counter.

Before Ruby had time to say anything, she heard a hissing sound and watched a pair of hands poke through the bead curtain and part it, the plump fingers pressed together as if their owner was about to dive through. Ruby caught a glimpse of a hallway, a thick red carpet and dark wallpaper, confirming that there was indeed a house attached to the back of the shop. And then a matronly woman appeared through the beads and stood behind the counter.

Ruby recognized Mrs Easton immediately and she managed to stop a little gasp escaping her mouth.

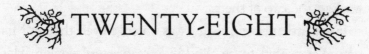

TWENTY-EIGHT

The Witch smiled at Ruby. It was a full-bloodied, all-toothy smile, full of pink gums and bright red lipstick.

'Wanna read your horoscope, Mrs Easton?' asked the shop girl as she pointed at the newspaper on the counter.

'No thank you, Sophie.' Mrs Easton's voice was as brittle as dead leaves. 'I'm not sure I believe in all that hocus-pocus, dear. It's almost lunchtime: why don't I serve this young lady and you get off for your break?'

Sophie slid off her stool and grabbed her coat from a peg on the wall behind her. Clearly, she could not leave fast enough. 'Thanks. See you later then, Mrs Easton.'

The woman took a step back to let Sophie past and smiled at Ruby. 'What can I get you?' she asked, as she took hold of the glasses hanging on a chain around her neck and set them on her nose.

'Eclair. Small one.' Ruby pushed a five-pound note across the glass counter as Sophie's shoes squeaked behind her on the floor.

Mrs Easton looked at Ruby as if something in the tone of her voice had interested her immensely. The shop door opened and banged shut, making Ruby flinch. And then it was just the two of them.

Every little nerve in Ruby was on edge even though Mrs Easton appeared to be the kindest, sweetest woman. Her cheeks looked as soft as peaches. A rich mound of brown hair was tied back in a bun without a curl out of place. Her fingernails were pared into perfect semi-circles. Everything about her suggested she was a clean, virtuous woman as Ruby caught a whiff of soap and lavender.

But Ruby saw through it all. She thought of what Jones had told her about the Badlands on the first night they'd met; the scary things that lurked on the edge of ordinary people's lives and right under their noses sometimes.

Mrs Easton picked up a small pink cake box and opened it. She smiled as she reached for a pair of tongs and flexed them, making a clinking sound as the ends tapped together. Her eyes flicked to Ruby's face and back to the picture on the front of the newspaper which was still on the counter.

'I think I know who you are. You're that runaway girl, aren't you?'

Ruby's heart screamed.

She thought she was shaking her head and saying 'no'. But she wasn't. She was just staring into Mrs Easton's face, and then she nodded in agreement as if someone had taken control of her neck.

'I knew it!' said the Witch. 'It's the eyes. They're a window into a person; they let you glimpse who someone really is if you look deep enough into them. And I can.' Ruby noticed that Mrs Easton smelt different now, like hot metal, but she could not remember when the change had happened. Her blue eyes, magnified by her glasses, were much brighter than before and Ruby could not stop staring into the big black pupils. 'A person's eyes are very, very special indeed,' said Mrs Easton. She pushed her glasses higher up her nose. The lenses were doing something, making her eyes shimmer. All thoughts Ruby had of running out of the shop like Jones had told her to do were starting to vanish. Her mind kept slipping like the gears on an old, broken bike.

'Who else knows you're here, dear?'

Ruby summoned all her strength to lie. 'No one.'

Mrs Easton observed her like a schoolmistress dealing with a naughty child. 'Are you sure?'

Ruby licked her lips. It was difficult to lie when the woman was looking at her like that through those glasses. But she managed to slip her mind sideways and tell the truth. Sort of.

'Not one adult knows I'm here except for you and Sophie.'

Mrs Easton studied her, tapping a finger on her lips. And then she smiled.

'So you're not with anyone else?'

Ruby clenched her toes inside her trainers to try and help her concentrate on what she wanted to say. She was not with anyone here in this shop. So that's what she focused on.

'No,' she said quietly, her voice wavering as she struggled to say what she wanted. Mrs Easton observed her for a second, and then walked out from behind the counter. By the sound of the woman's shoes on the floor, Ruby guessed she was going to look out of the window. But she could not turn her head to look because her body did not seem to be hers any more. There was no way of reaching for the gun in her pocket.

The bell over the door tinkled as Mrs Easton opened it, and then again before the door clicked shut. A lock snapped, a bolt was drawn, and Ruby heard the hiss of a window blind being drawn down. When the woman came back and stood beside her, she nodded, apparently satisfied.

'Well, then, little girl, or should I say . . .' Mrs Easton craned her head to look at the newspaper, 'Ruby Jenkins, I think you'll do very nicely indeed.' She raised a hand and gestured towards the bead curtain. 'After you.'

Ruby's legs started moving for her and she found herself walking without wanting to do so.

After Ruby had left, Jones had followed his nose until he was on the street that ran behind Mrs Easton's shop. Walking towards it, he could see there was definitely a house attached to the rear. But what intrigued him was the very tall brownstone wall extending out from the back of the building. It surrounded what he presumed was an extremely large back garden, judging by the tall chestnut trees he could see.

As he approached it, the road he was on ended and he walked through a gate onto a footpath. Stretching out ahead of him was a great expanse of grass dotted with trees and scrub and he recognized it as Hampstead Heath from the tour Simeon had given them. The brownstone wall extending out from the house behind Mrs Easton's shop was more than triple his height, making it impossible to see over. He started counting his steps as he marched quickly beside it, aware that Ruby might be back in the coffee shop already. By the time he reached the far end, he'd counted 300 paces and estimated the garden must be about 250 metres wide. He stood at the corner and estimated the garden to be longer than its width across. In other words, it was a very big garden indeed.

He retraced his steps beside the wall, looking for any obvious footholds that might make it easier to climb over. But there were none. Neither were there any chinks or holes that allowed him to see what was beyond the wall, into what he presumed was a garden. Because it backed onto the heath, there were no houses overlooking it. There were no trees tall enough to afford a view into it either. It was, he realized, completely hidden from view, meaning anything could be in there.

He stuffed his hands in his pockets and was about to walk back to meet Ruby when he saw the same ginger cat that had been sitting on the sill of the shop window earlier.

'Hello, cat,' said Jones as it rubbed up against his leg. 'Where'd you come from?' When he picked it up to give it a stroke, it didn't seem to mind and looked longingly at the top of the wall before coiling itself against his chest and leaping out of his arms. It did not quite reach the top but scrabbled up the remainder of the wall, looked back at Jones and then leapt down out of sight.

Instead of walking on, Jones listened very carefully for any sound that might give him a clue about what was behind the wall: paws padding along a gravel path . . . a body winding through long grass . . . claws being sharpened on a tree stump. But all he could hear was the cat purring contentedly. He imagined it sitting on the edge of a large lawn, washing its ears. And then he heard a terrible shriek. The cat's yowl died down to an awful lingering whisper that faded away. Jones waited a little longer, holding his breath, and heard a soft chattering sound. When no other clues were forthcoming, he started marching back to find Ruby. A moment later, he started to run.

Ruby was standing in the hallway of the house attached to the shop, the beaded curtain behind her. Some distance ahead of her was a doorway to what she presumed was a kitchen because she could see a sink. Above it was a window through which she could see a huge garden. It looked extremely overgrown. The grass was waist high. Thorny bushes had spread out of control. Ruby glimpsed a very high wall surrounding the garden. Various types of trees had grown up so tall they were towering over it.

'Just a few more steps, dear,' said Mrs Easton in an encouraging tone, sweeping past Ruby and stopping in front of her. The woman pressed her hand flat against the wall and pushed. There was a *click* and a hidden door popped out and swung open, revealing a set of dark stairs.

Ruby shook her head. She gritted her teeth and managed to speak through a slit her mouth had made. 'I'm not going down there.'

Mrs Easton smiled. 'Of course you are. You *must* do what I say.' Her blazing blue eyes looked so large behind the glasses they were like two huge marbles. Ruby could not look away. 'It'll all be over very soon. Then you won't have to worry about anything again. Ever.'

Ruby heard soft chattering sounds drifting up out of the cellar and she realized something was coming up the stairs as they creaked.

Ruby was desperate to reach for the gun in the pocket of her jacket. But her arms were as stiff as sticks and her fingers were like twigs that she couldn't move: there was no way of reaching for it.

'Come on,' cooed Mrs Easton at whatever was coming up the stairs. 'Come and see what I've got you, you lucky thing.'

A long black and bristly leg emerged out of the dark and landed gently on the topmost stair—

BANG! BANG! BANG!

A rapid hammering started up on the door at the front of the shop. The hairy black leg darted back down the stairs into the dark and Mrs Easton swung round to see what was happening. But it was impossible to make out much through the beaded curtain.

'Mrs Easton!' came a distant voice from outside. 'It's

Sophie. I forgot my wallet. It must have dropped out my bag.' **BANG! BANG! BANG!** 'Are you there? Mrs Easton? I'm supposed to be meeting someone for a drink at The Feathers.'

Straps seemed to loosen from Ruby's body, and from her mind, as the Witch was momentarily distracted. But a moment was all Ruby needed and she ran as hard as she could down the hallway.

When something slammed into her backpack, she heard the scrying mirror shatter before the impact felled her and she hit the floor. Ruby was up again quickly, looking back as Mrs Easton cursed. A long chain with a sharp hook on its end lay between them. Ruby could still feel the impact of it in her back. The chain retracted quickly, disappearing back into the open palm of the Witch's left hand until she was holding the hook, and then it shot out again, towards Ruby. This time she saw it coming and dodged, but the sharp tip caught the arm of her jacket, nicking her left shoulder as it flew past and struck the door frame ahead of her. Mrs Easton cursed again as she tried to retract the hook, which was embedded in the wood, and then she gave up and whispered a word and the hook and chain vanished. Ruby didn't bother waiting to see anything else and raced through into the kitchen.

She didn't stop when she saw spoons whirling round huge mixing bowls suspended in mid-air, without anyone holding them. Knives were cutting and slicing fruit on boards on their own. Icing was being piped onto cakes out of bags floating above them. A couple of clay Poppets turned to look at her as they stood on the counter, busy rolling out dough.

Ruby threw open the back door and ran into the garden. Fresh air. The scent of wild roses. Dead leaves gently composting.

The garden swallowed her up as she ran down a path, snaking through the tall grass. She kept running, the broken mirror clinking in her backpack, afraid Mrs Easton would appear behind her or even in front of her, or worse, that a large bristly black leg would poke its way out of the grass. When she felt a pain starting to throb in her shoulder where the Witch's hook had caught her, she gritted her teeth.

Ruby was breathless by the time she reached a large clearing in the centre of the garden where a table was set with twelve chairs around it. On each place setting was a card with a name written in black curly handwriting. Ruby decided not to hang around, but, as she reached for the bottle of Slap Dust in her pocket, she noticed something that made her stop.

A large cage was standing to her left, its top covered by a green waterproof canvas. Inside were two large objects wrapped up in foil. But not everything was covered. Ruby could see two heads, and she recognized the faces immediately.

As she stood there, breathing hard, Ruby could hear the gentle crackle of foil as Jones's mother and father breathed too.

The cage was locked with a dirty iron padlock, meaning there was no way in.

Beside it was a large clay oven with an iron door and below it a hearth piled with a stack of wood ready to be lit. It looked like a giant pizza oven, but Ruby had already guessed this oven wasn't for pizza. Set on a metal trolley was a large cookbook, open at a page with a set of instructions. A note written in spidery handwriting had been paper-clipped to the page:

Mr Davison – 165lbs 8hrs cooking –
approx. 2pm IN!
Mrs Davison – 120lbs 6.5hrs cooking –
3.30pm or thereabouts

Ruby checked her watch. It was a little after midday. She looked up when she heard a noise. Someone or something was moving in the tall grass. She didn't bother hanging around to find out what it was and sprinted on until she reached the end of the garden and stared up at the tall wall.

There was no way over it. But that was okay.

As she reached into her pocket for the Slap Dust, she noticed something beside her. It was wrapped up like a parcel in white silk. Looking closer, Ruby could see a cat's ginger head, the whiskers squashed flat. The green eyes weren't blinking.

She heard a rustle in the tall grass to her left and then she felt a *thunk* on her foot that almost knocked her over. Looking down she saw a line of white sticky thread stuck to her trainer. A chattering sound started up and a huge black spider the size of a horse crept out of the tall grass on long black, bristly legs, the thread on Ruby's trainer attached to the spider's spinneret. A row of eight glossy eyes stared at her and in each of them was reflected Ruby's startled face. She kicked off her trainer as the spider scuttled towards her, trying to reel her in. Her shoulder was more sore than before. She was panicking. But Ruby managed to pour out a measure of Slap Dust and slap her hands together, just in time, as the spider lunged at her, its fangs glistening.

She felt the now familiar *whoosh* as she left the garden and reappeared on the other side of the wall, where she found herself on Hampstead Heath, breathing hard. Quickly, she followed the path through a gate and out into a road, kicking off her other trainer so she could sprint faster. Ahead of her she spotted the figure of Jones running away.

'Jones!' she shouted. 'Jones!'

He stopped and turned around, hands on his head as he stood panting, a smile forming on his face when he saw she was safe.

But the smile soon disappeared when she told him what she'd found in the garden.

TWENTY-NINE

The cut on Ruby's shoulder was sore and she felt a great heat welling up in it Thomas Gabriel dabbed at it with a cloth, making her wince.

'I've got something for that in here,' said Jones, delving around in the chest of Commencement gifts that Maitland had left for him, which he'd lugged in from the van. He held up a jar of blue powder, with Deschamps & Sons stencilled on the front. 'It's Phoenix Powder.' He popped the lid off the jar and took out a spoonful.

'Is it going to hurt?' asked Ruby.

Jones shook his head. And so did Thomas Gabriel. But Ruby found out they were both lying and she yelled as the Phoenix Powder fizzed and burnt.

When it was over, Jones inspected her shoulder. The wound had healed perfectly, leaving a small blue mark which Ruby could just about read, twisting her arm to see it more clearly:

Courtesy of Deschamps & Sons.

'That'll go,' said Jones. 'But they like to advertise, so it may take a few weeks.'

The boys made her eat a piece of bread sprinkled with something that looked like sugar but tasted earthy, telling her it would give her some strength back. Jones's leg was pumping up and down the whole time as he watched her.

'Jones, what are we going to do?' asked Ruby after she'd finished eating and Thomas Gabriel had found her a new pair of shoes. 'How are we even going to get close to Mrs Easton and use the Dark Bottle? She'll stop us with her mind tricks.'

Jones shook his head. He looked at his watch and saw that it was almost one o'clock. His leg pumped harder and harder. And then suddenly it stopped. He seemed to think for a moment more before leaning forward to sort through the gifts in the chest. He took out a piece of wood about the length of a forearm. It looked like any old stick you might see on the ground.

'I know,' he said, tapping the piece of wood against his palm. 'I know what we'll do.'

Thomas Gabriel nodded as he seemed to understand what Jones was thinking. 'It might work. If you time it just right.'

Ruby folded her arms. Gave them both her best knowing look. 'I'm guessing that's not just a stick, right?'

She was right. It wasn't just a stick.

It was an 'In and Out'.

'It works like a passageway,' said Jones as he made Ruby stand up.

'A passageway?'

'Yeah, because it goes from one place to another. And you're going to use it.' Jones put the piece of wood in her hand, but Ruby wasn't convinced: even up close it looked as if it was … well … just a stick. 'I need you to think about Mrs Easton's garden.' Ruby raised her eyebrows at that because there was nothing about that place she wanted to remember at all. 'Please, Ruby,' said Jones. 'It's fine. Nothing's going to happen, honest.'

'Okay,' she said and cleared her head and started thinking about it. As soon as she did, the stick began to vibrate very gently in her hand as if there was something powerful contained in it that couldn't wait to be released.

'Can you feel it?' asked Jones.

'Yeah, kind of,' said Ruby nervously, wondering what was going to happen.

'Good. Now I want you to focus in a bit more detail on a particular spot.'

The stick was starting to tug a little harder in Ruby's hand and she wasn't quite sure why. 'What do you mean? Jones, what's going to happen?'

'Just focus on the cage you saw. The padlocked door. I want you to imagine you're standing in the garden in front of that door.' Ruby tried to hold the image of the cage's door in her mind. 'Can you see it?'

'Yep.'

'Okay, now I want you to imagine going there.'

'Jones, that is not—'

'Don't worry, nothing bad's gonna happen.'

The stick was vibrating, making Ruby's whole arm shake.

'I am not going to do this—'

'Ruby, you have to do this,' growled Jones. 'You're the only one who's been in the garden, so you're the only one who can make the "In and Out" work the way I need it to. This is the only plan I can think of. There's no time to try anything else. You want to be a Badlander, don't you? You want to help kill a Witch like Mrs Easton, don't you, and prove you're as good as any boy?'

'Yeah.'

'And we're supposed to be helping each other, ain't we?'

'Yes . . .'

'Then do what I'm asking.' Ruby stared into Jones's eyes. 'Trust me. I'd never let anything bad happen to you. Never. Not now, after everything we've done to get this far. You believe me, don't you?'

Ruby could feel the stick tugging harder and harder. 'You'd better not be lying this time, Jones.'

'I'm not.' He looked at her without a flicker in his face.

So Ruby let her mind go and imagined going back to Mrs Easton's garden to exactly the spot Jones had mentioned.

The picture of the place in her mind seemed to stretch down into her arm, as if her blood was carrying it, and went on out of her into the stick, which exploded out of her grip. Ruby screamed, thinking her hand had blown up, but any noise she made was lost in a great whooshing sound as the space directly in front of her swirled and spun in a vortex that stretched out across the room. Faster and faster it went and Ruby saw colours appearing inside it, and as the swirling began to slow she saw grass and sky and garden. And then she was staring down a cloudy, roiling tunnel that stretched the length of the room. At its far end, Ruby could see the cage door and two figures lying wrapped in foil. She could hear birdsong. The faint hum of traffic.

When she turned to look at Jones, he was beaming. 'In one end and out the other. That's how a passageway works, right?' Ruby nodded. ''Cept this is one-way so no one at the other end can see it and come through.'

'Not even a Witch?' asked Ruby.

'Not even a Witch.'

All three of them waited by the entrance of the 'In and Out', watching for Mrs Easton to shuffle into view to open the cage and start cooking. Jones checked the Dark Bottle in his overcoat pocket from time to time, reassuring himself it was still there. Thomas Gabriel leafed through pages of *The Black Book of Magical Instruction*, trying to learn new spells he thought might be useful when the time came. Ruby practised drawing the gun out of her waistband, and aiming it.

'So how big was this spider exactly?' asked the gun.

'Too big to squish,' replied Ruby and the gun laughed.

'If it comes to it, just make sure you aim straight and keep your eyes open,' it advised.

Thomas Gabriel started checking the clock on the mantelpiece more often as it ticked closer to two o'clock. And then everyone seemed to hold their breath as Mrs Easton walked into view at the far end of the 'In and Out', and stood in front of the cage, ready to unlock it.

Jones licked his lips, waiting for exactly the right moment to surprise the Witch. He crouched, ready to launch himself through the 'In and Out' with the Dark Bottle, his fingers tightening round the hilt of the dagger inside it.

But then Mrs Easton turned suddenly and seemed to look straight at them, her nose sniffing the air.

'Jones,' whispered Ruby nervously. 'I thought you said it's only one-way, that she wouldn't know about us.'

'I lied about that last bit,' he said, inching closer to the edge of the 'In and Out'. Ruby and Thomas Gabriel glared at him. 'Did either of you have a better plan? Look, at worst, she might be able to sense something, but there's no way she can see anything or know what's coming. No Witch could manage that,' and he crouched, ready to leap. 'We've still got the element of sur—'

His final word was lost as the hook came flying out of Mrs Easton's hand and up through the 'In and Out' and snagged Jones's overcoat with its sharp curved end. There was very little time to react as the chain attached to the hook yanked him hard through the passageway. Thomas Gabriel and Ruby screamed his name as he travelled, but the speed and force of the journey ripped the sound of their voices clean from his ears and all he heard was the rattling of the chain.

He landed hard on the grass in the garden beside the cage, with the hook still snagged on his overcoat.

Mrs Easton looked down at him as the hook retreated back into her hand and she grinned a smile so sharp it cut his mind loose from his body for a moment. And then all at once he was fumbling with the Dark Bottle, trying to pull out the dagger in it and stand up. But, before he could do either of these things, the Witch whispered something and the long grass surrounding them shot out like tentacles and wrapped around his body, pinning him to the ground with his arms tight to his sides, rendering him motionless, except for his short, sharp breathing.

When Mrs Easton saw the Dark Bottle in his hand, his fingers around the neck, she frowned. 'Someone's been busy,' she growled, walking towards him, as Jones struggled to get free.

Before Mrs Easton could take the Dark Bottle from him, a blood-curdling scream rang down out of the sky, and Thomas Gabriel came flying out of nowhere, from the 'In and Out', knocking the Witch back against the cage with a *clang!*

Thomas Gabriel rolled as he landed and stood up. He muttered some words and his fists started to glow blue, and he pointed both hands and shouted the final part of the spell.

'*Déapspere!*' A flash of white sparks streamed from his fingers, sharpening into a long white spear that flew towards the Witch. But the point of the weapon stopped centimetres from Mrs Easton's throat and dissolved.

The Witch cackled and waved a hand dismissively towards Thomas Gabriel, whose fists were already glowing blue again, his One Eye fluttering up out of his pocket and urging him on. But, before Thomas Gabriel could utter another word, his mouth disappeared, leaving in its place a bare patch of skin. Unable to release the charge in his fists with a command, the colour in his hands seeped away.

Thomas Gabriel felt for where his mouth might be, his eyes almost popping out of his head with the effort of trying to scream. As he looked up again, a black point of light came rushing at him from the Witch's hand and caught him side-on as he tried to turn away. He hit the ground hard, but without a mouth there was no cry, so he fell silently. He didn't get up. In fact, he didn't move. His One Eye vainly tried to wake him as the shadow of a huge spider crept over him. The creature had emerged from the tall grass and now it stood over Thomas Gabriel, studying the boy, wondering what to do.

Mrs Easton brushed herself down then folded her arms and shook her head as she looked at the two boys, one caught up in the grass and the other being wrapped up in silk spun from the spider's spinneret.

She walked towards Jones, her eyes fixed on the Dark Bottle in his hand. But, before she reached the boy, something else came flying from the 'In and Out', just missing her head, and landed in the grass in front of the cage.

Mrs Easton whirled round to see what it was. A silver revolver lay on the ground.

'Cooking and eating these folk wrapped in foil is going to put on a few pounds, isn't it?' said the gun. 'Not such a good idea at your age. I mean, who are you kidding? You're not the woman you were, not even your *Wiccacraeft* can hide it. You can't keep time at bay for ever, not even a Witch like you. The wrinkles get deeper eventually. The hair turns greyer, the double chins turn into triples—'

Mrs Easton growled like an angry bear.

'Hmm, looks like someone's got anger issues. You're gonna give yourself a heart attack if you're not careful.'

Mrs Easton shouted a stream of words and pointed an arm which this time stretched out like a piece of gum until her hand grabbed the gun and started to squeeze it, making it buckle and bend.

'Ow,' roared the gun. 'Ow.' And then it shouted at the top of its voice, 'Behind you, love!'

The Witch felt something hit her in the back, and the last thing she heard before everything went black was the gun shouting, 'Told you!'

'One ...' counted Ruby nervously as she knelt beside Jones bound up in the grass ...

'... two ...' she shouted as she felt the Slap Dust still ringing in the palms of her hands ...

'... three ...' she said as she withdrew the dagger from the Dark Bottle that Jones was holding ...

'... four ...' she said calmly at the blurry circle in front of her ...

'... five ...' she whispered as Mrs Easton came hurtling back through towards her.

Ruby held up the dagger and speared the Witch with the end of the blade as they collided. The force knocked her off her feet and Ruby landed on her back on the grass with Mrs Easton on top of her.

She could smell the Witch's foul breath. See right into her eyes. And, for a moment, Ruby wondered if the dagger deep in the Witch's heart was going to work.

'Ruby Jenkins,' gasped Mrs Easton.

'That's Ruby Jenkins the Badlander, actually.'

The Witch gasped again and began to tremble. The tremble grew into a wobble and then her whole body began to swirl as if she was made of smoke. Ruby heard a very faint scream as the formless, swirling shape that was now Mrs Easton was sucked down into the open Dark Bottle still in Jones's hand.

Other things were sucked down into it too . . .

. . . the giant spider standing over Thomas Gabriel . . .

. . . another one that was lifted out of the tall grass.

The oven went too.

And out the house came Poppets, screaming as they flew through the air . . .

And the cage was swallowed up too, leaving behind two figures wrapped in foil.

Thomas Gabriel's mouth returned and he shouted with joy as he tore apart the threads of silk binding him. The revolver, having returned to its normal shape, started hollering too.

The grass wrapped around Jones released him and he set down the Dark Bottle as he stumbled to his feet and rushed over to his mother and father. He watched them slowly opening their eyes, blinking in the sunlight, waiting to see how they were as an inky black cloud uncoiled from each of their mouths and sailed towards the Dark Bottle.

'Not too shabby for a girl, right, Jones?' said Ruby, dusting herself down.

Jones gave her a thumbs up and nodded. Before he could say anything, a blurry hole formed in the air and Victor Brynn came hurtling through and landed on the grass. The No-Thing just had time to grin his pointy, black-toothed smile before his body convulsed and a black billowing cloud was sucked out of his body through his mouth. Just like Mrs Easton, the cloud swirled round and round in the air before being pulled down into the Dark Bottle.

Victor Brynn lay on the ground, blinking up at the blue sky. He was no longer a No-Thing but a man again. His teeth were not pointed and black. His bald head was now covered in grey hair. His face glowed with a healthy pink colour.

Victor Brynn propped himself up on his elbows and looked at Ruby and Jones and they could see that his brain was ticking over.

'We killed Mrs Easton!' shouted Ruby. 'All her *Wiccacraeft* is going into the Bottle. It looks like it even brought you back to cure you too.'

Victor Brynn nodded. 'That Dark Bottle is stronger than any magic you can do,' he said and smiled as he watched the Dark Bottle absorbing more and more of Mrs Easton's *Wiccacraeft*. 'Thank you,' he shouted to Ruby and Jones as a whole mass of cakes came flying noisily out of the house in a great cloud of colour and was sucked down into the

Bottle. When Jones saw more inky black clouds come sailing over the wall surrounding the garden, he knew the other people Mrs Easton had cursed must have been saved from the Witch too.

'What about my parents?' asked Jones. 'Are they going to be all right? Will they recover from the Witch's curse?'

Victor Brynn nodded. 'I can help them. But you need to cancel your spell on me whilst you have the chance.' He pointed at the blurry circle in the air in front of him and Jones rushed towards Ruby with his hand outstretched.

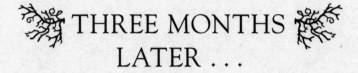

THREE MONTHS
LATER . . .

THIRTY

Thomas Gabriel smoothed back his hair in a ridiculous quiff as he studied his reflection in the bedroom mirror. He struck a couple of poses, making sure he looked good from all angles. Satisfied, he checked his teeth too. Gave them a rub with his finger. They looked good. In fact, all of him looked good. He nodded admiringly as his One Eye swooped down from the top of the mirror and landed on his shoulder.

Thomas Gabriel winked at himself before he turned round and reached for his herringbone coat, lying on the bed. As he put it on, he patted the right-hand pocket to check for *The Black Book of Magical Instruction*. He never went anywhere without it now. Because it had saved his life, he considered it his lucky charm.

Taking it out, he ran his finger over the leather-bound cover, exploring the tiny crater where the blast of Mrs Easton's magic had hit. Somehow the book had absorbed the full force and stopped it going through into his body.

All he had felt was a jolt so hard it had knocked him to the ground. The next thing he remembered was looking up at a huge spider.

He kept the Dark Bottle on his desk as a memento of everything that had happened. It would no doubt strike fear into the hearts of any apprentice he eventually took on. They would worship him for it.

As he let himself out of the house, he took a deep breath. The night air had the usual drone of traffic noise wafting through it. Thomas Gabriel found it comforting, not just because it was always there like an old friend, but it made the streets seem alive, ready and waiting for him to come and explore them. He couldn't understand how Ruby was so comfortable with the quiet of the countryside.

Putting up his collar to keep out the chill of the air, he walked on down the street, alert for anything that might be lurking in the Badlands of Hampstead tonight, his One Eye flitting like a bat in front of him.

Ruby was out in the Badlands too. She was lurking in the dark beside the whitewashed wall of a thatched cottage she knew well. As she looked back down the drive, she imagined the ordinary girl she'd been once, struggling to ride over the gravel on her bike, not knowing Maitland was about to appear, followed by Jones – the boy with one name who'd changed her life. And how it had changed. Now she had her own house where everything worked with magic because

Thomas Gabriel had wanted her to have it as a *'thank you'* for saving his life.

She'd received most of the money that Maitland had left for Jones too because he hadn't wanted any of it, but Ruby had made him take some. It meant she could buy pretty much anything she wanted although there was really no need for much. The garden produced far more fruit and vegetables than she could eat on her own. All she ever spent money on was the occasional bill from the baker or butcher in the nearest village who sent over the odd delivery, no questions asked, just as they had done when Maitland was alive. Jones had tried to give her the VW van too. But, as he'd handed over the keys, she'd seen his hand shaking, so she'd told him that teaching her to drive when she was ready wouldn't mean he was still a Badlander, just that he was being a friend. He'd grinned at that and put the keys back in his pocket.

'Remembering the first time around?' whispered the gun in her hand.

'Something like that.'

Ruby crept down the path beside the cottage and continued on beside the fence until she reached the door.

'Careful,' whispered the gun.

Ruby nodded as she lifted the latch. All her senses were alive. Opening the door, she saw the lawn in front of her. Sitting cross-legged in the centre of the grass was a man wearing a dark suit with his back to her. He was looking up at a sharp-pointed crescent of moon.

'Moon-bathing,' whispered the gun. 'I told you there was something about this place. Careful now,' it said as she stole quietly across the grass.

When Ruby was just metres away, the man looked round, a look of surprise on his face as he took in the girl and her gun that was currently pointed at his face.

'Evening,' said the revolver.

The man blinked. Ruby could see his brain trying to work out what was going on.

'Just to clear things up. I *am* a Badlander.' But the man just looked more confused. Ruby sighed. 'I've killed a Witch, you know, a Wretch, blah-blah-blah. So, I'm not afraid of you, mister man. Whatever you are.' Her finger tightened on the trigger.

'Don't shoot,' he said quickly.

'Why not?'

'Because I can tell you something every Badlander would want to know about this place.'

'Go on.'

But, before the man could say anything, a third person emerged out of the dark. A man. Grey-haired. Wearing a dark overcoat. He tutted loudly and shook his head.

Ruby sighed. 'What's wrong now?'

Victor Brynn hefted the large axe he was holding higher onto his shoulder. It had become his weapon of choice after Ruby and Jones had cancelled their spell on it. He wasn't entirely sure why he felt such kinship with it, and had been wondering about researching the effects of magic on people and objects affected by the same spell.

He cleared his throat. 'Before conversing with *any* creature, you should bind it securely.' He pointed to the silken rope hanging from her waist. 'I didn't give you that rope as a fashion item.'

'But—'

'Ruby, what's the point in me teaching you things if you don't do them?'

'But there's so *many* rules.'

'And rules save your life.'

Ruby sighed. She started to bind the other man's arms behind his back. 'Sorry about this. We're still figuring out the whole teacher-pupil thing.' She leant in as she pulled the rope tight. 'You wouldn't think *I'm* the one who saved his life,' she whispered.

Jones was sitting on the doorstep of his parents' house, the street lights throwing down cones of yellow light, when Thomas Gabriel turned up.

'Still can't sleep?' he asked and Jones shook his head. 'It's bound to take some getting used to after working with Maitland. At least you look like an ordinary boy.' Thomas Gabriel frowned. 'I still can't get used to seeing you with your new haircut or without your overcoat.'

'I've had to get used to a lot more than that.'

'Like what?'

'My new name for starters. And all the things people use. How they speak. What they do.'

'But you like it?'

'Yeah.'

Thomas Gabriel looked at him and wondered if he was telling the truth. 'What about school?' he asked.

'It's not as hard as learning to be a Badlander. The teachers ain't as strict. And it's not as dangerous either.'

'And no one's asked any more questions about you? Where you've come from?'

Jones shook his head. 'I'm good at making up stories if anyone asks why I was adopted. Ruby taught me what to say. And my mum and dad don't mind telling people that's how they got me. I think they're just so happy to have me back. They want to feel like normal people again.' Jones shrugged. 'I think they're slowly improving, anyway. At least from how they were at the start.'

'Wasn't pretty, was it?'

'No.' Jones sighed. 'Victor Brynn's potions have helped a lot, though, and I keep explaining things to 'em about the Badlands so they don't feel like they're losing their minds. It's going to take time, though.'

'Are they still having nightmares?'

'Yeah. I hear 'em. And not sleeping much means they argue a lot.' He sighed, shuffled his feet and hung his head.

'Mrs Easton cursed them for a long time,' said Thomas Gabriel, sounding slightly concerned. 'No one really knows what the long-term effects of a Witch's *Wiccacraeft* are on acolytes. There aren't any books on it. Not many people survive.'

Jones nodded and then smiled as something occurred to

318

him. 'Love helps with anything bad, I reckon. At least, that's what Ruby told me.'

'Any problems, let me know. I've got the Order keeping an eye on me and my territory now I'm not an apprentice any more. Apparently, if you lose your Master, you're on probation for the first few years after you Commence. I have to go to classes to replace everything Simeon would have taught me. I think some of the old Badlanders are jealous. It's a prime patch. And I got Maitland's house too because of the way the *Ordnung* works, seeing as you and Maitland are both dead.' He grinned as he thought about that. 'But I see the way the older ones look at me sometimes. They're watching. Waiting for me to trip up.'

'What about your Commencement?'

'What about it?'

Jones shrugged. 'Just wondering, that's all.'

'I need to get to work,' said Thomas Gabriel, standing up as if the last question had annoyed him. When they shook hands, Thomas Gabriel looked into Jones's eyes. 'Any problems with your parents at all, tell me. Okay?'

After Thomas Gabriel had left, Jones crept back into the house and shut the front door. He stood in the quiet dark of the hallway. He reminded himself he wasn't on the lookout for a creature now, that there was no reason to hunt through the house for anything beastly or dangerous. But some habits were hard to break.

He made his way upstairs to his bedroom. A couple of days earlier he'd slipped into Deschamps & Sons and bought the largest scrying mirror he could find with all the money he had left. It was full-length and encased in oak. It was going to be a difficult item to wrap, but he was determined to do it. The tag was already written out. It read:

Dear Ruby, thanks for everything
Love Ed

But, after reading it again, he crossed out his name and wrote Jones instead. It seemed right to sign it that way because that's who he'd been when he'd met Ruby and that's who he was whenever he remembered everything they'd done together. There was something about his old name he missed. Ruby had told him it was because it was a part of him and always would be. He'd denied it, telling her he was someone new now. But deep down he knew she was right. And sometimes, in the quiet of the night, when he lay in bed, with the dark screen of the television his parents had bought him staring at him, he thought long and hard about what that really meant.

GLOSSARY

of

BADLANDER

TERMS

Æhteland (ANGLO-SAXON)

Translates as 'territory' or 'landed property'. The term refers to a territory managed by a Badlander in a city, primarily London, which is split into a number of different patches. Only a Badlander who manages his æhteland is allowed to hunt on it and he is responsible for the safety of all ordinary people who live within its boundaries.

Andweardnes áflíeheþ (ANGLO-SAXON)

Translates as 'time flies' with *Andweardnes* meaning 'presence', 'presentness' or 'time' and *áflíeheþ* being the third person singular of the verb *áfléogan*, meaning 'to fly', 'flee away from', 'escape'. It is one of the 'Ten Easy Spells To Get Started' offered in *The Black Book of Magical Instruction* to newly commenced Badlanders. Anyone casting the spell needs to declare what time differential is to be used otherwise results will be random.

Apprentice A young

male Badlander trained and assessed over a period of time to see whether they are fit for Commencement. Apprentices are taken on by senior Badlanders who then become their Masters. Each Master only takes one apprentice at a time and only a small number eventually go on to be Commenced, usually at around the age of 12-13 years of age. The majority of those who do not Commence die in the Badlands during training. Those who survive but are not considered suitable for Commencement are returned to normal society with their minds and memories wiped by magic to be looked after by ordinary people. It is generally accepted that many of those returned to normal life suffer from mental disorders and depression as they grow up. The other option open to failed apprentices is to become a Whelp (see separate entry).

Badlanders find their apprentices in a number of ways, but by far the most common method is through the use of a secretive network that removes very young children from public care who have been placed there after being orphaned or abandoned. However, some apprentices are stolen straight from their families although this is a much rarer practice than it used to be.

The Badlands The Badlands describes any location where creatures might be lurking. It normally refers to places on the edge of normal people's lives. However, it is a name that encompasses a wide variety of areas, from a distant valley to a park in the heart of a city, or even to a house in the suburbs. Wherever a creature is found then that location is considered to be a part of the Badlands.

Badlander The given name for members of the Badlander Order, a secret society of monster hunters. The Order evolved in Great Britain during the 5th century after the arrival of Anglo-Saxons from continental Europe who brought with them their own secrets and methods of fighting monsters. Ancient Britons adopted these techniques as they gradually embraced the culture and language of Anglo-Saxons. The teachings and organised living of early monks also helped to create early Badlander practice. Initially, Badlanders were trained in the earliest monasteries until the Order began to emerge with its own established set of rules in approximately the second half of the 7th century. The influence of monasteries may explain why the Badlander Order is exclusively male.

The Badlander Bestiary - The Pocket Book Version A small, portable reference guide to all the various monsters found in the Badlands. The pages are blank until the user demands to know information about a specific creature at which point all the relevant information will be revealed. Because of this function it is usually used as a field guide on hunts and particularly valuable for apprentices who are learning about creatures.

'Be Prepared' An old motto used by Badlanders to ensure that they are always ready for whatever they may encounter in the Badlands. This phrase has been adopted into the larger society of ordinary people too (for example, the Scout Movement).

The Black Book of Magical Instruction

Presented to every apprentice during the act of Commencement, *The Black Book of Magical Instruction*, can only be read by those who have Commenced and been given the gift of magic. This ensures the secrets of spell-casting are reserved only for those deemed special enough to Commence. The book is vital as a teaching aid for young Badlanders, allowing them to learn how to use magic. It is interactive, leading apprentices through various lessons and answering their questions.

Charms Charms are often used by Badlanders to adapt or customise an object to make it more useful. Using magic is the only way to create a charm.

Charles Du Clement

(1770 – PRESENT) Born in Bordeaux, France in 1770, Charles Du Clement grew up as a member of the Badlander Order in France, although he was itinerant and travelled widely, researching a vast array of creatures across Europe. Eventually, he settled in England in 1820, preferring the English way of life to that of continental Europe. After being bitten and infected by a *Lich*, captured from a Bronze Age round barrow (burial site) in Dorset, Du Clement was imprisoned in the crypt of the chapel of St Crosse College, Oxford (see separate entry on the St Crosse for more information) for the benefit of Badlander scholarship because of his vast and detailed knowledge of creatures and monstrous beings. Despite being an important asset, Du Clement's imprisonment is kept a secret by high-ranking members of the Order because of his transformation into a *Lich*, a creature Badlanders are sworn to destroy.

As well as advising on creatures, Du Clement has the final say on whether the thesis of the Badlander research fellow at St Crosse passes or fails.

Cæg (ANGLO-SAXON) Translates as 'key'.

Commencement The

act of advancement of an apprentice Badlander by which he is given the gift of magic. Commencement is entirely at the discretion of the apprentice's Master who will formalise the Commencement by handing over a silver key. This key is worn around a Master's

neck for the duration of the apprenticeship and unlocks an oak chest that has the properties to set an apprentice's Commencement in motion.

The term Commencement was agreed upon by the Order in the early 17th century prior to which various terms had been used to describe the process and its different elements.

Dark Magic - *áglæccræft* (ANGLO-SAXON)

A relatively unknown form of magic, understood only by those who change and become warped enough to use it. It is considered a low form of magic by Badlanders because of the need to drink blood to cast spells. Many Badlanders are aware that the magic inside them can change, becoming rotten, of its own accord and try to tempt a person to use Dark Magic, thereby corrupting them. Therefore, many Badlanders practise forms of mediation to protect against this and avoid any temptation that magic presents to them.

Déapspere (Anglo-Saxon) A very basic spell that translates as 'deadly spear'. It allows the person casting the spell to hurl out a magical spear from their hands.

Deorcan Flascan

(Anglo-Saxon) Translates as 'dark bottle'. A Dark Bottle is a very private object that can be created by only the most powerful Witches, making them almost invincible. The actual process of making such a bottle is mired in secrecy because it requires the use of powerful *Wiccacraeft*. What is known about the bottles is that each one is the repository of all a Witch's fears. Having been placed in the bottle these fears are locked inside by a dagger lodged in the neck of the bottle. This dagger is then the only means by which the Witch can be killed and it must be driven through her heart.

For safekeeping, Dark Bottles are always buried with a powerful monster to protect it making it very difficult to steal – specifically the Dark Bottles of English Witches are buried together in one graveyard in the county of Herefordshire for greater security. Once a Witch has renounced her fears and buried the Dark Bottle she has no connection to it and must trust in the monster to guard it, as well as the *Wiccacraeft* designed to protect the bottle.

Deschamps & Sons

Deschamps & Sons is a large department store in London that sells everything a Badlander might need. It prides itself on providing the highest quality products, catering for a range of tastes. Deschamps began life as a small shop in the late 16th century, founded by Monsieur Deschamps, who had recently arrived from Paris. Over the years it has grown into a much larger business with several stores across the globe. Precise locations of the shops are known only by Badlanders who are all given an information brochure about the store after they have Commenced. Most of the London store is concealed underground with the entrance at street level, to what seems, at least to the ordinary person, a small tobacconists called Deschamps & Sons.

Door Wurm A very useful creature employed to open locked doors, however big or small. Wurms are very easy to use and once inserted into any lock, they will change into the required key. Door Wurms were originally just ordinary garden earthworms charmed by Badlanders but over time they have been bred specifically for their current purpose.

Fœcce (PRONOUNCED 'FETCH') (ANGLO-SAXON) Derived from the Anglo-Saxon word *fæccan* meaning 'to fetch'.

A *fæcce* is very similar to a doppelganger, namely, the magical 'double' of a person. On the rare occasions a Badlander steals a child from a family to be his apprentice he will create a *fæcce* to replace it. Usually, the *fæcce* will not live long after its creation, but in some instances, they have been recorded as living up to three or four years.

However, they do become progressively more sickly and unwell over the time they are alive.

Flying Rowan Staff
A flying rowan is a rowan tree that is not rooted directly in the earth. For example, it might be found growing on a cliff or on a large boulder or even in the boughs of another larger tree. The lack of direct contact with the earth increases the magical powers associated with the rowan tree. Badlanders are well aware of the magical properties of the tree and a staff made from a flying rowan is a very powerful weapon against creatures in hand-to-hand combat.

Forhwierfende (ANGLO-SAXON) Translates literally as 'changing'. *Forhwierfende* is the present participle of the verb *Forhwierfan*, meaning to change, transform or pervert. It is usually used by Badlanders to refer to the changing undergone by any shapeshifter.

Gebíed mé glæm (ANGLO-SAXON) A spell, which translates literally as 'Give me a bright light'.

Gebíed is the imperative form of the verb _Gebéodan_, which means 'to command', 'order' or 'give', and _Glæm_ is a noun meaning 'brilliant light' or 'splendour'.

Ghosting A Ghosting (called a _betreppende_ in Anglo-Saxon which translates as 'catching') is a ritual undertaken by a Badlander to capture a _Gást_. There are a variety of different ways to perform this rite although light is usually at the heart of any Ghosting. This is because light holds a great fascination for a _Gást_ and can lure the creature from its own plane of existence, forcing it to reveal itself. The various symbols used to trap a _Gást_ in a bottle, jar or whatever container is used are thought to derive from the ancient practice of imprisoning genies in bottles, a custom which originated in the Middle Eastern world.

Hazel Stick A Y-shaped hazel stick can be used to divine the location of a _Scucca_'s lair. In the same way that a person might dowse for water. The hazel stick must be charmed first for this to work. It fairly easy to use the stick as long as the person using it keeps their mind clear and free from other thoughts.

Heaton's Old Familiar Scrying Polish This polish is highly recommended for scryers to use, particularly beginners. Adolphus Heaton invented the polish in the early 17th century and it is still used today in exactly the same form, although its exact constituents are a well-kept secret. Prior to his death, Heaton set up a charitable trust that ensured the proceeds of sales of the polish would be invested in a fund to explore and promote the ongoing use of scrying within the Badlander community.

Imitator An imitator is an empty tube with a removable cap that is used to copy passages of text from a book. After a passage of text has been sucked up into the tube it can be revealed by removing the cap, then squeezing the tube, and squirting out the copied text into the air enabling it to be read easily. The earliest imitator was invented by Nicholas Gardiner in the early 20th century and is now widely used, especially by apprentices as a way of learning passages of text by rote.

In and Out A passageway compressed down into a manageable, easily portable form and is usually disguised as a stick to make it less likely to be stolen. The passageway, when released by the user, will create a magical portal to wherever the Badlander wants to go, the one main restriction being that it must be to a place that the user has visited before.

The In and Out provides a useful means of surprise because whilst the opening can be viewed by the user the exit is invisible. The limitation of an In and Out is that it only works one way.

Juicing 'Juicing' is a slang term for eliminating the bodies of dead monsters. It involves the use of a magical brown dust (its mixture of elements a closely guarded secret), which is sprinkled over a corpse, reducing it to a foamy white substance. Removing evidence of monsters is an essential part of any Badlander's kill.

Badlanders who have been killed in action are also disposed of in the same way but they are honoured with the *Wyrd* rhyme which is recited as the body melts away.

Learning Book A notebook commonly kept by apprentice Badlanders. It is a simple way of way keeping notes about the things they learn that are useful and important to know.

Louis Greizmann

(1763–1845) Louis Greizmann
was a renowned academic
who much preferred studying
and researching creatures than
hunting them in the Badlands.
He was born in France, in Paris,
and spent his whole life there,
cataloguing all the various
creatures he encountered. He
would often ask for accounts
of hunts by Badlanders to be
written up and sent to him in
order to build up as complete
a picture as possible about
monsters.

Greizmann was well known
as a drinker and playboy
on account of the money he
inherited from his Master,
Pierre Choux-Champ. However,
his thirst for the high life led
to the single most important
discovery of his career when,
after a heavy night of partying
(rumoured to be with Charles
Du Clement), he decided
to creep into a graveyard to
sleep off the booze (a highly
dangerous act) and ended up
doodling on the gravestones in a
drunken state. Whilst randomly
doodling symbols for various
magical acts he was studying
at the time, Greizmann was
surprised when one character
made the gravestone on which
it was written speak to him,
informing him what was buried
in the ground below. Despite
being an accidental discovery it
went on to become an extremely
valuable tool for Badlanders and
secured Greizmann's legacy in
Badlander history forever.

Magic The most important
tool in the Badlander's armoury
for tackling monsters, magic
is fundamental to surviving
the Badlands. It is also vitally
important because it allows
for the creation of charms that
make everyday life easier for
Badlanders given the lifestyle
restrictions placed on them by
the Ordnung, allowing them to
co-exist in the modern world
alongside ordinary people.
The gift of magic is granted at
Commencement and becomes
'fused' with the apprentice
receiving it.

Magic is a natural element
that Badlanders have managed
to control through ancient
means, drawing it from the

heart of the land and forcing it to work for them. Therefore, magic is always looking for a way to release itself from being controlled by the Badlander Order. This means magic can be fickle and unpredictable, attempting to lead Badlanders astray if they are not disciplined in how they use it. As a result, Badlanders are taught to treat magic with great respect at all times.

Memory Bush This plant is usually grown by someone in order to relive particular memories they may have forgotten or that might have become clouded through time, and even for a Badlander who may have been cursed by another to forget things. However, a memory bush is very difficult to grow. It requires a lot of love and attention to flourish and bear fruit, small purple berries, each of which recalls a memory when eaten.

An individual can only grow a memory bush after they remove their personal seed for it from their own body, which requires making a small incision in the belly button. A seed must be planted in a cool, quiet place and requires regular watering as well as a weekly feed of a few drops of blood by the person whose body has produced it. Only the Badlander who has planted the seed, taken from their body, may see the memories produced by the fruit that the plant grows. The berries are pungent and sharp tasting and eating one will reveal whatever memory the grower of the bush asks to see. The memory can be watched repeatedly over the course of a few minutes – up to an hour in some cases – until the effects start wearing off.

A memory bush is very protective of its berries and can defend itself by excreting a strong acid that is highly corrosive.

Mearcunga (ANGLO-SAXON) Translates as 'markings', 'brandings' or 'characteristics'. *Mearcunga* is the plural of the word *Mearcung*.

The formal name given to the

mark that a Badlander will make after killing and disposing of a creature to make it clear to other Badlanders what has happened in a particular location. It is also a way for Badlanders to show others how successful they have been in the Badlands, and promote their legacy.

Memory Leech Memory leeches are used to remove the memories of people, when required, by literally sucking them out of the brain. To do this they must be inserted into the head of the subject, usually through the ear canal. They are very clean and efficient removers of memories. Leeches work according to the amount of time they are instructed to remove from a person's memory so they are most commonly used to remove only very recent memories. Various rare sub species of leeches can work to remove older memories if they are given precise instructions about the date and time of the exact memories to be eliminated. After deleting memories, leeches will excrete a hallucinogenic substance that causes a false memory to be created, accounting for the missing time in a person's memory.

Mistletoe and Rowan A specific mix of berries from both the mistletoe plant (white berries) and the rowan tree (red berries), which can be used to inflict damage on certain creatures in the Badlands. The mix can be used in form of a paste, as a dried powder or even as pellets.

Moon-Bathing Moon-Bathing is an act performed by all types of shapeshifters whereby they bask in the moon's light, using its power to transform from human to creature and back again whenever they wish. Therefore, shapeshifters do not need a full moon to change into a creature but merely need to keep the effect of moonlight on their bodies 'topped up'.

Moon Globe Moon globes are very rare with only a handful thought to be in existence. How they came to exist is mired in mystery. They are spherical as the name suggests and about the size of a small apple. The glow that a moon globe emits is akin to the pearlescent light of the moon, hence the name. Quite what makes them glow is not known given that the scarcity of the objects makes study almost impossible. However, various Badlanders have postulated theories about them. The most detailed studies on moon globes were carried out in the early 20th century by Piers van Anhelm who came to the conclusion that they are fashioned from fragments of meteors that have landed on earth. Very few Badlanders have ever used a moon globe and ownership of them is kept a secret. The reason they are so valued is that they can be the only way to open certain concealed doors or entrances, meaning that something extremely valuable can be locked away securely.

No-Thing A No-Thing is a term for any Badlander when the magic inside them has become corrupted. Magic may change to something dark and subversive if a person is bitten by certain types of creature (most commonly a Witch), or if the magic itself warps into something rotten because of evil intent within the Badlander themselves. Once corrupted, the magic will allow its user to perform Dark Magic, known as *áglæccræft*. This type of magic has not been examined by Badlanders very often because the study of it can be very dangerous and lead to infection. Therefore, its power and potential is little known or understood. One thing that is well known, however, is that Dark Magic requires blood to 'power it' up and allow the No-Thing to use it. Thus, No-Things are always on the lookout for people or animals to drain of their blood. It is thought that there is some connection between No-Things and Vampires but so far there has been no conclusive proof for this.

One Eye A One Eye is one of the very few creatures the Ordnung allows Badlanders to use to help them on their hunts, having the skill for sensing unnatural and dangerous things. They are akin to a sprite or fairy (*ælf* in Anglo-Saxon), having wings and a diminutive stature. However, there are two key characteristics that differentiate a One Eye from these types of creatures: the big single eye in the centre of its forehead and a set of large, sharp teeth, which only come to prominence when bared. The colour of the eye is used to define the various types of One Eye that exist. In the wild the creatures are aggressive and have to be tamed by Badlanders using a four-leaf clover. Over time, One Eyes can be trained to become obedient and willing servants to their owners.

Ordnung (GERMAN) A German word, meaning 'order', 'discipline', 'rule' or 'system', *Ordnung* is used by Badlanders to describe the strict code of rules their Order must follow.

It was a term adopted by Badlanders in the early 15th century when new rules for the Order were established.

Phoenix Powder A regenerative powder used to heal wounds and clean out any nasty magical infection that might be lingering. The powder is created by removing a small portion of a Phoenix's ashes after it has combusted into flames, and died, before regenerating. This ash is then mixed with a variety of different elements to allow it to be suitable for human use. It is thought that high demand for the powder has led to the near extinction of the Phoenix.

Poppet A small doll or figurine that is created to represent a person with a view to controlling or cursing that individual. It can be made from a variety of materials such as clay, wood or metal. Poppets are usually used by Witches to control their acolytes. The most common type of Poppet that Witches use is the Blood Poppet, a hollow clay figure, which is filled with the blood of the person it represents.

Rosemary and Salt

A common mixture of two substances that Badlanders use as an all-purpose weapon against many creatures. It can cause burns on a variety of monsters. If sprinkled on the ground around the user it can also form a protective ring that repels many different creatures.

Rye drops/Bluebell Syrup/Rose Petal Powder

A variety of natural substances used in different forms to protect against the many types of Witches.

St John's Eve

Falling on the 23rd June, on the eve of Midsummer's Day, although a Christian celebration (taking its name from St John the Baptist), St John's Eve is also closely associated with the summer solstice, which means it incorporates pagan traditions. It is considered a most auspicious day for Witches and their *Wiccacraeft*. Many Witches will perform celebratory rites on St John's Eve to enhance their magical power, with the hour after midnight considered to the most symbolic and powerful time to do this (For further reading on the subject try *The Power of the Hour* by CJ Larssen).

St Crosse College, Oxford

St Crosse College, founded in 1450, is one of the colleges that make up the University of Oxford, one of the oldest universities in the world. The college admits undergraduate and graduate students. It has groomed four prime ministers as well as numerous lords, clergymen and scholars. What is not written in the guidebooks of the college (available for four pounds and fifty pence from the black wire shelves inside the main gate) is the legacy of its Badlander scholarship.

Ever since the foundation of the college a Badlander research fellowship has always existed. The Badlander holding the position of 'resident research fellow' is entrusted with the primary aim of researching rare creatures, studying the combat techniques, weapons and magic that might be most effective against them.

No questions are ever asked about the fellowship on account of a generous and anonymously run Trust that funds the position. The Trust also donates generously to the college, and even the University, whenever there is a need. The research fellow is resident for three years at the college and is required to be discreet at all times about Badlander affairs given that he is living amongst ordinary people. He is allowed to participate fully in normal life as required however most keep themselves to themselves.

The position of research fellow, despite being highly regarded is considered by some to be a 'poisoned chalice' (a direct quote from *Getting Cross with St Crosse* by AJ Heap) because adaptation back to life as a Badlander after living

amongst ordinary people can prove difficult and there is a history of mental health issues associated with fellows in later life. The Badlander research fellow also has the difficult duty of looking after Charles Du Clement, a *Lich* (See Charles Du Clement).

Scrying Scrying is the act of observing a person or location. It is an ancient skill that is largely vocational, meaning those Badlanders with a natural talent for scrying are drawn to trying it, usually through feeling an urge to hold a scrying object that is nearby. However, scrying still requires a great deal of practice and years of learning to perfect it. A person may only scry on a person they have met before or on a place they have visited previously.

The most common tool for a Badlander to use when scrying, is a mirror made for the purpose, although other objects such as glass balls, polished tabletops and fragments of glass can be used. Scrying mirrors come in all shapes and sizes and can be used as communication devices and even as portals if the scryer has sufficient skill. A mirror usually works more effectively if a polish is applied to the glass (See Heaton's Old Familiar Scrying Polish).

Sing-Songs Sing-Songs contain pieces of music that have been written down and then transformed into audio through magic. When its hard outer shell is cracked open, the Sing-Song will release the music inside it, which traditionally has a dreamy and magical quality to it that induces sleep. Badlanders will use Sing-Songs as a defence against creatures to lull them to sleep. Some Badlanders will also use them at night if they are struggling to sleep, a common side effect when working too hard or suffering trauma from their work. However, when employed for personal use, a low strength Sing-Sing must always be used since high strength ones can lull a person into a sleep from which they might never wake up.

Silver Silver is a useful and effective substance against a wide range of creatures in the Badlands and can inflict serious damage. It can be used in a wide number of ways, for example, as bullets for a gun or fashioned to make silver spikes or indeed items that can be worn by Badlanders such as knuckledusters. Ball bearings fired by catapult are one way for apprentices to use silver as a weapon when magic is unavailable to them.

Slap Dust A way of travelling from one place to another instantaneously. After a small amount of dust has been placed in the palm of one hand, all the user has to do is announce where they want to go, then slap their hands together, and they will travel to their desired location. The dust originated from a combination of charms that were mixed together by early Badlanders in the late 9th century and has been used ever since. It is particularly useful for apprentices who have not yet Commenced and cannot therefore use magic to travel. There are many different grades and strengths of Slap Dust available to purchase.

Although the dust offers a lightning-fast and efficient mode of transport, it does have its problems. Common issues are judging the right amount of dust required for a particular journey, materialising in too confined a space, lack of secrecy because the user must announce where they are going and being seen by ordinary people by accident (see Memory Leech for a useful way to combat this problem). There is also some evidence to suggest that using the dust has an unhealthy effect on the body if used too often (A good source for more information on this subject is *Why Dust Might be Bad for You* by J Heaslip).

Swamm (ANGLO-SAXON) Translates as 'fungus' or 'mushroom'.

Whelp Whelps are rare and generally tend to be failed apprentices who have shown

particular traits of loyalty and who are considered too useful by their Masters to be returned to the care of normal people. In very rare situations a Whelp may be Commenced later in life if they have shown great aptitude and deserve their chance at using magic.

Wiccacraeft (ANGLO-SAXON) Translates as 'Witchcraft'. It refers to the magic that a Witch uses, which is considered to be evil and corrupt compared to the magic that Badlanders use.

Wuduæppel (pl. *wuduæpplas*) (ANGLO-SAXON) Translates as 'wild apple'.

This is a very controversial object because it allows the person eating the fruit to transform temporarily into a creature of their choice. This can be very useful in times of combat or for investigative purposes but it is considered a highly contentious act because becoming a creature, whatever type it might be, is considered to be a deviant act by many

Badlanders. Because of divided
opinion among Badlanders,
the *Ordnung* states that eating
the fruit requires consent of
the Order first and without it a
person is open to punishment.
Trees that produce the fruit
are grown in highly secret
and well-guarded plots and no
Badlander is allowed to grow a
tree themselves. The fruit can
only purchased from Deschamps
& Sons where each purchase is
recorded and a list of owners
is available for consultation by
high-ranking Badlanders.

Wyrd (pronounced like the
common English word 'weird')
(ANGLO-SAXON)

Wyrd is the name in Anglo-
Saxon given to the concept of
fate or personal destiny, which
cannot be resisted. It is a noun
formed from the verb *weorþan*
(pronounced we-or-than) which
means 'to come to pass', 'to
become', or 'to happen'.

ACKNOWLEDGMENTS

Books are never written alone even though the author's name is the only one that appears on the cover so I would like to thank the people who have helped me to write this novel.

For all their input and time spent reading various drafts a big thank you to Bella Honess-Roe, Nick Roe, Cavan Ash and Davina Morgan-Witts. Thanks also to my students at Falmouth University for teaching me a few things. In particular, thank you to Daniel Hunt, Abigail Martin and Alice Benham for reading my manuscript.

I am indebted to my editor Jane Griffiths for all her guidance and wisdom about how to improve the story from its first beginnings all the way through to the final draft.

Thank you also to Jack Noel who designed such a fantastic cover.

Many thanks too to my agent, Madeleine Milburn, for all her help in making sure my idea became a book.

I could not have written this story without support and love from Diana, Katherine and Joanna.

Thank you, most of all, to Priscilla for all her belief, patience and love.